words

words

R. J. SUNDEAN

RJSUNDEAN.COM

Chapter 1

REBIRTH

Arden reaches out, grabs the top of his laptop's screen, and closes the lid. *Finally*, he thinks.

He takes a deep breath, leans back in his leather desk chair, and stretches his arms to the side, trying to push the soreness out of his back. Over the years, the long hours of sitting in front of his computer and working haven't done his body any good, and now he has to force himself to be cognizant of the time and to take breaks accordingly.

The final chapter for this manuscript took him longer to write than any of his prior novels; maybe because it was a long-anticipated closure to the series of novels that has kept him on the New York Times bestseller list for several years, or maybe because it was a welcome release from a hexalogy that absorbed all his creative effort, locking him into a set path and not allowing him to stretch his writer's muse into different genres.

He looks around his study. His writing room, as he likes

to call it, when he has guests over. The room is a modest size, as rooms go. A plain wooden desk sits in the middle of the room, upon which rests his usual requirements for writing: his laptop, his cellphone, a notepad with a pen, and a lowball glass of bourbon. The walls are lined with bookshelves, and each bookshelf is filled with a wide array of literature that he has collected over the years. The room has a permanently musky, but slightly sweet, smell to it as the books continue to age. It's a smell that beckons to him and encourages him every time he opens up the door to resume work on his latest creation. His desk and chair both face the only other way for natural light to make its way into the room beyond the doorway: a solitary window that breaks up the wrapping of bookshelves around the room. Under the window is a small table with a couple of lowball glasses and a decanter of bourbon on it.

A flash of light pierces the darkness beyond the window and briefly illuminates the room. The light is followed shortly after by a heavy rumble of thunder, which causes the ground to shake, sending vibrations throughout the house. The news this morning mentioned there would be heavy thunderstorms this evening, and it appears they have arrived.

Arden pushes himself out of his chair and stands up, stretching his legs in the process. He grabs his cellphone from its usual location on the desk and checks it—almost eleven at night. No calls, no messages. He stuffs the phone in his right pocket and grabs the empty glass from the coaster it calls home. The glass was emptied hours ago, and he was too engrossed in finalizing this last chapter to refresh it from his stockpile of bourbon. He takes one more deep breath and walks over to the decanter, removing the glass stopper so he can pour a new drink. After a quick splash of the amber liquid into his glass, he replaces the stopper and sets the etched crystal glass container back down. He picks up his glass to take a quick sip just as another bright flash of light chases away the dark of the night and fights to make its way into his home. The hair on his arms raises slightly when the accompanying thunder makes itself known—an odd and unexpected feeling of unease sets in. *Get a grip, man; it's just a storm*, he tells himself.

Glass in hand, he walks out of the room and into the main living room, making a beeline for the kitchen. A rumble from his stomach reminds him that he hasn't eaten dinner yet. Reaching the fridge, he sets the glass down on the counter and opens the fridge door. The fridge is mostly empty: the entire contents consist of some random condiments and a few takeout containers from lunch he had delivered this afternoon. Arden reaches in, grabs the nearest container, and sets it on the counter next to his bourbon. He closes the door to the fridge and grabs a fork, choosing to stand at the counter and eat versus sitting down at the dining room table or on one of the bar chairs at the breakfast bar. Sesame chicken with white rice, drizzled with more soy sauce than any health professional would ever recommend. He eats it cold, not wanting to wait the time it would take to reheat the meal, and the concoction has formed into one giant mass that requires him to stab at it with the fork to break it apart.

"Whoever said writers make a lot of money has never met me," he says out loud to the empty home around him. As if in response, the house illuminates once again, and the accompanying deep rumble with vibrations soon follows.

Arden shakes off the uneasy feeling still settling in and continues on his leftover adventure for dinner. Thirty-seven weeks in total on the bestseller list, and he barely makes enough to scrape by. Hopefully, this latest manuscript which brings his popular series to its finale, will be the push he needs to catapult him into financial freedom. He pauses in his meal and takes a sip of his drink. *Of course, it's not solely about the money*, he tells himself. He loves to write. He loves to see how much joy his creations bring to his readers, both new and old alike. But for him to enjoy more than just cold, leftover Chinese food for dinner? Well, it has to be about the money a little bit.

The approaching storm makes its presence known again, and Arden finishes up his meal, tossing the fork in the dishwasher and the empty container into the trash. He picks up his glass of bourbon, sets his cellphone down on the counter of the breakfast bar, walks over to his living room window, and looks outside. The dark is all-encompassing, due to the cloud cover, and there are no streetlights to penetrate the black beyond the window.

His house is located at the end of a long, private drive, with his nearest neighbor at least a mile or so away. The sky lights up once more, pushing away the dark and bringing the outside back from the void. For a brief moment, he can see his Wrangler parked in the front of the house where he always parks it, and the trees that line the driveway are all still where they were this afternoon. The Jeep is a necessity, since his luxurious long private drive is not paved, but instead dirt with ruts that have formed over the years of use.

Arden likes the solitude, though. No sounds of the city or the suburbs to distract him from his writing. No unexpected neighbors knocking on the door or helicopters flying overhead. He even appreciates the driveway, as it keeps most people from trying to visit him as their vehicles are unable to make it the entire way. His agent, Saphina, has even offered to pay to have the road paved out of her own pocket, so she doesn't have to park her Mercedes at the end of the drive and walk to his house every time she comes to visit. Of course, Arden has the business card of a local tow truck company taped to the side of his refrigerator for the times when the daring few try to drive too far down the road and find themselves stuck.

He smiles, still staring into the black void outside, and takes another sip of his bourbon.

There is a certain satisfaction of watching Saphina wobble back and forth down the dirt road in her ridiculously high heels and unnecessarily tight pencil skirts. Maybe it's just because he likes to cause her a little frustration in return for the frustration she causes him with deadlines and events. Arden has a good working relationship with her, though, even if he mildly dislikes her as a person. She's all about appearances and displays a sense of entitlement that he never really understood, but she was also the only agent willing to take a chance on him years ago when he had just finished his debut novel and was at his wit's end from the nonstop stream of rejections.

A fledgling novelist, his first foray into the literary world was a tale about a monster that would terrorize its victims and feed off their fear before it would ultimately kill them. An overplayed concept, sure, but Arden found more pleasure in writing about how the monster created the fear in its victims and how his characters handled that fear, how they reacted to that fear. How that fear may have, in part, been the cause of their demise. It was this same aspect of his writing that Saphina found promising and the reason why she signed him on. *Your writing is very cerebral, and I think readers will love it*, he remembers her telling him at their first meeting.

Little did either of them know just how popular the first novel would become. That its popularity would then lead to another four novels about the monster and its fear-inducing journey through so many different characters' lives. And now this sixth novel, the final novel, of the series. The novel that finally provides the readers with a protagonist to counter the monster's reign of terror. A protagonist worth cheering for. One that might be, in some small way, modeled after Arden himself, the hero Arden can only be through his writing. But then, all writers put pieces and parts of themselves into their writing, whether it is through their characters or through the soul of their writing.

He wonders what Saphina will think of how he ended the series. *Will she appreciate how the hero finally vanquishes the monster? Will she agree that this hero offers something that none of the other characters ever did?* She was the one who pushed him to continue writing about the monster after his debut novel took off. The one who pushed him with deadlines and expectations, causing him to spend day after day expanding upon this horrific character that only exists for fear. For death.

He wonders what his readers will think. *Will they be happy with the outcome? Will they like the new characters? Will they feel the same satisfaction and closure that I did when I wrote the last sentence?*

Another smile crosses his face and interrupts his thoughts. He should give Saphina a call and let her know he just finished the manuscript. Ahead of schedule, at that. *Who doesn't want a phone call at almost midnight on a Tuesday?* he contemplates, chuckling a bit at the thought of waking her up just to tell her the manuscript is completed.

Still smiling, another thought enters into his mind. *What about me? Will I be able to move on with my writing after all this time, or is this it? Will my readers be interested in anything else from me beyond what they know me for?*

The outside world is lit up once again by the angry sky, and Arden feels the sense of unease return. He turns from the window and tries to shake the feeling away.

He wonders where the feeling is coming from. An unexpected feeling of dread, as though something is off. As though something is about to happen. *Maybe this is how you are supposed to feel when you bring a large chapter of your life to a close?* He wonders. He would have expected more feelings of relief and elation instead of this strange discomfort.

He takes another sip of his bourbon and heads to the living room couch, sitting down and allowing himself to sink into the plush brown cushions. Grabbing the remote from the coffee table, he leans back and kicks his legs up in front of him, resting them in the same location the remote was previously occupying. He turns on the television and changes the channel to the weather channel. A pleasant, heavyset man in a blue suit is pointing at the various days in the five-day forecast and talking about how the weather will be ideal after the storm blows through. The map switches to the radar, and a good portion of the area where Arden lives is covered in various shades of red, yellow, and green. The red and yellow areas of the radar, which signify the more extreme conditions of the storm, are slowly approaching where he lives. As if on cue, the sky flashes from the window behind him once again. The weatherman talks of power outages and for residents to stay inside as there is a high volume of lightning strikes within the red section of the radar.

Arden figures he has about forty minutes or so before the bulk of the storm is upon him. He looks around and wonders if he should turn everything off and unplug everything. His house is older and has had electrical problems previously. When he first moved in, he blew out half the breakers and started a small fire the first time he used his microwave. That was an adventure he would be sure never to forget as he watched the electrical socket the microwave was plugged into burst into flame ten seconds into heating up his microwaveable meal. It took an electrician the better part of three days to dig out the old, frayed wiring from most of the house and replace it with wiring that met current code guidelines. Arden still has the electrician's business card stuck on the side of the fridge, right next to the tow truck company's card, since the gentleman did tell him he wasn't able to fix all the bad wiring and that Arden may have issues again in the future and to be careful.

Not feeling like getting up from the couch just yet, he continues to watch the weather channel talk about the approaching storm. Talk about how many power outages there already are and the wind damage that has occurred in nearby towns. Minutes slowly pass, and soon his eyes begin to get heavy. The voice from the television begins to blend in with the sound and rumble from the thunder, and soon his eyes close as he drifts into his dreams.

*

A loud, explosive boom abruptly rips Arden from his sleep on the couch. His heart now racing, he quickly sits upright and looks around. The house is completely dark, and the hair on his arms is standing straight up. The air feels as though it is electrically charged, and he can smell the distinctly sharp odor of ozone. The wind outside the house is howling, and with each powerful gust, the walls of the house groan in resistance.

Not sure if he turned everything off before he passed out or if the storm knocked out the power, Arden reaches over to the table lamp and flips the switch.

There is no response from the table lamp. *Power must be out,* he surmises; *at least, I hope it's just the power and not some shitty wiring on fire again.*

Just at that moment, a second loud, explosive boom makes the house shudder, and Arden practically jumps off the couch, a metallic taste suddenly filling his mouth. The electricity in the air is almost palpable now. *Did lightning just strike the house?* He asks himself.

Once more, a heavy gust of wind howls like a freight train, and the old house groans again, as if in pain while it struggles to stay upright against the storm's relentless assault. A loud succession of cracking noises from somewhere outside echoes through the surrounding trees.

A third loud, explosive boom reverberates throughout the house. Out of the corner of his eye, Arden can see blue tendrils of electricity shoot out of the wall outlet near the door to his writing room. A sudden moment of panic and fear races through him as a new thought comes to mind: *Did I unplug my laptop from the wall?*

A fourth loud, explosive boom fills his house, and several of the lightbulbs in the overhead ceiling fan begin to glow, getting brighter and brighter until they explode, raining small shards of glass down on and around Arden. His eyes are beginning to burn from the built-up energy in the air, and his ears are ringing. He can no longer hear the wind outside or the house's complaints from the storm's onslaught. He can feel the electricity in the air in his lungs with each breath he takes, and he can taste the current across his tongue, which now feels as though it is completely dry.

Two more loud, explosive booms, almost back-to-back, rock the house to its core. Arden can feel the built-up energy inside the house racing across every inch of his skin. Afraid to move from the couch for fear of being electrocuted, he waits and hopes that whatever is happening will quickly pass. The burning sensation in his eyes has caused his vision to go blurry. He tries to blink his living room back into focus, but every move of his eyelids feels like sandpaper across his eyes.

For a moment, through his blurry vision, it almost looks like the wall outlets are beginning to glow a light blue when another loud, explosive boom adds to the massive amount of built-up energy within the walls of his home. Arden's skin starts to feel like it's on fire. A jumbled cascade of thoughts race through his mind, the worry about his laptop forgotten. *How many times can lightning strike the same spot? Is this how it feels to be electrocuted to death? Am I going to die?*

Arden struggles to breathe; it's as though his lungs are unable to pull any oxygen out of the air, which now feels as if it has been replaced by pure energy. The pale blue light he thought was coming from the wall outlets is now coming from inside his writing room. As the blue light coming from the room gets brighter and brighter, Arden's vision gets darker and darker until he doesn't feel the fiery current ravaging through his body anymore, and he slumps over on the couch, unconscious.

The ringing of his cellphone pierces through the darkness Arden is floating in, and he slowly opens his eyes. His living room gradually comes into view, albeit sideways. He blinks several times in an effort to get rid of the gummy feeling caked across his eyes. He sits up straight on the couch, and sharp pain in his lower back lets him know he must have been slumped over for quite a few hours. The living room is bathed in daylight, with the sun beaming in through the windows. As his phone falls silent, indicating it sent the caller to his voicemail, he can hear birds chirping outside.

He looks around, afraid to see how much damage was caused by what happened during the storm. Small shards of glass from the overhead light bulbs are scattered all over the coffee table, couch, and surrounding floor. He doesn't see any other immediate damage from where he is sitting. A quick glance at the clock on the wall tells him that it's ten in the morning. He stands up, every muscle in his body sore and aching, as though he spent several hours doing an extreme full-body workout yesterday. A few pieces of glass fall off his clothes and onto the floor. He looks over at the wall socket and the doorway to his writing room, trying to remember if he really saw a blue light emanating from there or if it was merely a hallucination. *What the hell happened last night? How many times did the house get hit by lightning? Was that even lightning?* These questions dance through his thoughts while he looks around and decides he better get this glass cleaned up before he embeds one of the random shards in the bottom of his feet.

Watching where he steps, Arden maneuvers out of the living room and into the kitchen, grabbing the broom and dustpan from the pantry where it is stored. He pauses on his way back to the living room, grabs his cellphone from the counter, and checks to see who called. Ben, his closest neighbor who lives about a mile down the main road from the turnoff for his driveway. *Must have heard all the noise last night*, he thinks. He makes a mental note to call Ben back once he is done cleaning up the house and surveying the rest of the property. He is pretty sure he heard a tree falling over last night at some point, but with luck, it didn't fall across the driveway. He heads back into the living room and carefully sweeps up as much of the glass as he can find, then gingerly removes the bases of the broken bulbs from the overhead light, taking care not to slice his fingers open on the jagged edges. He digs through the cushions of the couch and collects any remaining shards he can find before he surveys the area and determines it is all cleaned up. After emptying the dustpan into the trash and putting the broom away, he grabs some spare light bulbs from under the sink and heads back into the living room, replacing all the missing bulbs. Satisfied, Arden takes a moment and looks out the front window. Branches are scattered all over the driveway, with a couple of them even resting on top of his Jeep. A runaway lawn chair is lying on its side about eighty feet away on the left side of the parking area. He doesn't see anything blocking the driveway, but he will need to either drive or walk the length of the road to be sure. "A job for later today," he says to the empty house.

He glances over towards his writing room and hesitates. He hopes that he merely imagined the strange blue light during the storm and that nothing has happened to his laptop and the manuscript contained within. Arden tries to think about the last time he backed up the work in progress on his thumb drive. Normally he would do it at the end of every chapter, however he was so engrossed in crafting the last couple of chapters last night that he can't remember if he did that simple step or not. *Chapter 14? Maybe Chapter 15? Did I back it up after the final chapter at all before I closed the laptop last night?*

Arden sighs and figures it's better to know sooner than later, especially if it means he has to recraft and recreate the final chapters. Before he heads into his writing room and finds out what might be waiting for him beyond that doorway, he grabs the remote from the couch and attempts to turn on the television. As he expects, there is no response, which hopefully just means the power is still out and not that every electrical circuit in his house is fried to a crisp.

He takes a few steps towards the doorway to where almost all his novels were created, and the troubling feeling of unease from last night sets in again. He pauses and takes a deep breath, suddenly afraid of what he might find waiting for him.

Arden laughs and shakes his head. "Arden, buddy, you are not a character in one of your novels. There is nothing in there to be afraid of. Man up!" he tells himself. Smiling, he proceeds across the living room and towards his study.

With his hands slightly shaking in contrast to his smile of false bravado, and almost convinced everything in the room is somehow burned to a crisp, he steps through the doorway and immediately exhales a deep sigh of relief. The room looks completely normal and exactly as it was when he left it last night. He glances over at the decanter and wonders if it's too early for a drink. One to celebrate the room looking normal or maybe just to steady his nerves a bit.

Still smiling, he walks over and sits down in his office chair, rotating the chair towards the desk and reaching out with his right hand to open his laptop. As his fingertips touch the top of the laptop, a sharp jolt of electricity erupts from its surface and races through his fingers and up his arm. He jerks his arm back and grabs his right hand with his left hand.

"What the actual fuck?" he loudly exclaims as he rubs the fingers of his right hand that made contact with the computer in front of him. A barely visible arc of blue light races across the surface of the laptop and then disappears at the spot where the power cord is plugged in.

Shit. I did leave it plugged in. And the lightning must have fried it.

Arden's brow furrows, and he wonders if computers can hold a residual charge, like a static electricity buildup when you scoot your sock-covered feet across a carpet and then touch something. He waits a few moments to see if there are any other visible signs that the laptop might shock him again. He wonders if he should get an oven mitt and then touch it.

He starts to stand up out of the chair to go get one of the mitts stored in the kitchen and then abruptly stops. *It's not a hot sheet pan coming out of the oven, dumbass. The oven mitt isn't going to help.* He promptly sits back down.

He takes a deep breath. He is going to have to touch it again anyways, so may as well do it now, shock or no shock. Arden reaches his right hand out again, fingers still slightly tingling from the initial shock, and pauses his hand about four inches from the surface of the laptop. In one swift movement, he quickly taps the top of the computer with just his index finger and quickly jerks his arm back.

Nothing. No shock this time. He sits there for a moment and stares at the laptop, almost expecting it to start talking or reach out to him with blue-colored plasma tendrils and grab him so it can drag him into some terrifying electrical world.

"Fuck, Arden, it's just a laptop. You need to give the imagination a rest sometimes," he tells himself.

He reaches out again for the laptop and grabs the top, involuntarily wincing just in case of another shock. The computer remains just a computer. He opens the lid and hits the power button, hoping for the best.

To his surprise, the laptop boots up as it normally does with no issues. He smiles. *Must have just been a static discharge, after all*, he surmises. After the computer is fully booted up, he opens up the manuscript, hoping that when it loads, he will be staring at the final page of the final chapter, just as he left it.

The manuscript loads, but what is displayed on the screen is not what Arden is hoping it would be.

A blank page greets him, the cursor line steadily blinking on the top of the page, waiting for input. Frowning, he flips back a few pages. Nothing. No words. He flips back even more pages—all blank. No chapters. Nothing. The only page with anything written on it, out of over three hundred pages, is the title page. Arden sits back and stares at the blank manuscript a moment.

"Well, that's fucking strange, isn't it?"

His only response is the quiet inside the house. He leans forward again and tries a document recovery. No luck. He tries loading from the last save. Still nothing but blank pages beyond the title page. Frustrated, Arden reaches over and opens the desk drawer to his right, pulling out a small thumb drive that he uses to back up his work. He puts the thumb drive in the USB port of the computer and opens the manuscript folder once the small storage drive boots up. The manuscript on the thumb drive opens and displayed in front of him is the beginning of Chapter 14.

Shit. So much for calling Saphina and letting her know I am done with the manuscript today.

Arden copies the file on the thumb drive to his desktop, overwriting the now blank file with the backup. He pulls the thumb drive out of the computer and returns it to its location in his desk drawer. "Well, at least the computer isn't fried, right?" he asks the silent room, trying to find the positive in the situation. It will take him a bit to retrace his steps and rewrite the last three chapters, a task he doesn't feel like starting just yet. In addition, without the power on in the house, the battery will only last a few hours before it dies. He closes the laptop and stands up, making sure to unplug the power cord this time. He walks over to the small table under the window and grabs one of the lowball glasses. He pours himself a small drink from the decanter and takes a sip, looking out the window. The sky is clear, with no indication of the violent storm from last night. He finishes the remaining amber-colored liquid in the glass and sets it back down on the table. He might as well go get dressed and head outside to clean up, then walk the driveway to ensure there are no trees blocking the road.

He turns and exits the study, heading through the living room and into the kitchen, checking his cellphone on the way. Ten percent left on the battery. That will teach him to make sure he plugs the phone in to charge on occasion; since most of the time, the phone dies while he is working because he never remembers to charge it. Arden sets the phone back down on the counter. "Sorry, Ben, can't waste the last of the juice on a phone call with you, so you are going to have to wait."

He smiles. Ben, although nice, likes to talk Arden's ear off when he is on the phone. One call to Ben would easily kill the rest of the power on the phone, and Arden may need that to call a tree removal service or even possibly the electrician again.

Arden nods to himself.

Time to head outside and see what else he may need to fix.

Chapter 2

Arden takes off his safety glasses and wipes the sweat from his brow with the right sleeve of his shirt. He grabs the jug of water sitting in the back his Jeep and takes several swigs from the container before he sets it back down. Putting the safety glasses back on, he bends down and picks up the chainsaw from the ground and starts it back up, intent on finishing the job of cutting up the tree currently blocking his driveway.

The damage outside was not as bad as Arden expected. After coming to the conclusion that the house, for some reason or another, was hit last night by a freakishly high number of lightning strikes, he expected to see all sorts of damage to the shingles on the roof from each of the strikes. Once he was on the roof, he saw that instead of multiple areas of damage, there was only one spot that was damaged.

A large, circular section of badly burned shingles and

charred plywood, about two feet in diameter, located directly above his study.

Arden wasn't sure what the odds were of lightning striking the same spot multiple times, but he is pretty sure his house set a Guinness World Record last night. After making a mental note that he might need to replace the plywood and definitely all the shingles around it, and checking to make sure there were no immediate major leaks, he cleaned up all the branches on the roof, as well as all the branches scattered around his house and yard. With all the debris now piled in a large pile in the fire pit in his backyard, to be burned at a later time, he put back the errant chairs and rehung his wind chime on the back porch.

The real work presented itself after he had walked the length of his driveway. Not one but two trees had fallen over. The first was about halfway down the driveway: a large oak tree, which meant Arden would have to spend some time cutting it up just to clear the road, although he would be able to salvage most of the wood for firewood. The second tree was at the end of the driveway, and he wasn't about to go near this one. This tree, which had had its branches cut off a long time ago—before it was installed—did have several power lines attached to it, as it was the electrical power pole that split the main line from the road and provided the power down to his house.

That one will be the electric company's problem, and seeing it gave Arden comfort at the thought that it was the power lines going down that caused his power outage and not a massive circuit failure in the house that might cost him thousands of dollars to fix.

It was also probably the reason Ben had called him earlier this morning, since that specific pole also provided power for Ben's house and beyond, further down the main road.

At least Arden isn't alone in his powerless misery.

The chainsaw catches a knot and jerks Arden back to the present and out of his thoughts. He backs the blade up a small amount and changes the angle, finishing the cut through one of the last sections of the tree he needs to clear out. The tree was a good size, and he will have firewood for quite some time once he is done. He finishes the last few cuts and turns the chainsaw off, setting it next to the water jug in the back of the Wrangler. He takes off the safety glasses and tosses them next to the chainsaw. Leaning against the back of his vehicle and admiring his handiwork, he thinks it will take several trips with the Jeep to get all the wood back to the house. Arden expects he should be done within an hour or so, just in time for a late afternoon lunch. The protein bar he ate for breakfast was good, but not a substitute for real food. He momentarily wonders how long it might take the power company to get the power back on, and if the fridge will stay cold for that long, provided he doesn't open it up very much.

He reaches over and grabs the jug of water, taking another drink. "Looks like dinner tonight will be cooked over a fire," he announces to the surrounding trees and any potential wildlife within range of his voice. He smiles. "That's the one drawback to a solitary life, ladies and gentlemen. You end up talking just for the sake of talking."

Setting the jug back down, he moves the chainsaw to the far right side of the back of the Jeep. With the back seat flipped up, he should be able to load a good amount of wood for his first trip. He sets himself to loading the logs into the back of the vehicle until he is unable to fit anymore. He closes the rear tailgate and then the spare tire rack. To ensure he is able to move the maximum amount of wood per trip, he even puts a couple of logs on the front passenger floorboard and in the passenger seat.

As he stacks the second log on the passenger seat, he grabs the seatbelt and buckles the two logs in. "Always wear your seatbelt!" he tells the two logs, chuckling at his own humor as he walks around the front of the vehicle to the driver's seat.

Three trips later and Arden has moved all the cut-up wood from his driveway to his backyard, where he neatly stacks all the logs along the back of the house so they can be chopped into firewood later. He takes a quick shower, using the last of the hot water in the water tank; he's not looking forward to his next shower, which will be ice cold if the power still isn't back on. After getting dressed, he heads into the kitchen and looks at what he has available in the pantry to eat.

His pantry inventory consists of six cans of chicken noodle soup, a can of tomato paste, a jar of peanut butter, three flavored tuna packets, two protein bars, a large container of whey protein powder, a box of turkey stuffing, a box of devil's food cake mix, a box of pasta shells of an unknown age, and two boxes of tuna helper. Arden sighs and makes note that the next time he is in town, it might be a good idea to actually buy some food. He grabs one of the cans of chicken noodle soup and checks the date on the bottom to ensure it has not expired. Content the soup won't kill him if he eats it, he sets the can on the counter next to him and retrieves one of the cooking pots from the cabinets below.

For a brief moment, he considers eating what remains of the takeout Chinese food from yesterday afternoon, but decides that might be a gamble with his stomach he's not willing to take since the power has been out for so long.

He grabs the can opener and a spoon from the silverware drawer and puts them in his back pocket. He puts the can of soup in the pot, and after putting on his shoes, he grabs the pot and heads out of the kitchen and through the door in the dining room, which leads to his backyard. His kitchen and dining room are both the same room, an open-air design that was popular when the house was built. A breakfast bar and a short wall are the only things that separate the kitchen from the living room. At the back of the dining room, near the pantry, is a wooden door with a window that leads to the back porch.

Arden's back porch is one of the nicer features of the house and easily one of his favorite places, besides his writing room. The porch runs along most of the back of the house and has a roof over its entire length. He had the whole thing screened in a few months after he moved in to help stave off the furious blitzkrieg of hungry mosquitos in the summer evenings. He has spent many rainy nights and clear sunsets sitting out here, a small glass of bourbon in hand, either listening to the rain as it plays its song upon the roof and ground or just watching the setting sun paint its bright evening colors across the sky and through the canopy of the trees behind his house. About thirty feet from the back porch is a large fire pit that he built for debris disposal, as well as for cool autumn nights where sitting around a fire outside just feels right. Cinder blocks ring the outside of the pit to contain the wood and ash, and Arden used the excess blocks to create some seats around the pit as well, each makeshift chair about three feet away from the ring of the fire pit.

It is on one of these cinderblock seats that he sets the pot down, with the unopened can of soup still resting inside it. The debris from last night's storm is stacked a couple of feet higher than the top of the cinder block ring. Arden hopes the sun and heat today were able to dry out the wood as much as possible so it won't be too difficult to light on fire.

He turns and heads back into the screened porch to retrieve a lighter and some newspapers he normally keeps on hand to get a fire going. Once back at the fire pit, Arden crumples up several of the newspapers and stuffs them deep into the center of the debris pile. He maneuvers the lighter to the newspapers, and after setting them on fire, he pulls his hand back. He watches as the flames grow, eating through the crumpled paper and growing in size. Stepping back as the heat intensifies, he hopes the branches will catch. If not, he may have to assist the fire by tossing some of the spare gasoline that he has stored away near his tool chest on the back porch onto the pile.

The fire catches, though, no gasoline needed, and soon the flames are leaping several feet above the fire pit, and the debris pile has substantially decreased. After locating and tossing a couple of dry logs from his log pile on the back porch onto the fire, he returns his attention to the pot and soup still on the cinderblock seat. Using the can opener from his back pocket, he removes the lid from the soup and pours the contents of the can into the pot, setting the now empty can to the side. He sets the pot on the cinderblock ring and sits down on one of the other seats. The smell of the soup is making his stomach rumble. He figures it should only take about ten to fifteen minutes for the soup to warm up enough to be eaten, although he is no stranger to eating cold soup out of the can either.

While the soup is heating up next to the fire, Arden heads back inside and into the study, grabbing his glass from earlier this morning and pouring another small drink of bourbon. He exits the study and heads back out to the fire pit, glass in hand, while taking a seat on one of the cinderblock chairs after glancing into the pot to see if the soup is warm enough yet.

Evening is quickly approaching as the sun sets, and Arden will need to remember where he stored his flashlights and candles after he is done with dinner. He won't get any work done tonight rewriting the lost chapters, but he can at least write out what he remembers to help him when he does start.

He will also need to make a trip into town for some more food sometime tomorrow, provided the power pole at the end of his driveway has been cleaned up, as he's not about to drive over any downed electrical wires any time soon.

After last night, he's had about as much fun with electricity as he ever wants to for the rest of his life. Every one of his muscles is still sore, and not because of his work on the tree today. The current surging through the house from the repeated strikes must have caused him to tightly tense up every muscle the entire time it was happening. The feeling of unease from yesterday evening creeps its way back in while he thinks about what happened during the storm. The feeling that something has changed. That something has been released. He takes a deep breath and tightens his grip on the glass, his hands slightly shaking as the feeling runs through him.

Must just be my mind trying to deal with finishing the manuscript, but then realizing I am not done yet and now have to recreate the last few chapters. He shakes the feeling off as best he can and takes a sip of his bourbon. Arden hopes he can recreate the final struggle and ultimate triumph of his protagonist as well as he did before.

Once the power is back on, he will have to do some research to determine if what he experienced and felt is actually possible. He will also have to research how many times lightning can strike the same location. If anything, it might be good fodder for a future manuscript down the road.

He makes a mental note to see if there are any small

generators he can pick up tomorrow if he is able to make it into town. This way, he can at least charge his phone and his laptop, allowing him to continue to work and maintain contact with the few people he stays in touch from the outside world. Saphina will be expecting a status update soon, and with the setback from last night, Arden isn't sure if he will be able to make the deadline in time now.

A bubbling noise from the pan next to the fire pulls him from his thoughts. He stands up and takes a quick look in the pan. The soup is lightly boiling, indicating it is definitely ready to eat. He carefully grabs the handle of the pan and relocates it to one of the cinderblock chairs, giving it some time to cool down before he digs in.

While Arden enjoys his elegant dinner of canned chicken noodle soup by the fire, the sun starts its journey below the horizon, using the sky as its canvas to paint vibrant shades of red and pink as it says goodnight.

*

"Mr. Carleigh, your vehicle will be here at eight a.m. sharp as you requested, and the jet will be ready for departure as soon as you reach the airport. Will you need anything else this evening, sir?"

Erick waves his hand dismissively towards his assistant. "No, that will be all." He glances down at the watch on his wrist—nine in the evening.

He continues to look out the large picture window of his penthouse room and waits until he hears the door behind him open and then close, announcing that his assistant has left. He looks out across the rooftops and lights of the city spread out below him and smiles. *My city*, he thinks.

He turns from the skyline view and walks over to the bar, checking to make sure the hotel provided the bottle of scotch he requested. As he expected, a bottle of Macallan M Single Malt is sitting on the bar counter, a small handwritten note card next to the bottle. *Compliments of the house.*

Erick opens and uncorks the unique crystal decanter which holds the scotch and pours himself a glass of the dark amber liquid. He swirls the scotch around in the glass and turns from the bar, walking back over to the picture window and opening the glass door, which leads out to the balcony. He steps through the door frame and walks over to the railing, leaning on the wrought iron bar and looking out over the city. It took Erick a long time to get to where he is now. Years of hard work, backroom business deals, and strategic elimination of his competition. But now here he is, CEO of one of the biggest pharmaceutical companies in the world. He has more money than he will ever know what to do with and continues to make more every single second.

Life is good, he thinks. He takes a sip of the six-thousand-dollar scotch and listens to the sounds of the evening city below him—the sounds of the rats scurrying around with their daily lives, only surviving because of the drugs his company provides and only existing to flow their wages all the way up the ladder to his satin-lined pockets. He takes a deep breath and allows the crisp air fill his lungs. *The air tastes better when you are at the top, doesn't it?* He asks himself, smiling.

As he takes another sip of his scotch, a heavy pounding comes from the direction of the door to his suite. A slow but heavy strike that seems to echo throughout the room before falling back into silence. Erick pushes himself off the railing and turns towards the room, a furrow forming in his brow. There isn't anyone in this world that should be banging on his door like that. Not anyone who wants to continue living, that is. He waits a moment to see if they do it again. The room remains silent. He shakes his head, irritated, and turns back towards his view of the city, taking another sip of his drink.

The pounding from the front door echoes through his room once again. He looks down at his watch. Ten at night. He wonders what moron in the hotel doesn't understand what "do not disturb" means.

Erick turns once more from his view and walks into his suite, closing the sliding glass door of the balcony behind him. "Whoever you are, you will be fired for disturbing me once I open that door."

He reaches the entrance to his suite and transfers his scotch from his right hand to his left hand so he can grab the doorknob. He can feel his anger building that someone has the nerve to bother him, especially in this sort of manner. Not bothering to look through the peephole, he turns the knob and pulls the door open.

What he sees in the small hallway puzzles him.

The entryway is empty. The elevator doors are closed. The indicator for the elevator tells him the elevator is on the ground floor, fifty-two floors below him.

Erick closes the door to his suite and steps back. The only way to access his floor is by keycard, as there are no other rooms on the top level beyond his. He turns, wondering if he merely imagined the noise, and heads back towards the balcony. Before he can reach the glass door which leads outside, the heavy pounding on the suite door resumes and then stops again.

Erick takes a deep breath and finishes the remaining scotch in his glass before he turns back towards where he just came from.

"If you think this is funny, you better enjoy your last few laughs," he announces to the quiet room and to whoever is on the other side of the door.

The only response is the heavy pounding once more. Slow. Deliberate. As though the person on the other side of the door was purposely mocking him. Purposely trying to piss him off.

"That's enough!" he says forcefully, as he storms across the room towards the suite door, setting his empty glass on the bar counter as he passes it. He reaches the door and grabs the handle, ripping the door open, ready to confront whoever has the balls to think they can disrespect him like this.

The entryway is again empty. The elevator doors are still closed. The indicator on the elevator shows that it is still on the ground floor.

Erick steps from his room into the entryway, confused.

There is no way whoever is hammering on his door could have made it to the elevator and then down to the ground floor in the time it took him to walk to the door and open it.

He returns to his suite and walks over to the telephone next to the bar, slamming his room door in frustration behind him as he goes. He grabs the phone and calls down to the receptionist. A cheery voice on the other end of the line greets him. "Yes, Mr. Carleigh, how may I help you?"

"There has been someone pounding on my door. I need to know who has accessed my elevator, and I need to know now. Then, I need them fired immediately."

Erick waits while the person on the other end of the line registers what he just said and then responds. "Mr. Carleigh, I am so sorry to hear that someone has bothered you. Our records indicate that your assistant was the last person to utilize the elevator. Their keycard was swiped at nine o'clock, and they took the elevator down to the fifteenth floor, where their room is located. The elevator then returned to the ground floor level and has been on the ground floor level since then. Do you want us to send someone up to your room or notify your assistant for you?"

He waits a moment before responding, an unsettling fear beginning to set in. *Who is banging on my door if the elevator has not been used?* He pushes the thought from his mind.

"Is there any way your system is wrong and someone could have used the elevator?" he asks.

He hears the receptionist typing on their keyboard in the

background. "No, sir, the system is accurate. The elevator has not moved since it returned to the ground floor an hour ago. Is everything ok, Mr. Carleigh?"

"Yes, everything is fine. Thank you."

Erick hangs up the phone, not waiting for a response. He looks over at the suite door and wonders if he is imagining it all when another idea surfaces. He walks the length of the bar and over to the bottle of scotch sitting on the counter. He picks up the cork and inspects it for any indication that someone may have used a needle to inject a hallucinogen into the bottle in an attempt to drug him, a trick he used himself several years back to take care of a rival. The cork shows no indication of any tampering.

As he sets the cork back down on the table, the slow and steady pounding on the suite door fills the room again. Three heavy raps on the door, and the room returns to silence.

Erick takes a couple of steps back from the bar and away from the direction of the pounding, staring at the stark white door with the gold-plated door handle. He can feel his pulse racing and his anger quickly turning to fear.

"This isn't funny anymore, and the police are on their way."

He hopes the forced bravado in his voice will deter whoever is at the door, so they just leave. He turns and quickly crosses the floor of the main room and into the bedroom, where his briefcase is resting on the bed. He hurriedly unlocks the briefcase and opens it up, revealing its contents. From one of the pockets, he retrieves a small handgun and checks to ensure it's loaded. Closing the briefcase, Erick walks back into the main room of his suite, his right hand by his side and tightly holding onto the gun. The pounding on the door reaches his ears once again.

"Listen here motherfucker. I have a gun. I will fucking kill you! Do you have any idea who I am? How powerful am I? I could kill you on stage in the middle of Times Square on New Year's Eve and get away with it!"

Erick's right hand begins to shake a little as he approaches the front door. Once he reaches it, he pauses before he grabs the gold-plated handle and instead looks through the peephole.

The view beyond his door through the small peephole increases the feeling of fear that has been taking over. His eyes try to make sense of what they are seeing. Instead of being brightly lit up, the entryway is now dim, covered in shadows, as though the lights are being suffocated by darkness. Near the elevator doors, Erick can vaguely make out a shape shifting back and forth in the darkness.

He pulls his head away from the door and steps back. *Why are the lights like that?* He wonders.

He steps back a few more steps, and the steady, rhythmic pounding on the door resumes. One thump. Two thumps. Three thumps.

Erick turns from the door and heads right to the room's phone, grabbing the headset with his left hand and setting his gun down on the bar so he can dial the lobby. The line rings repeatedly, but this time, no one answers. He hangs up the phone and tries the receptionist again.

The line rings once more with no response.

As Erick is hanging up the phone and getting ready to dial his assistant's room, the heavy pounding echoes through the room once more, and this time, after the third thump, the suite door slowly begins to open. Erick drops the headset of the phone and grabs the gun from the bar counter, stumbling back several steps away from the door, which is still slowly opening.

Fear has taken over every ounce of his being. Erick aims the gun towards the hallway and tries to regain his composure.

"I will fucking shoot you!" he yells towards the door and the dark entryway beyond.

Erick stares at the hallway until the door has opened all the way, allowing him to finally see his tormentor. The dark outline of a figure is standing in the doorway, its features concealed by darkness even though the lights in the penthouse are still on and are fighting to cascade light around his unwelcome guest and push the growing shadows away. Two red eyes are the only things he can distinguish on the figure's face. It's in these eyes that Erick can feel his fear take over. An irrational fear that scrambles his thoughts and instantly saps away any bravado he may have left.

He continues to stumble backward, away from the person in front of him that his mind can't seem to comprehend. A raspy, guttural voice reaches his ears.

"Erick."

Still moving backward, the gun in his hand almost forgotten, his left leg suddenly hits the coffee table, and he falls back over the table and onto the floor. As he tries to put his hands behind him to stop his fall, he lets go of the gun, allowing the weapon to sail away from his right hand and through the air, landing on the floor somewhere to his right.

The lights in the penthouse begin to dim, as though the shadows from the figure in front of him are expanding and overpowering the bright white bulbs above.

Erick scrambles backward along the floor, away from the individual approaching him until his back hits the glass of the door to the balcony. The figure continues to move towards him, still shrouded in darkness, the red eyes focused intently on Erick.

He opens his mouth to speak, but his fear chokes him, and he is unable to say anything. Every cell in his body is screaming for him to run. For him to escape. He scrambles to his feet and yanks open the glass door to the balcony, racing out the door and to the metal railing. He looks over the railing to see if he is able to climb down to any of the rooms below him so he can get away.

The only thing below his balcony is a long fall to the ground below.

Erick turns around, his heart racing, his back against the metal railing. His guest, now in the middle of the main room of the suite, continues to move forward. Erick briefly leaves his position on the balcony so he can slam the sliding glass door closed and then quickly returns to the spot against the railing.

He watches as the unknown individual continues to approach him. As their red eyes reach the glass door, an arm shrouded in darkness reaches out and wraps its fingers around the handle. Long fingers that end with sharp claws. His uninvited guest slowly slides the door open and what appear to be tendrils of darkness from around the figure begin to move across the balcony floor and through the air, now only a couple of feet away from him.

Run Erick, now! he tells himself, trying to force himself into action. His mind, still unable to make sense of what he is seeing, refuses to will his legs to move. He remains frozen in place against the metal railing of the balcony.

Erick watches as it gets closer, the expanding darkness around it slowly beginning to envelop him and start to dull the lights of the city he can see in his peripheral vision. The red eyes continue to move closer until they are only a couple of feet away.

The pounding of his heart is the only sound he can hear now. The sounds of the city below him have melted away, just as the lights seemed to have done.

Erick wants to scream for help. To beg for mercy. To know what this person wants and who they are. To know why they are after him.

The voice reaches his ears once again; at the same time, the figure reaches out with its clawed hands and places them on his chest.

"Because you are the first."

As he is falling, with the cool evening air whipping around him and the occasional lighted balcony zipping past, Erick tries to remember what the two arms of his assailant looked like as they reached out from the dark shape standing in front of him and pushed him backward over the railing. He wonders if this is all a dream and his scotch was a lot stronger than he expected it to be. He wonders if he really was drugged, and this is all part of the hallucination.

Once he hits the ground, Erick doesn't wonder anymore. Or ever again.

Chapter 3

RESTART

Arden opens his eyes and looks at the ceiling of his bedroom. He yawns and stretches his legs out underneath the covers, waking up his still sleepy muscles. Out of habit, he looks over to his left at the clock on the table to see what time it is. To his surprise, the clock is flashing two in the morning at him.

The power must have come on a couple hours ago, he surmises. He throws the covers back and gets out of bed, stretching once again after his feet hit the carpeted floor. Daylight is coming in through the window in his bedroom, so clearly it isn't two a.m. He stumbles out of his bedroom and into the living room, and looks at the clock on the wall—nine in the morning.

He must have needed the sleep, as he didn't stay up too much longer after he finished his dinner last night and washed the dishes. Normally he's up well before this time in the morning.

Grabbing the remote, he turns on the television. The screen

powers on, and soon the weatherman's voice fills Arden's living room, reporting about the widespread damage from the storm the other night. He briefly watches the television for a moment before heading into the kitchen to plug in his cellphone, which died sometime yesterday. He will have to call Saphina today and let her know about the setback. He will also have to head into town in a bit and get some groceries, as well as replace anything that might have spoiled in the fridge.

Arden takes a deep breath and pauses in his thoughts of the day as his morning breath hits him. First, he needs to shower and definitely brush his teeth. Happy to see his phone is now charging, he heads through the living room and towards the bathroom, quickly stopping by his bedroom to grab some clean boxers.

One very welcome hot shower and a good sonic cleaning of his teeth later, Arden emerges from his bathroom refreshed and ready for everything he will need to do today. The news anchor on the television is talking about the power outages and which areas are still without electricity. Arden heads to his bedroom and tosses on a T-shirt and jeans, noting that he will need to do laundry soon as well.

A trip to the kitchen allows him to grab his cellphone. The phone is now charged up to sixty percent, which will be plenty of charge for the time being. He powers on the phone and waits for it to boot up. He sets the phone down while it is turning on and heads into his writing room, where he grabs the power cord to the laptop and plugs it in. May as well get the laptop charged back up as well while he is out and about today, just in case he feels like cracking it open and getting started on recreating the lost chapters later this evening. Arden momentarily contemplates having a small glass of bourbon but decides against it, and heads back into the kitchen to see if his phone has powered up yet.

Now fully up and running, his phone announces to him that he missed five calls and six text messages. Two calls from Ben, one call from Saphina, and two calls from a restricted number. And all six text messages are from Saphina. She must have heard about the storm and the damage in the area as most of her messages were asking if he was alive and ok. And of course, what the status of the manuscript is.

Arden hits the return call button and puts the phone to his ear, waiting for Saphina to pick up. A couple of rings later and her familiar voice is on the line, immediately asking him how he is doing.

"I'm fine, Saphina," he tells her, "The power is back on and besides just a bit of damage on the house from some lighting strikes, everything is almost back to normal."

He waits while she goes on her usual tirade about how he should live in the city and not in the middle of the "boonies," as she likes to call it. When she is done, she gets right to business and asks about the status of the manuscript.

"I had a setback. The storm somehow erased the last three chapters and now I have to rewrite them. My last backup was at the start of Chapter 14."

Once again, Arden waits patiently while Saphina's next rant is about how he needs to back up his manuscript every couple hours and not just when he remembers to do it. She complains he is just like her contractor who is redesigning her kitchen. Promises results but fails to deliver.

You would think she would get sick of complaining about this after the last four novels, he thinks.

He waits until she is almost at the end of her rant before he interrupts her. "Saphina, calm down, it won't take me that long to rewrite the chapters. I might be two, maybe three days behind schedule for the first edit."

This seems to calm her down a bit and leads her to her next request. She wants to see the current manuscript and where he is at with it. Arden agrees to send her a copy as soon as he is off the phone so she can review it, but makes it clear that he already has the ending planned out and isn't going to change it. After she agrees, he hangs up the phone.

Figuring Saphina can wait a few more minutes before he emails her, Arden calls Ben to see why he called yesterday. Ben picks up after the second ring.

Looks like Arden isn't the only one who had to deal with a downed tree. Ben explains how one of the large oaks next to his house came down in the storm and, in the process, crushed the front of his truck. He was hoping he could get a ride into town if Arden was able to take him so he could get some supplies. Arden agrees and lets him know that he will swing by to pick him up in just a bit, as he was about to head out the door anyways. Ben expresses his thanks, and he hangs up the phone.

Arden smiles. That might have been the shortest phone call he has ever had with Ben. Of course, the trip into town might be the longest trip he will ever have, since he knows Ben will have a million things to talk about with Arden as a captive audience.

Still smiling, he sets his phone back down on the counter and heads into the living room, grabbing the remote and turning off the television, silencing the weatherman as they talk about the next five days and how great the weather is going to be now that the storm has passed. He walks into the study and sits down in front of his laptop, grabbing the lid and opening it up. The computer powers up quickly, and soon Arden is looking at the desktop screen. He opens his email and, after checking to make sure the manuscript is still at the beginning of Chapter 14, sends a copy to Saphina.

Satisfied that should keep her busy for a few days, Arden sits back and stares a moment at the blinking cursor, currently waiting for input just under the heading for Chapter 14. He is going to have to take some time tonight or tomorrow to write down and summarize everything he can remember from the lost chapters before he starts to recreate them. He stares at the blinking cursor a few more minutes, wondering if he can will the missing words back into existence. The cursor maintains its position and merely continues to blink at him. *Guess not,* he thinks. A brief wave of the uneasy feeling he had the night he completed the manuscript washes over him, causing him to frown. Something still feels as though it's off. The hair on his arms stands up as a brief flashback to the bright blue glow emanating from his study during the lightning storm crosses his mind.

He gets up from the chair and heads back into the kitchen, taking another look in the pantry to determine what he will need to pick up to last him a few weeks. Arden also opens the fridge to see what survived while the power was out. The moment he opens the door, his remaining leftover Chinese food from a couple days ago lets him know it is not happy anymore. Or edible. He tosses the container of spoiled food in the trash, as well as a few other items which did not survive. Although he is already confident about what he will find when he checks the freezer side of the fridge, a quick glance inside reminds him that beyond his dish of reusable plastic ice cubes, it is still empty. Arden sighs. *Gotta love the bachelor life*, he tells himself.

Content that he knows what he will need to pick up while in town, he tosses on his boots sitting next to the back door. The smell from the unhappy Chinese food is beginning to take over the kitchen, so Arden grabs the plastic bag for the trash and pulls it out of the storage bin. He ties the drawstrings of the plastic bag tightly closed, and takes the bag outside to the large garbage can at the side of the house. Tossing the bag inside the almost full container, Arden reminds himself to wheel the trash can down to the end of the road tonight when he gets back so it will be ready for garbage pickup tomorrow. He does appreciate that although he lives off the beaten path, he doesn't live so far off the beaten path that he has to haul his garbage to the dump on his own. Although, he does tend to forget what day the garbage truck drives by and more often than not, he doesn't get the trash can down to the main road quick enough for them to pick it up. With the can almost at max capacity now, he needs to make sure he doesn't miss this week's pickup. *At least, I think pickup is tomorrow, right?* he asks himself. He pauses a moment by the trash can while he remembers what day it is and what day the pickup is. He's pretty sure collection is tomorrow, but figures he can confirm with Ben when he swings by to pick him up.

Arden steps away from the trash can and heads back inside the house, grabbing his phone off the counter and swinging by his bedroom to get his wallet. The sooner he gets the trip over with, the sooner he can get back to working on the manuscript, and finally close this chapter of his literary life.

Closing and locking the front door after he steps through it, Arden heads over to the driver's side of his Jeep and gets in. He starts the vehicle up and after a moment, his satellite radio finds its signal and the sound of alternative rock fills the cab. He lowers the volume a bit and puts the vehicle in first gear, easing off the clutch and slowly making his way down his driveway towards the main road. A brief and bumpy ride later, Arden is at the intersection of his driveway and the main highway. The power pole that was previously knocked over across the exit to his road has been cleaned up and a new pole now stands where the old pole used to be. The power company was pretty quick to get these repairs done, and Arden surmises that they were flooded with complaints about the power outage all the way down the line past his house. He can imagine Ben with phone in hand, calling over and over, asking when the power will be back on with each and every call.

Arden smiles at this thought and makes the left turn onto the main road, towards Ben's house. A couple miles later and he is making the left turn into the driveway. Ben's driveway, unlike his, is much shorter and nicely paved. He pulls his vehicle up behind Ben's truck and hits the horn. Ben wasn't kidding. One of the large oak trees that are scattered around the front yard is currently overturned, with a large portion of the thick tree trunk casually resting right across the front of Ben's truck. Broken branches are scattered all across the rest of the driveway beyond the truck. Ben's wife, Cassie, appears at the open door and waves at Arden. "Hey Arden, Ben will be right out," she calls over to him. Arden waves back and gives her a thumbs-up. He points at Ben's truck and grimaces. Cassie laughs and nods, shrugs her shoulders, and then disappears back into the house. A moment later, Ben appears, quickly crossing the distance between the front door and the passenger side of the Wrangler. He opens the door and hops in.

"Thanks Arden, I appreciate it. Damn storm killed my poor truck and left debris all over the place. Insurance folks said they can't get out here until tomorrow, and we were running low on supplies."

Arden smiles, and nods. "Yeah, I had a tree come down as

well across my driveway, plus lightning struck the house a few times. Made for one interesting night."

Arden laughs when he sees Ben staring at him with wide eyes. "I'm fine, Ben. It hit the house, not me. Lost a little work on my computer, that's all. Plus, I have to replace some shingles and probably the plywood underneath where the strikes hit. Might have to get an electrician out to make sure it didn't fry any of the house wiring, but so far, everything seems normal."

Ben seems satisfied with his explanation and then begins to talk about when his cousin was struck by lightning while jogging on the beach one night several summers ago. Only partially listening, as he has already heard this story a couple of times, Arden turns the vehicle around and pulls back onto the main highway, heading into town. As Ben launches into great detail about how his cousin now can't see out of his left eye and what his left arm looks like from where the bolt made impact, Arden wonders how rude it would be if he was to turn the radio up as loud as it can go for the duration of the trip.

*

After Arden drops Ben off at the hardware store, he heads on over to the supermarket, and it is here where he now faces one of life's difficult decisions. Feeling the cold on his face that is emanating from the large, glass-windowed freezers, he studies the various boxes of frozen dinners displayed in front of him and wonders what he should select. *Chicken pot pie or turkey pot pie? Maybe a couple Salisbury steaks? What about this meatloaf with mashed potatoes? All the photos on the boxes look delicious but which ones actually taste good? Which ones are the ones where the boxes they come in taste better than the food contained within?*

"Sir, finding everything ok?"

The voice coming from his right side pulls him from his thoughts, and Arden glances in the direction it came from. A young store clerk is standing near him, smiling.

"Actually, would you happen to know which one of these doesn't taste like cardboard?" Arden asks, motioning towards the variety of frozen meals in front of him.

The clerk laughs and points at the pot pies. "That brand is pretty good and they taste a lot better than most of this other stuff."

Arden smiles and thanks the clerk. He opens the large glass door and grabs several boxes of the chicken pot pies and adds them to his cart. He normally doesn't buy frozen meals but after taking stock of how little food he has at home, probably best to keep a few of these on hand in the freezer for the future. He allows the glass door to close behind him and grabs the handle of his shopping cart, proceeding down the aisle. A bag of frozen dinosaur chicken nuggets, a box of frozen hamburger patties, and two packages of bacon later, Arden finds himself standing in front of the deli meats. He grabs a variety of lunch meats for sandwiches, as well as a couple of packages of pepper jack cheese slices, and adds all of them to the growing pile of groceries in his cart. Continuing his journey through the aisles, he picks up a loaf of bread as well as a dozen eggs. Satisfied that he has gathered enough groceries to last him for a couple weeks, he heads towards the registers to check out. On his way there, his cellphone rings.

Arden brings the cart to a halt and digs his phone out of his pocket to check to see who is calling. Ben.

"What's up, Ben?" He listens as Ben tells him about this great sale on chainsaw blades. "Yeah, sounds like a good deal. I will have to check it out later." He continues to listen as Ben suggests they grab a quick bite to eat at the diner before heading back. Ben's treat, since Arden was nice enough to drive him into town. "Sure, Ben, sounds like a plan. I am about to check out, so I will meet you at the diner." He ends the call and puts the phone back in his pocket.

Arden resumes his trip towards the checkout register, but detours down the general supplies aisle first. He grabs one of the medium-sized Styrofoam coolers and adds it to his cart. He then grabs a bag of ice from the ice cooler and adds it to the cart as well. He forgot to bring one of his coolers from home and if he's grabbing food at the diner, he will need to make sure his cold groceries stay cold.

Arden gets in line and waits until it is his turn to check out. He exchanges the usual pleasantries with the cashier and heads off to where he is parked, pushing his shopping cart full of bags to its next destination. Once Arden reaches the back of his Jeep, he opens the spare tire rack and then the tailgate. He grabs the cooler and sets it down on the floor behind the rear seat. He breaks up the bag of ice by dropping it a couple times on the ground and then puts the bag in the bottom of the cooler. After filling the cooler with his perishables, he secures the lid on top and then puts the rest of the bags next to the cooler. He closes the back of the vehicle up and pushes the cart to one of the cart return stalls.

Arden turns to walk back to the vehicle and pauses. The diner is just across the street. It doesn't make any sense for him to drive over there when it would be just as easy to walk over. A few minutes later, Arden is walking up to the door of the diner and pulling it open. Most of the seats and booths are full, as it appears many of the people who live around the area decided to come into town today as well. Arden spots Ben in a back booth and maneuvers around the other customers to the booth, sitting down on the opposite side. Ben is on the phone when Arden sits down. He smiles at Arden and continues talking. "Yes honey, I did. Yes, five cans, just like you wanted. I know, sweetie. In a little bit. We are going to eat first. Yes, I can bring you some loaded fries. Sure. Ok. Yes honey, I love you too. Ok. Yes. I will. Kisses. I gotta go, love you."

Ben sets his phone down on the table and looks at Arden. "I love her, but she can drive me crazy sometimes."

Arden laughs. "Yeah, it sounded like a fun conversation. To summarize, five cans of loaded fries with love and kisses." Ben chuckles and nods. "Pretty much. Any idea on what you are going to order?"

Arden shakes his head no and grabs one of the menus at the end of the table. The fare is typical diner fare, and Arden has eaten here several times before. Not the best food in town, but the coffee is great and the wait staff is always pleasant. Their signature dish is a country fried steak sandwich with a side of fries drizzled with gravy. Arden's cholesterol levels start to rise just thinking about it. The waitress on duty makes her way over to the table and asks them what they want. Ben orders the heart attack special, complete with extra gravy on the side to drizzle all over his sandwich. Arden orders a bacon cheeseburger and a side of steak fries, hold the gravy. Both men order a cup of coffee for their drinks: black for Arden and one with cream and sugar for Ben.

The waitress heads off to put in their orders and get their coffee while the two men make small talk. Well, Ben does most of the talking. Currently, he's telling Arden about Cassie's latest hobby, painting. Which is what the five cans of paint are for. Arden tries to pay attention to the conversation as best he can while he watches the various patrons go about their day. He wonders what their stories are. What adventures they have had lately. What experiences they could captivate the world with. That's probably what Arden loves about writing the most. Creating the adventures and experiences for each of his characters. Crafting their personalities and their interactions with every situation they end up in. Maybe for his next foray into the literary world, he can write about this town and the people in it. He wonders if his readers would read something like that.

Ben's voice breaks through his thoughts. "Arden? Earth to

Arden. You still with us buddy? You sure that lightning only hit your house and not you?"

Arden looks over at Ben and laughs. "Yeah, sorry about that. I was just thinking of some ideas for future writing projects." Ben smiles and asks the usual question about how his current work is going. While Arden tells him about the setback with the lost chapters, the coffee is delivered. After he finishes telling Ben how much longer he estimates it might be before he is completed, Arden grabs his cup and takes a sip of the black nectar within while Ben adds a few more sugar packets to his. He shakes his head and smiles. Ben is one of those guys who can eat anything they want, whenever they want, and never gains a pound. On the other hand, Arden gains weight just by thinking about how many calories Ben is about to consume.

Ben notices Arden looking at him with a smile. "I know, I know, I shouldn't have so much sugar. Cassie, for about seven months, decided we were going to try a no meat, no sugar, and no carbs diet. About three months into it, I was convinced I was going to die. My mouth would water and I would get the shakes just watching people on TV eat chicken or steak. I found myself sneaking sugar packets to eat while in the bathroom. Sneaking a loaf of bread and then hiding in the barn to eat the entire thing before Cassie came looking for me." Arden laughs and takes another sip of his coffee.

"Trust me Arden, it was not fun. I don't know how anyone can live on what really was just lettuce and water. Cassie finally caught me one day in the barn while I was trying to inhale a can of spam and just laughed. Apparently, she had been sneaking food as well and showed me her stash of chocolate peanut butter cups hidden in her sewing room."

Arden chuckles and finishes his coffee, setting the cup down at the edge of the table for the waitress to refill when she comes back to check on them. Ben continues to talk about his wife's other hobbies that she forces on him and Arden drifts back into his thoughts. *Ben's adventures with his wife would make an interesting story*, he thinks, *Maybe I can incorporate that into my next creation. I can call it Adventures with Ben and Cassie and it would be all about Ben trying to survive the various adventures that Cassie would throw at him. It would be a comedy, of course.* Arden wonders if he could write a comedy after writing horror novels for so long. Once a writer becomes comfortable in a genre, becomes associated with a genre, it's hard to break free from it. Many writers have before, and very successfully, but Arden just isn't sure he would have that same success. He continues to think about possible plot lines for the Ben and Cassie story when the waitress appears back at their table, asking Arden if he would like a refill. He nods and watches as she fills his coffee cup back up.

"It's a shame what some people will do to escape their lives, isn't it?" she asks the two men at the table, as she motions with her head towards the television on the wall behind the counter.

"What do you mean?" Arden asks. The waitress looks at Arden a moment. "You didn't hear? It's been all over the news all day. Some super rich CEO jumped from his penthouse room and went splat all over the ground. You would think you wouldn't have any problems when you have that kind of money but guess everyone has some sort of demon to deal with inside them."

Arden nods in response and thanks her for the refill as she turns and walks away to go check on their orders. He focuses his attention on the reporter currently on the television, standing in front of some posh hotel in New York City with a couple of police cars and yellow crime scene tape in the scene behind her. The reporter is describing what happened and talking about the man that killed himself. Some bigwig pharmaceutical executive who decided to go over the balcony instead of the elevator to get the ground. As more of the details about the man's life are given by the reporter, the uneasy feeling Arden had from the other night begins to set in. A feeling of déjà vu rushes over him and for a moment he feels like he knows this story. Like he has seen this story before.

As quick as the feeling comes over him, it's gone. Arden frowns slightly and he can't help but feel that something isn't right. Something about all of this is just too familiar.

Ben's voice finds its way into his thoughts. "Damn, wonder if his wife was making him enjoy a lettuce and water diet as well?"

Arden laughs a bit at Ben's comment but the uneasy feeling remains. Before he has a chance to think about it more, the waitress is back at the table and is setting down two large plates of food, the burger and fries for Arden and the gravy-coated cholesterol express for Ben.

The news story is quickly forgotten as the two men dig into their meal. They eat in silence, allowing the sounds of the diner to take over. The sounds coming from the kitchen as food is prepared for the hungry customers. The sound of the pass-through bell as it announces an order is ready to go. The various conversations of the patrons around Ben and Arden, each talking about their day or the storm that recently came through.

Arden takes it all in, thinking about how he could best describe this scene to his readers. As he finishes the last bite of his burger and wipes his hands on the napkin in his lap, Ben's phone rings. Cassie again. Arden munches on one of his remaining steak fries while he listens to Ben explain he will be home shortly, and that he knows she needs the paint before she can get any further with her current painting. Arden finishes his last steak fry at the same time Ben is hanging up the phone.

"Arden, you sure you don't want a wife?" Ben asks him.

Arden laughs and shakes his head no. Ben continues on. "I don't have the heart to tell her that she's a terrible painter and that she should try something else. We have six of her so-called paintings now hanging up around the house. Arden, let me tell you, her paintings look like she was blindfolded while holding a paintbrush, and then was hit by a taser while she painted."

Still laughing, Arden adds the painting adventure to the story line of Ben and Cassie's book in his head. *Definitely a comedy*, he thinks.

With full stomachs, the two men get ready to head back to

their homes. Ben gets the check and pays the tab, hardware store bags in hand, and they both leave the diner, quickly crossing the road and into the parking lot of the grocery store.

As Ben puts his bags in the back of the Wrangler, he mentions he should probably hit the grocery store really quick. Arden checks to make sure the cooler is keeping his perishables cold and nods, letting Ben know he is going to swing by the hardware store as well to check on the cost of a bag of shingles to replace the damaged ones on his house.

The two men agree to meet back at the Jeep in a short time and quickly part ways to finish up their shopping. Arden briskly walks to the hardware store in silence, lost in thought about repair supplies and hoping he has enough room in the Jeep for everything, the uneasy feeling from earlier once again forgotten.

Chapter 4

REPAIR

After dropping Ben off at home, thanking him for lunch, and declining his invitation to come inside and see Cassie's artwork, Arden makes his way down his driveway and to his own house. The sun is working its way lower in the western sky and will be setting in another hour or so. The overall trip took longer than expected, and Arden hopes his frozen goods held up in the cooler. He pulls into his usual parking spot and turns off the vehicle.

As he is walking to the back of the Jeep, his cellphone rings. He pulls the phone from his pocket and checks to see who is calling. The caller ID indicates it is a restricted number. Arden briefly wonders if it is the same person from the other day and sends the caller to voicemail, putting the phone back in his pocket. *Probably some telemarketer randomly dialing numbers,* he thinks. He opens the back of the vehicle up and begins to haul his groceries and supplies into the house. It only takes a couple of trips to get everything inside the house and onto the kitchen counters, with the exception of the bag of shingles and a box of roofing nails, which he sets on the ground outside the front door. Tomorrow he will haul them up onto the roof and see what he can do about repairing the damaged section.

In the kitchen, he quickly transfers his perishable foods from the cooler to their respective locations in the fridge and freezer. He carries the cooler with the partially melted bag of ice still inside it to the back porch and sets it down outside the door. He puts the lid back on the top of the cooler and decides to leave it there for the evening. Another chore added to the list for tomorrow.

Arden heads back inside and finishes putting his groceries away. With the pantry now looking fairly respectable when it comes to stockpiles, he heads towards his writing room to grab a glass of bourbon in celebration. After pouring himself a small glass, he crosses the few steps from the decanter to his desk and grabs the notepad and pen from where they usually sit next to his laptop. *Might as well scribble down what I can remember from the lost chapters,* he thinks as he heads back into the living room and sits down on the couch, kicking his feet up on the coffee table. He sets the notepad and pen on the couch cushion to his right side and leans forward to grab the remote from the table. He turns on the television and changes the channel from the weather channel to one of the various movie channels included with his satellite package. Living this far outside of town, his only option for television and internet was via satellite. Thankfully, the provider he uses is reliable and only has issues with connectivity during heavy storms and power outages. A random action movie fills the screen of his television and he lowers the volume until it is almost barely audible. Although most writers prefer no distractions when they are writing or brainstorming, Arden likes the background noise. It provides a much-needed diversion at times when he is struggling with a sentence or a direction for a chapter.

He watches the movie for a few minutes and takes a small sip of his bourbon. On the screen, two charismatic police officers are shooting their way through what appears to be a never-ending supply of bad guys.

Arden pulls his attention from the television and reaches forward to set his bourbon down on the coffee table. He grabs the notepad and pen from the cushion next to him and opens it up. He flips past notes of timelines and story concepts until he reaches a blank page. Putting pen to paper, he starts writing down everything he can remember about Chapter 14.

Minutes turn to hours and soon the light streaming in the window behind him fades to black, leaving the television screen as only the source of light in his living room. He sets the pad and pen down, happy with his progress, and turns on the lamp to his left. The room fills with warm white light and chases the encroaching shadows away. He glances at the clock on the wall. Seven in the evening. Dinner time.

As if in agreement, his stomach growls. Arden gets up from the couch and grabs his empty bourbon glass. He finished the glass well over an hour ago, but was too focused on his task at hand to go get a refill. He heads into the study and pours several ounces into the glass from the decanter, taking a moment to look out the window after he sets the decanter back onto the table. The view beyond the window is black, with no outside lights on to push away the night. A light cloud cover overhead is holding back an otherwise bright moon, helping the dark on its mission to take over. Arden steps away from the window and walks through his living room and into the kitchen, turning on the kitchen light once he is there. He sets his glass down on the counter and opens the fridge, grabbing a package of deli turkey and one of the packages of pepper jack cheese slices. They find a resting spot on the counter next to his bourbon while he grabs the loaf of bread sitting on top of the microwave.

A few minutes later, Arden is enjoying some turkey and cheese sandwiches for dinner. He eats while standing at the counter, not bothering to get a plate or sit down at the dining room table. Once he finishes, he cleans up the few crumbs he left behind with a wet paper towel and tosses it into the trash. He pulls his cellphone out of his pocket and sets it down on the counter, takes another sip of his bourbon, and looks over into the living room. He wonders how much more he will be able to get done tonight before sleep takes over.

Bourbon in hand, Arden walks over to his front door and turns on his outside porch lamps, bathing his Jeep and the surrounding area in light. As he is looking out the door's medium-sized four-pane window, movement at the far left of his driveway catches his eye. He looks in the direction of the movement but is unable to see very well due to the angle. Arden moves from the door to his living room window for a better view. He takes a sip of his bourbon and watches for any other movement from where he saw it last. It's not uncommon for the occasional wildlife to visit from time to time, but then Arden did have an issue a few years back with an obsessed fan who stood outside his house one night, staring in his windows.

That was one experience Arden hopes to never have again, as turning on his front porch lights one night only to see someone standing next to his Jeep was almost enough to give him a heart attack.

Just as he is about to turn away from the window and get back to the couch, more movement pulls his eyes back to the edge of his driveway. This time, a small rabbit comes into view, cautiously looking around before it takes another hop.

"Another obsessed fan, I see," he says with a smile. "Stick around until tomorrow morning and I will autograph whatever you want. Some lettuce or a carrot possibly? You will have to bring your own, though, because I don't have any."

In response, the rabbit turns and hops back into the darkness, away from the house and out of Arden's view.

"OK, maybe no autographs then."

Still smiling, Arden turns from the window and heads back to the couch. He sits down and allows himself to sink into the cushions. Another action movie is playing on the television. He watches the movie for a short time, feeling his eyelids get heavier and heavier, and soon he is fast asleep.

The sound of his phone ringing pulls Arden from his slumber. He groggily rubs his eyes and yawns. The television is still on, and an overly cheery woman is talking about how amazing this air fryer is and how it can cook anything. It feels like he just dozed off a few minutes ago, but the daylight pouring in from the living room window behind him lets him know that he did get some sleep after all. He sits up straight and stretches his arms, the soreness in his back and his neck reminding him that he should probably sleep in his bed instead of on the couch. The ringing of his phone persists, prompting Arden to slowly stand up and stumble his way into the kitchen.

"I'm coming, I'm coming," he tells the ringing phone. He reaches the phone and picks it up, looking at who is calling him this early. Saphina. *Of course it would be her*, he thinks. He swipes the answer button to the left and puts the phone on speaker, setting the phone back down on the counter while he turns to the coffee maker and hits the power button to get it warmed up and ready to brew.

"Good morning, Saphina. Why are you calling me this early?" he asks the black rectangular device on the counter. Her voice erupts from the phone's speakers and fills his kitchen.

"Arden, my dear, I absolutely love what you have done with the new manuscript so far."

Arden shakes his head and grabs one of the coffee cups from the cabinet in front of him and places it on the tray of the coffee maker. Anytime she starts out with a compliment means she is going to have suggestions for changes. She continues on, "But that being said, I do think a few changes are necessary, namely in Chapter 2 and Chapter 9." Arden laughs and puts one of his coffee pods into the machine, hitting the brew button while Saphina goes into greater detail about what she thinks should be fixed in those two chapters. He watches as hot coffee slowly fills the cup, the noise slightly drowning out Saphina in the background. He waits until the cup is full and the machine notifies him that his coffee is done, then removes the used coffee pod and throws it in the trash.

"Arden, did you hear me about the changes?"

Leave it to Saphina to be pushy even when talking about feedback.

"Yes I did. I am still outlining the lost pages but I can go back and make some revisions to those two chapters afterwards." Although frustrating, Arden knows after his prior novels that Saphina's feedback is normally in the best interest of the manuscript. He takes a sip of his coffee and listens to her as she quickly outlines the estimated publishing date and press events. Of course, she makes sure to remind him that none of these dates will work if he doesn't finish the manuscript on time. He takes another sip of his coffee and voices his agreement. "I got it, Saphina. Get the script done on time. I will make it happen." Her response lets him know she is happy and they exchange their goodbyes. He checks to make sure the phone is hung up and then carries his coffee cup with him into the living room, stopping to pick up the remote and turn the television off. The clock on the wall says it is just after eight in the morning. Arden finishes his coffee and returns the mug to the kitchen, turning off the lights he left on last night as he goes.

After rinsing out the mug and setting it down in the sink, Arden heads into the bathroom to clean up and get ready for the day. It doesn't take him long to shower and brush his teeth, then toss on a pair of faded jeans and a T-shirt. *May as well get up on the roof and replace the damaged shingles before the rain comes back through again, he tells himself, then get back to work on the script.*

Back in the kitchen, he stuffs his cellphone into his pocket and then puts on his shoes sitting next to the back door before he heads out the door and onto the back porch. It doesn't take Arden long to drain the melted bag of ice from the cooler and toss the empty plastic bag into the trash, which is now at borderline peak capacity.

"Shit!" he exclaims. He forgot to take the trash to the end of the road last night when he got home. He wonders if the garbage truck has already been by yet. Pulling his phone from his pocket, he quickly calls Ben. Ben answers on the second ring and lets Arden know that the truck has not been by his house yet, which means he still has some time to get the can out there. He thanks Ben for checking and returns the phone to his pocket. Thankfully, his trash can has two wheels in the back, which allows him to tilt the can and push the large bin to its destination versus having to drag it there. Twenty minutes later and slightly out of breath, Arden has the trash bin sitting at the side of the main road, waiting for the garbage truck to come along.

Maybe Saphina is right and he should get his drive paved. *It would definitely be a lot easier to get the bin to the highway, that's for sure*, he thinks. Arden quickly walks the distance back to his house and around to the back porch where he keeps his ladder.

It only takes him a few minutes to get the ladder leaned up against the roof so he can carefully haul the bag of shingles up the rungs. He carries the bag to the damaged section and sets it down. Still amazed at how lightning can strike the same spot that many times, he heads back down to get a hammer and the box of roofing nails.

As he is climbing back up the ladder, hammer and nails in hand, he pauses right before he reaches the top and takes a deep breath. *It's going to be a long damn day.*

✳

About the same time Arden is finishing up the roof repair on his house, on the other side of the country, actress Ashanti Wylls is getting her two boys ready to spend the next couple weeks with their father. Although she hates to be without them, she also appreciates the time to herself. A bottle of wine is chilling in the fridge and the man she is currently seeing has already confirmed he would be over around nine tonight.

Ashanti smiles. *It's going to be a good night indeed*, she thinks, imagining what exactly they will be doing later this evening.

Her oldest boy's voice from his room down the hall interrupts her thoughts. "Mom, I can't find my earphones!" She sighs in response. "Did you check your backpack?" She waits a few moments until she gets an answer. "Thanks mom, found them."

She rolls her eyes and continues folding up the large pile of laundry in front of her. How two boys can dirty this much clothing in a week is beyond her. She makes quick work of the laundry and delivers the neatly folded piles to each of their rooms, only to see them rip through the piles to grab their favorite shirts or pants to stuff into their suitcases. As she heads downstairs, the doorbell rings.

"Your father's here," she announces. The noises of hurried shuffling can be heard coming from the boys' rooms upstairs behind her. She crosses the foyer and to the front door, glancing out the peephole to confirm it's him. She opens the door and stands in the doorway.

"What's going on, Ashanti?" he asks her, "The boys ready?"

She waits a moment before she responds. "I'm fine and the boys will be down in just a moment." Their father shifts his weight from his left leg to his right leg and smiles at her. "You gonna invite me in while I wait for, old times' sake?"

Ashanti scoffs and replies as she closes the door in his face. "No, you can wait right there."

"Boys, hurry up. Your father is waiting outside," she calls up the stairs. "OK mom," echoes from both of their rooms. As she heads into the living room, a stampede of heavy footsteps can be heard rumbling down the stairs as the two boys race down with their suitcases in tow behind them.

She pauses at the living room couch and grabs the two backpacks sitting there.

"Don't forget your books," she tells them while handing each of them their backpack. "I expect all your homework to be done by the time you get back. I don't want to see either of you trying to get it done the night before school starts back up." Both boys agree and she kneels down to collect her hugs and kisses. "Behave for your father and I will see you when you both get back. Call me if you have any problems." Another chorus of agreement and then out the door they go. Their father tries one last time to engage her in conversation by telling her she looks good and he really liked her last movie, but she doesn't respond. She watches in the doorway as they all load up in the SUV parked out front and both boys wave at her as the vehicle pulls away. She waves back at them and then retreats back inside the house, closing the front door behind her. She's sad to see the boys go, but happy their father isn't at her door anymore. It was his choice to cheat on her when the boys were still just babies, and she will never forgive him for leaving her to struggle with her blossoming acting career as well as having to take care of her babies on her own. If the boys' visits with their father weren't court ordered, she would be completely happy not having him in their lives at all.

Now standing in the kitchen, Ashanti checks the clock. Almost three in the afternoon. She has quite a bit of time before her date will show up, so she takes an hour or so and cleans up the house, putting the boys' toys away in their rooms and getting the sink full of dishes washed, dried, and then put away as well. Satisfied the house is back in order from the chaos of this morning, she opens the fridge up and grabs the now chilled bottle of wine. She uncorks the bottle and grabs a wine glass hanging upside down on the rack under one of the kitchen cabinets. She pours herself about a quarter of a glass and takes a drink. She stands a moment at the kitchen counter, enjoying her drink, when she decides a bubble bath would go great with this wine.

She grabs an ice bucket from under the counter and fills it partially with cubed ice from the ice dispenser on the fridge. After nestling the wine bottle in the ice, she proceeds upstairs towards her bedroom and bathroom with both the bucket and wine glass in hand. Once inside her bathroom, she sets the ice bucket and glass on the wide ledge of the tub closest to the vanity. She then turns on the water and waits for it to reach the temperature she likes before putting the stopper in and allowing the tub to fill up.

While the water level in the tub slowly rises, Ashanti places her cellphone on the vanity counter and connects it to the portable waterproof speaker she uses to play music on when in the bath or shower. Soft jazz music quickly fills the room from the speaker, fighting for control of the room over the sound of the running water. One bath bomb later and the surface of the water in the tub is a bubbly swirl of pink and orange, with a strong scent of pumpkin spice filling the air. Ashanti smiles as the tub reaches the desired level and she turns off the water.

She then grabs two towels from the linen shelf, one for her hair and one to rest her neck on, setting them both next to the wine bucket before she begins to undress.

Just as she removes the last of her clothing, the doorbell downstairs rings. Ashanti frowns. Her date would not show up early without calling her, and she wasn't expecting any other visitors today. *Maybe one of the boys forgot something?* she wonders, *maybe her ex is currently standing at the door once more, wearing his sleazy smile.*

She tosses on her robe that is hanging on the back of the bathroom door and heads out of the room and down the stairs. She reaches the front door and looks out the peephole only to see her front stoop empty. *Odd,* she thinks, *must have been someone who realized they have the wrong house.* She takes one more look out the peephole to confirm no one is there. As she turns to head back upstairs to her awaiting bath, she pauses a moment, making sure that she locks the deadbolt. Several stairs later and Ashanti is back in her bathroom, taking her robe off and re-hanging it on the back of the door.

Before she is able to step into the colorful, bubble-covered water, the front doorbell rings once again. "Are you fucking kidding me?" she exclaims over the sound of a saxophone solo currently playing from the speaker.

Ashanti sighs and repeats the process of putting on her robe and then heading down the stairs to the front door. Once again she looks out the peephole, only to be greeted by the same empty stoop. A slight wave of fear rushes over her as she steps back away from the door. *Get a grip girl, it's probably just some neighborhood kids playing ding dong ditch*, she tells herself as she turns from the door and returns to her bath upstairs.

With her robe back on its hook and the bathroom door closed, Ashanti gets into the hot bath and sits down, stretching her long legs out in front of her and allowing the hot water to wrap itself around her body. She grabs one of the towels to her left and wraps it around her hair, tucking up the edges so her hair will remain dry. She takes the other towel and rolls it up, putting it between the back of her neck and the edge of the tub. She reaches over and grabs the bottle of wine, uncorking it and refilling her glass. Once the wine bottle is back and resting in the ice, she grabs her glass of wine and takes a sip. As she does so, the doorbell downstairs rings one more time.

Ashanti frowns, another brief wave of fear washing over her. She will have to call the security company and have them do a drive by after she gets out of the bath to hopefully scare whoever is out there away. She sets her wine glass down next to the bucket and relaxes, closing her eyes and allowing herself to float away in the music.

As she begins to drift off, right at that hazy point between awake and asleep, a soft knocking noise comes from her bathroom door. Ashanti immediately sits up and looks at the door with wide eyes, a rush of panic causing her heart rate to drastically increase.

She stares at the door, frozen in place, breathlessly fixated on the doorknob. The song playing on the speaker changes, the trumpets from the last song replaced by a piano. Ashanti waits, still frozen, fear surging through her body, wondering if she merely imagined the noise. She takes a deep breath and tries to calm herself down. *You are just imagining things*, she tells herself.

Another deep breath and Ashanti slowly begins to lay back into her original position, cautiously glancing at the bathroom door as she does. She grabs her wine glass and finishes it off, setting the glass back down next to the bucket. The piano filling the room is joined by a guitar.

Ashanti nervously laughs and shakes her head, trying to force herself to relax, trying to allow the still hot water to calm her nerves. *Stupid doorbell has me on edge and imagining things*, she thinks.

She closes her eyes once more and focuses on the music currently echoing throughout the bathroom. Just as the haziness is about to take for a second time, she hears the creaking of the bathroom door as it opens. Her eyes open and she looks to the left towards the door, fear spiking across every inch of her body.

For a split second, she sees the dark outline of a figure standing in the doorway, its red eyes the only discernable feature on its face. Then the lights in the bathroom drastically dim, plunging the room into dark shadows.

Ashanti screams and tries to sit up. Tries to get out of the tub so she can escape. Her legs and arms have stopped responding. Her mind screams to run, but fear has paralyzed her body from answering.

Now only outlined by the light from beyond the bathroom door, the intruder slowly moves closer and closer to her. Each step it takes towards her causes her fear to intensify. Her panic becomes all consuming. *Run!* she screams inside, *Run!*

Once it reaches the edge of the bathtub, the figure leans over Ashanti and puts its hands on her shoulders, its face only about a foot away from hers. A raspy voice reaches her ears. "Ashanti."

She tries to force her body to respond. To force her body to fight back against the terrifying red eyes that are currently staring into her soul. Her body refuses to respond.

Please, God, please don't hurt me. Please don't hurt my babies, she thinks, as tears begin to stream down her face. The guttural voice makes its way to her ears once more, the figure's breath hot upon her face.

"Only here for you."

She squeezes her eyes shut and begins to pray that this is all just a bad dream. That she will wake up any moment, still alone in her bathroom, accompanied by only her wine and her music. The figure's hand on her right shoulder is lifted away and for a fleeting moment she hopes the assailant is leaving, until she feels the towel from behind her neck being removed. Several moments pass and then Ashanti feels the towel wrapped around her hair being removed. She continues to keep her eyes closed even as she feels the unwelcome hand once again return to its previous location on her shoulder.

The intruder's fingers tighten on her shoulders and suddenly she is pushed downwards into the tub, water quickly cascading over her face and head. She holds her breath, still unable to move, and opens her eyes.

Through the several inches of water now above her, the two red eyes seem to be glowing, their shapes distorted by the water's hazy, wavy surface. Still staring at her. Still staring into her.

Ashanti continues to hold her breath, panic and fear racing from her fingers to her toes, mingled with confusion as to why her body is not responding to her demands that it fights back, that it tries to save itself. Her lungs are beginning to burn. The heavily distorted sound of a trombone joins the hammering sound of her heartbeat in her ears. She tries to turn her head left and right in a vain attempt to escape, but like her body, it also refuses to respond to her commands.

Moments pass. Her mind is now screaming at her to breathe. Screaming at her that she needs oxygen. The fire in her lungs is an inferno and suddenly her diaphragm spasms, causing her to inhale. Except it isn't air that fills her lungs. Ashanti tries to scream but her voice is not there anymore. Only the fiery pain in her lungs, reaching out to every nerve in her body.

She inhales again, against her will, her body and mind no longer communicating with each other. Still no air. Her eyes dart back and forth in panic, her mind screaming for help. Screaming for air. The pressure of the grip on her shoulders is unrelenting, keeping her firmly pressed to the bottom of the tub.

Soon, the sounds of her heartbeat and the muffled music

from outside her watery prison slowly begin to fade. The distorted red eyes that now appear to be floating miles above her slowly begin to fade. Even the molten lava vice grip crushing her chest slowly begins to fade.

It all continues to fade until there is no more.

Chapter 5

REFOCUS

Arden sets the ladder down on the back porch and wipes the sweat from his brow. The roof repairs took a bit longer than he expected but luckily the plywood decking wasn't so damaged that it needed to be replaced. The most difficult part was replacing the charred underlayment as best he could without tearing up too many additional shingles.

Now firmly back on *terra firma*, he puts away all his tools and leftover shingles, and throws the ruined ones away in the now empty trash bin he retrieved from the end of his long driveway. *Hopefully that takes care of everything that was damaged in the storm,* he thinks to himself, *Besides the missing chapters of the manuscript.*

He looks to the western sky and watches a moment as the sun slowly works its way towards the horizon, teasing the upcoming sunset. *Might have to have a drink or two out on the porch tonight,* he surmises. Pulling himself away from the sky,

Arden turns and heads back inside the house, kicking his shoes off at the back door and proceeding into his bedroom to grab a change of clothes. As usual, it doesn't take him long to shower the day off, clean up, and put on a fresh set of clothes for the evening. His goal tonight is to wrap up the recall of the lost work and then actually start writing it all down again. But first, he is going to need some dinner and a celebratory drink. Not like Arden needs a celebratory reason for a drink, but it doesn't make any sense as to why he wouldn't enjoy a nice bourbon to top off the successful completion of the roof repairs.

Cleaned up and dressed, with his hair combed back out of his eyes, Arden heads into his writing room and pours a small glass of bourbon. He looks out the window above the table and raises his glass to the world beyond, paying his respects to a now repaired roof and a job well done. He takes a small sip and smiles, content with what he achieved so far today. Glass in hand, he turns from the window and heads towards the living room, stopping to turn on the television and then making sure the channel is set for the evening news.

Although he doesn't care for the sensationalism or political lean that a vast majority of the news has today, he does like to keep informed and up to date on the latest stories. Currently, the reporter on the screen is talking about an upcoming change in electricity rates for the county. *Figures*, Arden thinks, setting the remote back down on the coffee table, *Gotta pay for the storm damage somehow, right?* Not expecting his electric bill to change by much since it's only him at the house, he loses interest in the rest of the story and heads into the kitchen to determine something to eat for dinner. The temptation to dig into his frozen food stash is high, but since he intended that for backup, he chooses to have sandwiches for dinner once again before the bread reaches its expiration date. Two ham, turkey, and cheese sandwiches later and Arden is stifling a yawn.

He rinses off the plate he used for dinner and puts it in the bottom rack of the dishwasher. Grabbing his almost empty glass of bourbon, he heads into the study and refreshes his glass, then returns to the living room and sits down on the couch. Tonight's goal, prior to falling asleep, is to complete the outlining of the missing chapters so he can start rewriting them. He sets his glass of bourbon next to the remote on the coffee table, turns on the living room lamp to his left, and grabs the notepad and pen next to him.

The next hour and a half go by quickly, with Arden outlining as much as he can remember from what he wrote for the last two chapters, the news still playing on the television but now merely existing as background noise. Closing his notepad for the night, he glances at the clock. Almost eight-thirty in the evening. He sets the notepad and pen down on the couch cushion to his right and reaches forward to grab his glass, which still has a couple of sips remaining. As he is taking a sip and thinking about whether he should start working on Chapter 14 tonight, a news story on the television catches his attention.

The reporter on the screen is talking about the drowning death of an up-and-coming actress. He turns up the sound and watches as the reporter relays more information about the death, about how she was found dead in her bathtub by a maid from what the authorities are calling an accidental drowning, as there were no signs of foul play. The reporter continues, talking about the actress's two surviving children and ex-husband, and how the late actress's talent will be missed within the acting community as well as by her fans.

The uneasy feeling from before makes itself known within Arden, once again causing the hair on the back of his neck to rise up. *Why does this sound so familiar?* he wonders.

Arden continues to watch the news story, trying to remember if he ever met the actress before at a book signing or a press conference, in an attempt to determine why it feels like he knows her.

Before he can figure it out, his cellphone, currently sitting at its usual place on his kitchen counter, rings. The sound pulls Arden from his thoughts about the actress and he glances at the clock once again. *Who on earth is calling this late?* he asks himself. He gets up from the couch and heads into the kitchen to grab the phone. It goes silent by the time he picks it up and glances at the screen.

Another restricted number.

Arden frowns. His cell number is unpublished and he has only shared it with a handful of people. He hopes he doesn't have to change his number again. The last time he had a restricted number calling repeatedly, it was the obsessed fan who eventually ended up standing outside his house one night.

In the end, the fan was harmless, but the experience was enough to make Arden change his cell number the very next day.

He sets his phone back down and turns to head back into the living room. Before he can reach the couch, the phone rings again. He stops mid-step and looks out his living room window, almost expecting to see someone standing next to his Jeep once again. Beyond his window, the failing light has allowed the darkness to take over. The phone continues to ring as he detours to the front door from the living room and turns on the outside porch lamps, hesitantly looking out the door's window towards his Jeep. Much to his relief, the now-visible portions of his driveway are empty and his vehicle has no unwanted guests eerily standing next to it.

His phone persists and he makes his way once more to where it sets on the counter. He glances again at the caller ID, hoping it doesn't display restricted.

Cassie.

Arden is momentarily confused and then worried. The only reason Cassie would be calling him at this hour is if something had happened to Ben.

He quickly grabs the phone and swipes the answer button. "Hey Cassie, everything ok?" he asks, imagining the worst. Imagining that Ben finally succumbed to the water and lettuce diet, or that the heart attack special from when they had lunch at the diner actually caused a heart attack.

"Arden! I am so sorry to call this late, but I am here with a good friend of mine and I have an unusual question I want…

wait…yes, I know, shhhhhhhhh…WE…want to ask you." Two sets of feminine giggles erupt from the other end of the phone line as soon as she is done talking.

The voice in the background that Cassie is also talking to is definitely not Ben. Arden raises one eyebrow and suspects a setup is about to happen. "Ok, what's the question?" he asks, "Just know I am not going to answer any questions about how the current book ends."

"No book questions, we promise. Actually, I was having some wine with a friend when we realized that you both are authors and you both are single and that you both should go out on a date." The voice in the background can be heard telling Cassie to stop being so forward.

Arden laughs. His suspicions were right. *At least nothing bad happened to Ben,* he thinks, *hopefully.* A drunk Cassie is a force unto herself at times, as Arden has witnessed in the past. "And what is this mystery lady's name, if I may inquire?" he asks.

The voice in the background speaks up, almost drowning out Cassie as they both say the woman's name. "Lilly!"

Arden laughs once more, deducing he must be on speaker phone. The feminine voice in the background, who has been identified as Lilly, speaks up, proclaiming as sweetly as she can, "I promise I won't ask you about the ending of your current book or for an autograph." Both women erupt in another fit of giggles.

Afraid the call may take end up taking an awkward, but

probably entertaining, turn if he lets it go on any further, Arden sighs and agrees to a date. Cassie, still giggling, passes the phone to Lilly who gives Arden her cell number and promises she is not as crazy as Cassie might make her out to be. After some additional brief small talk, Arden excuses himself, promises both ladies that he will call Lilly tomorrow, and hangs up the phone. He double checks to make sure Lilly's number is saved in his phone and he sets his phone back down on the counter, making sure he plugs it in this time so it can charge overnight.

The smile on his face still there from the phone call he just had, Arden walks into his living room and grabs his glass of bourbon still sitting on the coffee table. He takes a sip and looks out his living room window, his eyes glancing across the portions of his driveway illuminated by his porch lamps. He wonders what Lilly looks like and then cringes. He should have asked before he got off the phone. Her voice sounded cute, which is a hopeful indication that she doesn't look like a female version of Chewbacca.

Arden laughs. Regardless of how she looks, it has been quite some time since he has been on a date of any sort and Cassie did mention that Lilly is a fellow writer. At the very least, he may end up with more creative material for a future character in one of his novels.

He nods to himself, as if in agreement with his logic, and returns his attention to his task this evening. Getting Chapter 14 back down on paper. Arden leans down and grabs his notepad and pen from the couch with his free hand and turns towards the study. A few steps later and he's settling into his office chair, the leather well-worn from days upon days of usage. He sets the notepad and pen down on the table, to the left of his laptop. He sets his bourbon down to the right.

Arden takes a deep breath and hits the enter button on the laptop's keyboard and waits for it to wake up from sleep mode. The screen comes on, bright white light filling the dark study and causing Arden to squint for a couple moments while his eyes adjust.

Displayed on the screen in front of him is his manuscript.

Chapter 14, in black letters at the top of the page, patiently reminds him where he has to start from. The cursor is two spaces below, steadily flashing its happy little beat, ready to lead the way with every typed letter.

Before he settles in to start, he gets up from his chair, walks over to the light switch next to the doorway, and flips the switch upwards. The light overhead turns on, filling the room with its warm glow. Arden returns to the chair and sits back down. He opens his notepad and flips to where his notes for Chapter 14 start. He leans forward and puts his fingers on the keyboard and begins to type.

Arden loses track of time as he works. Word after word appears on the blank lines, slowly bringing the chapter back to life. Slowly bringing the protagonist closer to the final confrontation by giving them a glimmer of hope that the monster can be defeated. Slowly bringing the monster closer to its ultimate demise. By the time he pulls himself away from the computer screen, he has completed just over two-thirds of the first lost chapter.

He leans back and rubs his eyes, a yawn settling in. He looks at the time displayed in the lower right corner of his laptop. A few minutes before one in the morning. Happy with his progress, Arden decides he should probably wrap it up for the night and get some sleep. Not willing to make the same mistake as last time, he saves the manuscript on the laptop as well as to his thumb drive.

After returning the memory stick to the safety of the desk drawer, he gets up out of the chair and grabs his bourbon glass. A quick trip to the kitchen allows him to wash the glass out and set it on the drying pad next to the sink. He checks his phone and confirms no messages or calls since Cassie called earlier in the evening. Another yawn and he heads into the living room to grab the remote to turn the television off. He pauses a moment before doing so, briefly watching the weatherman on the screen talking about the weather for the next couple days. The forecast is saying that the weather is going to be sunny and slightly cool. *Good, maybe my upcoming date would be interested in sitting around a fire while we chat*, he thinks, as he hits the power button and turns the screen black. He turns out the lights as he goes, leaving only the outside porch lights on before he heads into his bedroom and throws himself down on the mattress. He stretches out and contemplates getting back up to brush his teeth and change into some pajamas, something normal people do before they go to sleep. He yawns again and closes his eyes for a moment, deciding he can get up in a minute or two and try to be a normal person.

Arden is fast asleep before that minute or two arrives.

*

A distant ringing gradually pulls Arden from his dreams and back to reality. He slowly opens his eyes and stares at the ceiling above him. The ringing continues and it finally registers that his phone is the object making the noise.

Yeah, not going to be answering that one, he tells himself, not feeling like moving just yet. He continues to stare at the ceiling, his eyes following the random patterns made from the knockdown texture. The phone rings a couple more times and then goes silent. He wonders what time it is and why people always insist on calling him when he's not awake. *Who needs an alarm clock when I have a phone that only rings when I am sleeping?*

Turning his head to the left, he looks over at the clock sitting on the nightstand next to the side of the bed. Nine in the morning.

Guess it isn't as early as I thought, he tells himself.

Arden stretches out on his bed and tries to wake his body up. He lies there a few more minutes before finally finding the energy to get out of bed. He grabs a change of clothes and heads into his bathroom, quickly taking care of the usual morning routine. Forty-five minutes later, Arden emerges clean and refreshed from his bathroom, ready for some coffee. He tosses his dirty clothes into the hamper and makes his way into the kitchen, hitting the power button on the coffee machine and retrieving one of his usual coffee pods. He places a coffee mug on the machine's tray and while the coffee maker is warming up, he grabs his cellphone to see who called him.

A restricted number.

Arden frowns, the uneasy feeling coming back. *Even a telemarketer dialing random numbers would not be this determined*, he thinks, *unless my number was added to an automated dialing list.* He will have to answer the phone the next time they call. If it is an automated dialer, he can hopefully unsubscribe or at the worst, hop online to have his phone number changed.

The coffee maker indicates it's ready to go and he sets the phone back down on the counter, still trying to figure out why he feels like there is more to the calls than just a telemarketer. Putting one of the pods in the machine, he hits the brew button and waits for his mug to fill up.

Please don't be another obsessed fan, he thinks, *one of those is enough for a lifetime.*

After his coffee finishes brewing, he tosses the used coffee pod in the trash while picking up and carrying the hot mug into the living room and sitting down at his usual spot on the couch. He takes a sip of the coffee and leans forward, setting the mug down on the table. He grabs the remote and turns on the television, filling the living room with the visage and voice of the local news anchor who is currently talking about some random political fiasco. Arden sets the remote back down on the table and grabs his coffee, leaning back and taking another sip. He watches the various stories on the news as he enjoys his hot, heavily caffeinated beverage.

It doesn't take long before he is enjoying the last sip of coffee in his mug. *Why does the news only ever report the bad in the world?* he wonders. He gets up from the couch and heads towards the coffee machine for his second cup of the morning. While the machine brews him another mug, he grabs his cellphone and unlocks the screen. He flips through his contacts until he settles on the most recent contact added to his phone.

Lilly.

He hesitates a moment while her name is displayed on the small screen in his hand and smiles. *Why sir, are you nervous to call her?* he asks himself.

It has been quite a long time since Arden has had an actual date, or spent any time in person with someone who wasn't his neighbor, his agent, his editors, or his various fans at the occasional book signing. The coffee machine behind him lets him know that his brew is complete. He sets his phone back down on the counter and waits until the screen goes black, hiding the name and number from his view.

He repeats the process of retrieving his full mug and throwing away the used coffee pod, then turns his attention back to his phone setting on the counter.

Arden stares at the small device, holding his mug with both hands, letting the creative side of his mind wander, thinking about the wide variety of possibilities that could exist at the other end of the line when he calls her number. He has always been a bit of an overthinker, analyzing everything in excruciating detail and imagining every possible scenario, no matter how farfetched the scenario may seem. He likes to think that this is the reason why he got into writing in the first place. To allow his mind to put those scenarios down on paper instead of dwelling on them, replaying them over and over again, each time with a new outcome. He takes a sip of his coffee and nods. *Won't know how the story goes if I don't start writing it, right?*

Arden grabs the phone and unlocks it, the screen once again displaying Lilly's name and number. He hits the dial button and waits, switching it to speaker phone and listening to the phone ring throughout the kitchen. She answers on the fourth ring.

"Good morning, Arden," the voice on the other end of the phone states. Arden smiles. At least she remembers exchanging numbers. He wasn't sure since both she and Cassie sounded pretty tipsy last night.

"Good morning, Lilly. I wasn't sure if you would know who was calling, since you ladies seemed pretty happy last night when we briefly talked." The soft voice on the other end of the line giggles.

"Yeah, that kind of happens every time Cassie and I get together. Poor Ben ends up hiding in his den the entire time." Arden laughs as he imagines Ben, barricaded inside his den, while two drunken women bang on the door, trying to get in. "I am glad you called though. Saves me the awkward feeling of staring at my phone wondering if you were going to call me or if I should call you first."

A big smile crosses Arden's face. "It took me a bit to work up the nerve to call, I won't lie. At least a half cup of coffee." Another giggle from the other end of the phone reaches his ears. "I was wondering if you would be interested in dinner tonight? Say, my place around eight? If that isn't too forward or uncomfortable?"

Arden waits for her to respond. *Maybe inviting her to my place was too forward?* he wonders. *She doesn't know me beyond what Cassie may have told her.* Just as he is about to suggest something else, possibly dinner at the diner in town, she answers.

"That sounds like fun," she says, "It's been a few months since I spent several hours worried that I might be chopped up into little pieces or if I was about to spend the rest of my life chained up in someone's basement so they could turn me into a new skin suit."

Smiling, Arden doesn't hesitate with his answer. "Nah, I don't have a basement and I'm more of a chain you to a tree in the backyard for display versus a chop you up kind of guy."

Lilly's laughter fills the kitchen. "Well then, how could I say no to a good time like that?"

Arden joins her in laugher and he gives her directions to get to his place. She promises to give him a call if the drive gets too scary, since she is still over at Ben and Cassie's house and will be coming over from there. They exchange a quick goodbye and then end the call. He finishes off his coffee and rinses out the mug in the sink. *At least she has a good sense of humor*, he tells himself. *I still forgot to ask if she looks like a female Chewbacca though.*

He puts the mug back in the cabinet after drying it with the kitchen towel he hangs over the handle of the oven door. He turns to head towards the study to get some more writing done before she comes over later and hesitates, a new thought crossing his mind.

What the hell are you going to make for dinner?

Arden quickly looks in the fridge and pantry, refreshing his memory about the food he has available. He weighs the limited options and decides on either cheeseburgers with bread slices for the buns, or chicken pot pies. *Yep, this is how you make a great first impression*, he thinks. Nor did he have anything to drink besides water, coffee, and bourbon. *Hopefully, she isn't very picky.* He will have to play it by ear to determine if he should go with the burgers or the pot pies when the time comes to eat.

The thought of food makes his stomach growl, and it isn't very long before he has a pan on the stove and is cooking a couple of over easy eggs for breakfast. His meal is uneventful, and he washes and dries the dishes in the same manner as he did with his coffee mug, choosing to hand dry them versus stacking them on the drying mat still next to the sink. Stomach now content, Arden finds himself back in his writing room, laptop screen once again glowing white, the flashing cursor inviting more of his input.

He begins to type, transporting himself to the world he created over the last several years, and quickly loses track of time.

Just as he is finishing up Chapter 14, he hears the sound of a vehicle pulling up in front of the house. A momentary jolt of panic races through his system as he wonders who could be here, and he gets up from his chair, quickly walking into the living room to see who is outside. A black SUV is now parked next to his Jeep out front. He glances at the clock on the wall. Almost seven-thirty. The light outside is quickly fading as the night approaches, and Arden is surprised at how much time has passed since he started writing earlier this morning. The vehicle next to his shuts off and the driver's side door opens at the same time the headlights turn off.

For a breathless moment, while standing in his living room, Arden pictures Chewbacca in high heels, bright pink lipstick smeared all around his mouth, and wearing a short red dress getting out of the vehicle in front of his house. Thankfully, instead of the presently disturbing mental image of Chewbacca in Arden's head, a petite redhead in blue jeans and a pink tank top exits the vehicle. Her hair is tied back in a loose ponytail, and she grabs a large paper bag from the back seat of her vehicle before heading towards Arden's front door. The panic from a moment ago returns as Arden realizes he might look terrible and he didn't have a chance to put something nicer on than the jeans and T-shirt he is currently wearing. *Well, if I can't wow her with my wardrobe, I can wow her with the dinner selection,* he tells himself. He quickly turns from where he is standing and swiftly walks into his bathroom, flipping on the light and assessing how he looks. He fixes up his slightly disheveled brown hair a bit and splashes a bit of cologne on. As he does so, the doorbell rings.

He heads out of the bathroom, turning the light off as he exits the room. With the television currently the only source of light on in the house, Arden realizes it might be a good idea to have a few lights on so Lilly doesn't immediately turn and leave when he opens the door. He turns on the living room lamp and turns the television off. He also makes his way to the kitchen, turning on the recessed overhead lights once he gets there.

The doorbell rings again, several times in a row this time. The soft voice from the phone can be heard just outside his front door. "Hey, creepy killer, this bag isn't getting any lighter and I just saw you walk by the window. In fact, I can see you staring at me right now."

Arden laughs and pulls open the door to greet her. "Creepy killer, huh? Says the woman peeping in my windows at night." Lilly laughs and hands him the paper bag in her outstretched arms. "I come bearing gifts, since Ben and Cassie told me you might not have much of a selection." He takes the bag from her and steps aside so she can come in. Once she is inside, he closes the door and carries the bag into the kitchen, setting it down on the counter. Lilly, now standing next to the counter, extends her right hand. "It's a pleasure to meet you in person, Arden."

He takes her hand and shakes it. "It's a pleasure to meet you as well, Lilly." Her hand is soft, delicate, with well-manicured dark red painted nails. "So, what is on the menu for dinner tonight?" she asks as he lets her hand go.

Arden hesitates a moment before he answers. "Well, you have your choice of either homemade gourmet cheeseburgers or chicken pot pies individually prepared for us by world famous chefs."

Lilly smiles. "Sounds exquisite. I don't know if I can compete with that. I only brought a couple of store-made salads and a cheap bottle of red wine. I say let's go with the chef prepared pot pies since I don't eat a lot of red meat." Arden nods and turns to the freezer door, opening it up and retrieving the two frozen pies from the middle shelf. As he closes the door, Lilly's voice can be heard behind him. "I happen to have that same kind at home. Good choice."

While Arden preheats the oven and locates a sheet pan to put the pot pies on, Lilly unpacks the paper bag, setting two small side salads and a bottle of wine wrapped in a large neoprene koozie on the center island counter.

Lilly answers his question before he even asks it. "Yes, I brought over chilled wine. In case you were extremely ugly, I didn't want to have to wait to start drinking."

Handing her a corkscrew and two wine glasses, he smiles. "Well, you have been here about ten minutes, so there goes any self-confidence I thought I may have had about my handsome visage."

Lilly giggles and rolls her eyes at him. "Any man willing to make frozen pot pies for a first date dinner should have plenty of confidence, and I never said you were ugly. I'm just thirsty."

They continue to make small talk while Lilly opens the bottle of wine and pours each of them a glass. Once the pot pies are in the oven and cooking, they both sit down at the breakfast bar. Arden asks her about her work, and Lilly tells him about how she ended up writing poetry, and who some of her favorite poets are. A couple glasses of wine later and they are both sharing and laughing at their stories about Ben and Cassie. Arden tells her about his book idea involving them, as well as Ben's story about their latest diet, which causes Lilly to erupt in another fit of laugher. As she is telling him about Cassie's side of that diet adventure, Arden begins to realize he really enjoys Lilly's company. He finds himself stealing looks at her every chance he can. Her eyes are green, like his, but a lighter shade. Her long red hair, although pulled back into the ponytail, has several long tendrils that hang down on either side of her face, accenting her delicate features. Her nose is slightly upturned at the tip and her eyes sparkle and widen every time she laughs.

As the evening wears on, Arden tells himself he owes Cassie a big thank you and begins to wish the night will never end.

Chapter 6

REVEAL

"Taryn! Order up for delivery!"

The young woman gets up from where she is sitting in the kitchen and puts her cellphone in her back pocket. The cook sets two large pizza boxes down on the counter with a ticket sitting on top of them. Taryn grabs the ticket and looks at the address.

"Oh for fuck's sake, Cory. This is way out in the middle of nowhere. Don't you have anyone else you can send out on this one?" she asks.

"No, you are the only driver left for tonight. Quit complaining, grab the boxes, and get your ass on the road before they get cold."

Taryn huffs and gives Cory the middle finger while she grabs the two pizza boxes from the counter and heads off to her car. This will be her last year working for the pizzeria before she heads off to college and that time can't come soon enough.

Although she doesn't mind delivering pizzas because the tips can be pretty good on busy nights, the longer drives take forever and she almost always gets yelled at by the customers for the pizza being late or not hot enough. This particular customer, in fact. And they never tip her more than a dollar or two, which doesn't even cover the gas her car will use making the delivery.

Reaching the passenger side of her vehicle, she opens the door and sticks the two boxes into the insulated delivery bag sitting on the passenger seat that helps keep the pizza warm. She pulls her cellphone out of her back pocket and tosses it into the center console. She closes the door and heads around the front of the car to the driver's side, getting in behind the wheel and starting the car up. The radio comes on, blasting one of the latest top forty hits. Taryn turns the headlights on and puts the car in drive. The clock on the radio indicates it is a few minutes after ten in the evening. She will have to hurry if she wants to get back here before eleven when the restaurant closes.

She pulls out from where she's parked behind the pizzeria and makes a right turn onto the highway as she reaches the end of the parking lot. The cops are pretty lenient in this area, and she knows every one of them because the town is relatively small, so she accelerates up to ten to fifteen miles per hour over the posted speed limit. She doesn't expect to run into any other cars on the road at this time of night anyways, as most people are home by now. The sooner she can get this delivery over with, the sooner she can get home and call her boyfriend to come over for the rest of the night.

The miles begin to pass and as she expected, Taryn doesn't encounter any other cars while she drives. The song changes on the radio and a new popular hit fills the interior of her car. She starts to zone out, thinking about later tonight, as the tree-lined sides of the road create a repeating pattern within the range of her headlights. Lost in thought, she bobs her head back and forth to the beat of the song on the radio, oblivious to the smell of the pepperoni pizza permeating the cab of her small car.

Once she is about five miles away from her destination, Taryn is jolted out of her thoughts by what looks like the shape of a person standing at the edge of the right side of the road as she drives by them. She quickly looks in her rearview mirror in an attempt to confirm what she just saw flash by, but she only sees the black of the night behind her car, partially illuminated by the red of her taillights.

An odd feeling of fear surges through her. The only living things she ever runs into this far away from town are usually deer. Taryn shakes the feeling off and focuses on the last few miles before the turnoff to the customer's address.

A few seconds later and she can see another person standing along the right side of the road. Enveloped in darkness, with only their eyes visible, glowing red from the car headlights.

They reach out their left arm towards her car as she passes by, as though beckoning her to stop. The surge of fear from a moment ago returns, growing within her.

Another couple hundred feet and the shape of another

person, barely illuminated by her headlights, can be seen standing at the edge of the road. Shrouded in darkness, arm also extended towards her, with only their red eyes visible.

Suddenly afraid to slow down, Taryn steps on the gas, increasing her speed to get to her destination faster and away from the strange people standing along the road.

She frowns, trying to force the fear away. *Don't people have better shit to do than trying to scare people driving by?* she wonders. The trees are beginning to blur as the car's speed increases. She passes another shadowy figure, reaching for her. The fear inside her rising, Taryn briefly glances down at the dashboard and at her speedometer. Seventy miles an hour and increasing.

Another figure zips by on the right side. Their red eyes the only feature visible. Left arm outstretched. For a moment, over the sound of the radio filling her car, Taryn hears a raspy voice whisper her name.

"Taryn."

Fear, coupled with panic, explodes through her body. Her hands begin to hurt from gripping the steering wheel so tightly, knuckles white from the pressure.

The turnoff to the customer's driveway is quickly approaching, but Taryn is suddenly too scared to slow the car down. Slowing the car down means that whoever these people are might be able to get to her. There might be more waiting for her when she slows to make the turn. She glances at the speedometer again. Eighty-five miles per hour. Her car starts to shudder a little bit, reminding her that it is not in the proper mechanical shape to be going this fast.

As the customer's driveway appears within the range of her headlights along the right side of the road, she can see another shadowy figure standing there. Eyes glowing red. Left arm outstretched. Standing in the middle of the road she needs to turn onto.

Taryn maintains her foot on the gas and speeds past the turn, terrified to look behind her in the rearview mirror. Terrified that if she looks into the mirror, she will see those red eyes looking back at her. Tears start to form in her eyes. *Please just leave me alone*, she begs in her head.

The shuddering of the car intensifies with every increase in miles per hour.

Another figure passes by, a blur due to the speed of the car, but now standing just on the edge of the road. Tears freely race down Taryn's cheeks and to her chin while she maintains her iron grip on the steering wheel, now afraid to take her eyes off the road to see how fast she is going. The shaking of the car continues to escalate when the sound of her cellphone ringing reaches her ears. Out of habit, her eyes quickly glance down towards her center console where her phone is sitting and then right back to the road. The fear and panic inside completely consumes her when her eyes return to the road.

In the middle of the road, about thirty feet away and directly in the path of her car, stands one of the shadowy tormentors.

Taryn immediately jerks the steering wheel hard to the right to avoid the person in the road. The car lurches in the direction of the abrupt turn, but the sudden shift in the balance of the car's weight at its current speed causes the vehicle to overturn.

The next few moments feel as though they are happening in slow motion. Taryn watches as the world in front of her tilts to the right and continues to tilt until it is almost upside down. A loud crunching noise fills the interior of the vehicle, and the windshield in front of her shatters into a million spiderwebs as her head and left shoulder slam into the roof of her car, which is now several inches lower than before. Pain erupts from her left side and from the back of her neck. Beyond the shattered windshield, the world continues to tilt until another loud crunching noise fills the vehicle. This time, the passenger side window shatters inward, and the pavement from the road fills the view out the window. Taryn, unrestrained, is flung towards the concrete-filled view and tries to put her right arm out in front of her to stop her from going face-first into the passenger side door. She feels her right arm crumple under her weight and momentum, and a sharp pain explodes from her arm and elbow. The outside world beyond the shattered windshield continues to tilt, and suddenly, Taryn is free of the overturning vehicle.

For a brief moment, she feels as though she is flying, completely weightless. She sees her car continuing to roll down the highway without her, showering a trail of sparks when it makes contact with the concrete, its headlights creating a spiraling dance along the right side of the road that almost looks beautiful.

Then that moment is over and Taryn feels the cold, hard concrete of the road as she forcefully slams down onto it, back first. An excruciating pain races up her spine and then there is no pain at all. Taryn continues to roll down the road, each impact with the concrete slowing her momentum until she finally comes to a rest, lying on her back, staring up into the night sky.

The crunching sound of her car, much fainter now, continues for several moments longer until it finally stops, allowing the sounds of the nighttime forest to take over.

Taryn tries to move but nothing is responding to her commands. The throbbing from the left side of her face is the only thing she can feel. The rest of her body is as though it's not even there anymore. She tries to take a deep breath but instead coughs, wet droplets raining down on her face. Breathing is becoming harder with each breath. Tears fall from the corners of her eyes. *I don't want to die*, she begs the night.

She looks at the starry sky above her. From her left eye, the stars are all tinted red when she looks at them. She blinks a few times, trying to clear the red tint away, when a shadow appears standing over her, blocking out the stars beyond. Two red eyes that look as though they are glowing are staring down at her from the figure above her. The fear from before surges through her thoughts.

Taryn tries to speak, tries to ask why her, but it feels as though her throat is full of liquid. She coughs, once more raining droplets all over her face. She wants to ask this person who they are and why they would do something like this to someone else.

The figure above her kneels down, their knees on either side of her head. They sit back on their heels and then lean their face down towards hers. The darkness shrouding their facial features seems to extend outwards, overtaking any light, as though they have tendrils of black extending from a void that exists behind their glowing red eyes.

Taryn tries not to look into their eyes but she cannot force herself to look away. Her fear has overtaken any of her prior thoughts. Her tears continue to fall down either side of her head, disappearing into her hair. She coughs again, the warm droplets raining down on her face one more time.

The red eyes staring into her pull away as the person above her sits up straight again. Taryn feels their hand touch the right side of her face. A hand that feels as though it's too hot for the cool of the night. Too hot to belong to a person.

The raspy voice she thought she heard in the car earlier reaches her ears.

"He will know now."

The boiling hot hand leaves her cheek, allowing the night air to quickly cool her skin. The figure stands up and turns, walking away out of Taryn's sight and disappearing into the darkness, allowing the stars above her to return.

Taryn coughs once more, her breathing beginning to slow as each breath becomes harder and harder to take. She wonders how much longer she has and wishes she was able to tell her parents how much she loves them one last time. She tries once more to move, but her body is unresponsive. She looks to her left; quite a distance away from where she is laying, she can see the headlights of her car are still on, twin beams shining off into the woods. She looks to her right and only finds the dark of the night. Turning her head is painful, and causes more coughing, so she straightens her head back up and stares once more at the stars spread out above her.

She momentarily wonders if an approaching car will see her and save her. She blinks a couple more times, clearing away the blurriness caused by her tears, allowing the stars to come back into focus.

A new noise, one out of place with the sounds of the forest, reaches her ears. Somewhere nearby, her cellphone is ringing. As the stars above her get dimmer and dimmer, she wonders who is calling her. Maybe it's her boss Cory, trying to find out where she is and why the pizza hasn't been delivered yet. The customer would have definitely already called and complained. Maybe it's her boyfriend, checking to see if they were still going to see each other tonight and if he should bring anything over. Maybe it's her mom calling to check in on her and making sure she had a good shift with lots of tips.

These thoughts dance through Taryn's mind as the stars above her get darker and darker.

One last ragged breath escapes her lips, and then she wonders no more.

✳

Arden tosses the empty eggshells into the trash and turns his attention back to the two eggs now frying in the pan. He yawns, still tired from last night. Lilly kept him company until almost one in the morning before she finally had to leave. They made plans to see each other again later tonight provided neither of them was too tired.

He smiles while he watches the eggs cook. It has been a very long time since he connected so well with someone else, and he didn't want to see her leave last night. They talked until early in the morning about every possible topic, enjoying each other's company and the less than gourmet meal once it had finished cooking. They talked about work and about their current projects, and what they wanted to accomplish next. The conversation flowed freely, and Arden was able to find an ease with her that he has not had before.

Excited about the opportunity to see her again tonight, he grabs a spatula from the utensil rack and works it under each of the eggs, flipping them over one by one, taking care not to bust the yolks in the process. The oven timer dings, letting him know that the bacon is done cooking. He sets the spatula down on the counter and removes the foil-lined sheet pan from the over with an oven mitt. He transfers the bacon from the pan to a paper towel-lined plate to help absorb the excess grease, and then removes the pan with the eggs from the heat.

A couple slices of toasted bread later, and with a little layering of the cooked food, Arden is staring at his breakfast creation: a bacon and egg breakfast sandwich.

He eats his meal in silence, still thinking about seeing Lilly later. Once he is done eating, he washes the dishes and sets them on the drying mat. The plan today is to reread Chapter 14 and fix any errors he can catch, as well as ensure the chapter's pace is still on par with the rest of the manuscript.

The tiredness from earlier is now gone, thanks to his hearty breakfast and his usual two cups of coffee. He glances at the clock on the stove. Almost eleven in the morning. Satisfied it's not too early for a small drink; Arden heads into his writing room and pours himself a small glass of bourbon. He looks out the window in front of him as he takes a sip, the sun shining brightly across the parking area and through the trees beyond, with clear blue skies above.

He turns from the window and the welcoming morning sun and walks into the living room, picking up the remote and turning on the television. Arden sits down on the couch and takes another sip of his bourbon.

Doesn't hurt to let breakfast settle before I start working, he thinks.

The weatherman appears on the screen, talking about what kind of weather the region can look forward to for the next five days. He takes another sip of his bourbon as the morning news anchor comes on the screen, replacing the weatherman, and launches into a story about a fatal car accident involving a young woman last night. Per the anchor, a long-haul trucker came across the accident scene early in the morning. The authorities indicated that the young woman was delivering for a local pizzeria when she lost control of her vehicle at a high rate of speed and, because she was not wearing a seatbelt at the time, she was ejected from the vehicle during the accident. She died on the scene from her injuries.

Arden frowns. Not only at the tragic loss of a young life, but at a sudden nagging in the back of his mind. *Why does this sound so familiar?* he asks himself. An uneasy feeling of déjà vu settles in, the same feeling he had the other day when he was eating lunch with Ben. The same feeling he had when he watched the news story about the actress who killed herself.

Something isn't right, he thinks, *these stories sound too familiar.*

That's when a sudden realization hits him. *That's it. Stories. These deaths feel familiar because I wrote ones exactly like them in my novels.*

Arden picks up the remote and turns off the television. He takes a sip of his bourbon and speaks, as though he needs to hear the words to believe them. "These have to just be coincidences, right?"

He gets up from the couch and heads into his study, setting his bourbon down on the desk. He grabs a copy of his first novel from the middle shelf behind his chair and begins to flip through the pages until he reaches Chapter 2. He quickly scans the chapter until he gets to the part he is looking for. The part about a high-level executive who is thrown to his death from a high rise by his monster.

Arden marks the location by folding down the corner of the

page, closes the book, and sets it down on his desk. He stares at the book a few moments before he picks up his bourbon and takes a sip, trying to remember which one of his books involved the death of an actress. He sets the glass back down and turns again to the shelf, grabbing his second novel. He quickly flips through the pages until he reaches Chapter 4. He skims the paragraphs until he reaches the portion of the chapter he is looking for: the portion about a young actress who is killed in her home by his antagonist. By drowning. He folds the page down to mark the spot, and then skims through the rest of the book to see if any of the other deaths involve a young pizza delivery driver. Not finding the additional portion he is looking for, he closes the novel and sets it down next to the other one on his desk.

Must just be coincidences, right? he asks himself. *I wrote these novels years ago.*

He reaches forward, grabs his glass, and finishes the contents in one quick swig. He walks over to the small table and pours another glass, staring out the window at the sun-filled world beyond. Lost in thought, he tries to remember if it was the third or fourth book that involved the delivery driver. Confident it was his third one, he pulls his gaze from the window and returns to the shelf, putting his glass back down on the desk in the process. He grabs his third novel and begins to scan the pages.

Arden finds what he is looking for in Chapter 6. A young woman, delivering pizzas late at night, killed by his monster in a car accident. He marks the page and closes the book, setting it down on his desk next to the other two.

A chill runs down his spine. *Coincidences. Just coincidences.*

He sits down in his chair and reaches forward, hitting a key on his laptop and waking it up from sleep mode. He takes a quick sip of his bourbon and then opens a web browser on the computer. A few keystrokes later and the news article about the executive's death is displayed on the screen in front of him. Arden grabs his first book off the desk and opens it to where the page is folded over. He reads through the chapter, taking note of the details.

Turning his attention back to the computer screen, he reads through the details reported about the executive's death. About how it appeared to be a suicide as there was also an unregistered, loaded handgun found in the penthouse suite. The news article surmises that Mr. Carleigh chose to jump off the balcony to his death instead of using the weapon as there were no signs of forced entry or foul play.

The hair on Arden's neck rises up. The executive's death in his novel also describes a handgun, left behind and unused.

He sets the book down on the desk and takes a deep breath. *Still just a coincidence. Most people with that kind of money and power have handguns they carry, right?* he asks himself.

Returning his attention to the task at hand, he enters a few more keystrokes and brings up the news article about the actress. Per the article, the actress had drowned in her own bathtub and was found by a maid the next morning. The drowning appeared to be accidental as the house was locked and again, there were no signs of forced entry or foul play. Arden turns his attention from the news article to his second novel setting on the desk. He grabs the book and opens it to the dog-eared page he marked earlier, quickly reading through the chapter.

Similarities appear once more. A locked door with no forced entry. A drowning that appears accidental, with no signs of violence.

He sets the book back down on the desk, closed, and takes a deep breath.

Arden stares at the computer monitor for a few minutes before reaching forward and bringing up the news article of the young delivery driver's death. Her name is being withheld until her next of kin can be notified, but the article states it appears she lost control of her vehicle, which caused it to overturn multiple times. She'd been thrown from the vehicle and was pronounced dead on the scene.

He sits back in the chair, still looking at the article on the screen in front of him. He's familiar with the pizzeria the driver worked at, but he can't remember who his delivery driver was the last time he ordered pizza from there. He grabs his third novel from the desk and opens it to the earmarked page.

Once more, the similarities are glaring. Young female delivery driver, ejected from the vehicle during a rollover accident at a high rate of speed. Except in his book, the driver was attempting to get away from his monster that ultimately caused the accident when it appeared in front of the driver's car. The driver swerved to avoid the monster, and that's when they lost control of the vehicle.

Arden closes the novel and sets it down next to his other two. He closes the browser on his laptop and grabs his glass of bourbon, taking a sip.

What are the odds that this could happen? he wonders. *What are the odds that a bunch of deaths are happening that just happen to have this many similarities to the ones I created in my books? It's not possible, is it? Or am I allowing my imagination to run wild and create paranoia where there is none?*

He takes another sip of his bourbon and sets the glass down on the desk. Getting up out of his chair, he grabs the three books on the desk and returns them to their spots on his bookshelf. He returns to the chair and stares out the small window on the other side of the room for a few moments, lost in thought. He created a lot of deaths for a lot of different characters in his books over the last several years. These similarities are just freak chance, rolls of the dice of life matching up and nothing more. The feeling from earlier remains, as though he is still missing something. As though something is still not right. But Arden is satisfied with his presumption.

Just coincidences and nothing more.

Pulling his gaze from the window, he looks back at the monitor. He still has a deadline to meet, and two more chapters to recreate, and they won't get done with him playing detective by reading too much into what he sees on the news. He leans forward and brings up his current manuscript. The beginning of Chapter 14 awaits, and Arden will need to focus if he wants to finish a thorough proofreading while adjusting any developmental errors he can spot. He pushes the thought of the three deaths from his mind and throws himself into the edit of Chapter 14.

Lost in his efforts, the hours quickly pass until Arden reaches the last paragraph of the chapter. He finishes the edit and sits back, taking a moment to rub his eyes. Two more chapters to go, and then he can put this series to bed. Once again.

Ensuring he doesn't make the same mistake as before, he backs up the manuscript on both the hard drive and on his thumb drive. He picks up the notepad on the desk and skims through the notes he made about Chapter 15 and the direction he took it. He smiles while he refreshes his memory. This is the chapter where the protagonist realizes that he has found a way to finally defeat the monster. Although he's excited to get the chapter back down in writing, Arden's stomach reminds him that he needs to eat. He gets up from the chair and heads into the kitchen, glancing at the wall clock as he does. Almost seven in the evening. Lilly said she would come over around eight, and she would bring their dinner this time. Of course, she made the decision to bring their dinner with her after she looked in his fridge and his pantry last night to see what was available for tonight.

As he reaches the kitchen, he grabs his phone from the counter and checks it. A couple of texts and a missed phone call with accompanying voicemail from Ben asking him how last night went. Cassie's voice can be heard in the voicemail prompting Ben to ask certain questions like did he think she was pretty and are they going to see each other again. One missed phone call without voicemail from Saphina, who is probably just checking up on the status of the chapter rewrites. One missed call from a restricted number, which reminds Arden he may actually need to change his phone number soon if they keep continuing to call. The last message is a text from Lilly confirming she will be over around eight, and he better be awake when she shows up.

The last message puts a big smile on Arden's face, and he realizes he needs to get ready. Setting the phone back down on the counter, he heads off to his bedroom to get a change of clothes.

Less than an hour later, Arden is showered and dressed in a crisp white button-down shirt and blue jeans. His hair is combed back out of his face, and the edges of his medium-length beard are trimmed. A quick splash of cologne and Arden is back in the kitchen.

He grabs his phone, and before he is able to return the calls to Ben and Saphina, the doorbell rings.

Chapter 7

RECOGNITION

Dinner with Lilly flies by, and after several glasses of bourbon, Arden finds himself sitting on the living room couch next to her. Facing each other, almost knee to knee, they laugh and talk about their day and how much they were both looking forward to another chance to spend some more time together.

The conversation drifts to what he was able to accomplish on the manuscript today, and Arden tells her about how he finished up the edit on Chapter 14 and is about to start work on rewriting Chapter 15. He tells her that he really likes how this one initially turned out, and hopefully his readers will feel the same. Lilly tells him she can relate; she feels locked into her current poetry content and style since she has been doing it for so long. Arden listens to her talk about the current collection she is writing, mesmerized by her sparking green eyes. By how her soft red hair cascades down around her ears. By how her pink lip gloss accents her lips perfectly in the light from the living room lamps.

He wonders what it would be like to kiss those lips. To run his hands through her hair and hold her petite body close to his.

"Hey creepy killer, you still with me?"

Arden is pulled from his fantasizing and blinks his eyes a couple times. "Yeah, sorry, my mind's going one hundred directions at once lately," he responds.

Lilly laughs.

"I can see that. Well, while you're imagining chaining me up to a tree in the back of your house and possibly wearing my skin as a suit, would you please get me another glass of wine?" she says as she holds up her empty glass.

Arden laughs and takes the glass from her. "I'd love to."

As he makes his way to the kitchen, Lilly asks if he would like to watch a movie. He nods, and as he is refilling her glass, his phone rings. He glances over at the screen to see who is calling. Saphina. He forgot to call her back earlier after Lilly arrived. Grabbing the phone, he carries it along with Lilly's glass into the living room. He hands the glass to Lilly and nods at the still ringing phone. "My agent. Would you hate me forever if I took the call?" he asks.

Lilly smiles and shakes her head no, winking in the process. "This just gives me a reason to say nothing repeatedly in response to you as you ask me what's wrong later this evening when I have an attitude." She reaches forward and grabs the remote from the table. "Go on. I'll find us something good to watch."

Arden smiles and makes his way into the study to take the phone call. He swipes to answer the phone and puts the device to his ear. Saphina's voice fills his head, asking why he can't be bothered to return her calls during the day but is willing to answer her calls in the evening and what is the status of the manuscript. Arden reassures her that he was able to get some more work done on it and should be restarting Chapter 15 tomorrow.

While talking to Saphina, he hears the television in the living room turn on, the news station from earlier once again telling the top stories of the day. The voice of the evening anchor reaches his ears and reminds Arden of the deaths in the news and how they seemed to match what he wrote in his novels. As Saphina pauses to catch her breath in the middle of her current lecture on deadlines and complaining about her contractor's delay in finishing her remodel, Arden decides to tell her about what he has observed the last couple of days.

He tells her about the three deaths and how they match deaths he created in his first three books. He tells her about how something just doesn't feel right, and about the uneasy feeling he had both the night of the lightning storm as well as each time he heard the news reports. He also tells her about the sudden volume of restricted calls calling his cellphone and not leaving any messages.

Saphina is quiet on the other end of the phone for a few moments.

Just as Arden is about to ask if she's still there, her stern voice is in his ear asking him if he's been drinking a lot more lately or if he's been taking any kind of mind-altering drugs. She asks if he's gotten into conspiracy theories recently or if he thinks people are following him.

Arden is pretty sure he hears her use the words "don't go crazy" or "end up crazy" at least ten times.

He reassures her. No, he isn't going crazy. No, he's not seeing things. No, he doesn't believe someone is out to get him. And no, he's not taking drugs or drinking any more than usual.

Saphina repeats the same thing he told himself several times earlier today. It's all a coincidence. That the deaths in his novels were written a long time before the recent ones in the news. She tells him that his mind is probably just manifesting a relationship between the two because he is so close to wrapping up his current novel.

Letting her words sink in, he nods to himself. It would make sense that he is fabricating a relationship between his novels and the recent deaths in the news. His creative brain is constantly working on plot development and storylines, and he is bringing a big portion of his life to a close with the publication of this last novel in the series. Agreeing with her analysis, Arden brings the phone call to an end, reassuring Saphina that he should have the manuscript wrapped up within the week. He ends the call, sets the ringer to silent, and places his phone down on the desk, blankly staring out the small window and into the dark of night beyond.

Fabricated relationship. Makes more sense than the deaths in his books actually happening in real life. But that still doesn't explain the uneasy sensation, the coincidences in the details, and the feeling in the pit of his stomach that something isn't right. That something bad is happening. That something bad is coming. That something bad might already be here.

Lilly's voice can be heard coming from the living room. "You planning on coming back, or were you hit with some inspiration from my amazing company and have decided to write instead of watch a movie with me?" Her head appears in the doorway, peeking around the frame at him as he turns toward the sound. "Good phone call, hopefully?"

Arden smiles and nods at the beautiful redhead now standing in the doorway. "Yeah, good call. Just getting some things off my chest and reassuring my agent the book will be done soon."

Lilly nods, her green eyes sparkling with her smile, and points back towards the couch. "So, movie time? So we can tell all our friends how we Netflix and chilled?"

Arden laughs and nods, following her as she turns and returns to her seat the couch. "Netflix and chill huh? You know what that really means right?"

Lilly sticks her tongue out at him as she sits back down. "Yes, it means that if you suddenly get all handsy during the movie, I'll slap some teeth out of your head and then it will become dentist appointment and chill."

Arden sits down next to her, still laughing, and pretends

to write in an imaginary notebook. "Note to self, do not get handsy during the movie."

Lilly laughs in response and turns her attention to the television. As she does, she asks Arden if he has any popcorn and if so, would he be willing to be a gentleman and make some for them.

Arden agrees, instantly happy that he picked some up when he was in town the other day with Ben. He gets up from the couch, heading toward the pantry. As he does, he can hear the news anchor on the screen talking about the latest details in the death of the delivery driver.

The uneasy feeling returns and he tries to shake it off as he pulls the box of popcorn from the pantry. He opens the box and removes one of the bags, returning the box to the pantry and removing the plastic from the bag. As he is putting the bag in the microwave, Lilly's voice can be heard over the television.

"It's a shame what happened, isn't it? She was so young."

The details of the young delivery driver's death in his book and how they are so similar to the one from the news once again begin to race through his mind, escalating the uneasy feeling until it feels as though it is taking over. *No*, he tells himself, *don't let this ruin your evening. It's just coincidence. A fabricated relationship.* He forces himself to take a deep breath and push the thoughts away. Listening to the hum of the microwave while it heats up the popcorn, he focuses his attention on Lilly as she begins to scroll through the available channels for a movie to watch. Watching her occasionally shake her head *no* as she scrolls though the channels, as though the movie offered by the channel wasn't good enough for them to watch tonight, Arden's smile slowly returns and the uneasy feeling begins to diminish. Before the feeling is completely gone, the first few pops of popcorn from the bag in the microwave startle him, making him jump. Lilly, who must have caught his reaction from the corner of her eye, stops in her hunt for a movie and looks over at him.

"You ok? You look a little pale."

Lilly sets the remote down on the table and gets up from the couch, walks into the kitchen, and stops next to him. "You look like you have seen a ghost. What's going on?"

Arden nervously laughs and shrugs, not sure if he should tell her what is on his mind. "I would rather not have you convinced I am crazy on our second date. I was hoping we could make it to date four or five before that point."

Lilly laughs and nods. "No, I am pretty sure you are crazy. All of us are crazy in our own ways; it all really just comes down to how compatible our crazies are." She reaches out with her left hand and softly grabs his right arm. "Seriously though, what's up? You've had something on your mind all night, and I know it's not just inappropriate thoughts about me."

Arden's smile grows bigger at the last thing she says. "Hey now, you can't blame me for imagining what you'd look like, clothes all disheveled and torn, chained to the tree out back and begging to be let go."

Lilly laughs and rolls her eyes at him. "Seriously, Arden, what's on your mind?"

The popping inside the microwave slows, and Arden hits the cancel button, turning the microwave off.

"You'll think it's stupid. I think it's stupid. Just my overactive mind in hyperdrive, making things seem like they're more than what they really are." He opens the microwave door and carefully pulls out the puffed-up bag of popcorn. He pulls at the edges of the bag and opens it up, releasing the steam from the bag and filling the kitchen with the smell of butter.

Lilly lets go of his arm. "Well, this sounds like it might be a better movie than any of the movies I saw when I was trying to find one for us to watch." She reaches into the bag of popcorn he's still holding and grabs a small handful, popping a piece into her mouth and nodding towards the living room. "C'mon creepy killer, let's go have a seat and you can tell me all about it."

Arden nods and follows her into the living room, each of them sitting down at their previous spots on the couch. Lilly grabs the remote and lowers the volume of the television until it is just barely audible. She returns the remote to the table and grabs her glass of wine, leaning back into the couch cushions. She grabs another handful of popcorn and nods at him. "Ok, let me have it, both barrels."

He smiles at her and sets the popcorn bag down on the couch between them. Grabbing his own drink from the end table next to him, he begins to tell her the same thing he told Saphina.

About how the recent deaths in the news all seem to mirror deaths he has written about in his books. About how there is no way they can be related, but how the details of each death seem to mirror each other. About how he knows how ridiculous it seems but the feeling of unease he gets every time he thinks about it tells him that there might be something more to it than just a bunch of freak coincidences.

Lilly listens and nods as he speaks, occasionally grabbing some more popcorn and taking a sip of her wine. When he finishes, he waits to see her reaction, to hear her response. To see if she gets up from the couch and bolts out the door because of how crazy he sounds talking about it. Long seconds pass before she finally speaks.

"Yeah, that sounds insane. If you give me a moment, I need to make a quick phone call to the nearest loony bin so we can get you the help you need."

A brief wave of panic washes over Arden until he sees her smiling, her eyes twinkling in response.

"I'm kidding, Arden. It does sound crazy, but if I can play devil's advocate here, what if there really is something more to it. What if there is someone out there who is going around killing people like in your books? There are a lot of crazy people in this world."

Arden nods, relieved. "I wondered that as well, if there is some sort of insane copycat. But I wrote a lot of deaths into each one of my novels, and each of these similarities has only been one death from each novel so far. If it's someone intent on copying the deaths in my books, why just one from each book? That's what I can't seem to fathom and why I want to believe these are just coincidences and I'm imagining they're related to my books."

He grabs a handful of popcorn and takes a few bites, waiting for Lilly's response. Her brow is slightly furrowed, as though she is deep in thought.

The expression on her face softens and she looks at him. "Have you identified where the deaths are in your books? Like what books and what chapters?"

Arden nods, his mouth currently full of popcorn.

Lilly gets up from the couch, wine glass in her right hand, and stands in front of him, extending her left hand to him.

"So let's go see if there's a pattern. And if so, see if your uneasy feeling is right."

✳

After grabbing a chair from the kitchen for Lilly to sit on in the study, they reviewed what Arden has already made note of. The first similarity appears in his first book, in the second chapter. The second similarity is from his second book, in the fourth chapter. The third comes from his third book, in the sixth chapter.

It doesn't take long before the two of them are able to identify a pattern and determine that if someone really is mimicking his books, the next death would be from his fourth book, in the eighth chapter. It also doesn't take them long to deduce that if this is more than just a coincidence, the next death should happen soon since all the recent parallels have been within the last week.

Lilly sits back in the chair and finishes the last of the wine in her glass. "So now we just have to figure out who the next death might be and see if it really is something to be worried about."

Grabbing his fourth book from the bookshelf, Arden quickly skims through the related chapter and then sets the book down on the table. He takes a deep breath. "Well that presents a challenge, since there are six deaths in that chapter. A family of three, a police officer, a young male college athlete, and an airplane pilot."

Lilly taps the top of her wine glass, in thought. "Do you know anyone who fits any of those descriptions?"

Arden shakes his head no. "Not really. I briefly interacted with a few of the local cops because I had a stalker issue a few years back but other than that, I haven't had any contact with them in a while." He finishes his bourbon and gets up from the chair, walking over to the small table with the decanter on it to pour another glass.

"Sure, get yourself another drink while ignoring my empty glass. I see how it is." Lilly says. She picks up the glass and holds it out. "If you don't mind, good sir, I would appreciate another glass as well."

Arden laughs and nods, finishing a small pour of his bourbon into his glass. He turns towards Lilly and looks at her glass being held towards him and then at her, then back at the glass. He takes a quick sip of his own drink. "Well, since you put it that way, I would be happy to refresh your drink, my dear."

Lilly giggles and relinquishes her glass to Arden. She picks up his fourth novel from the table and flips to the earmarked page identifying the eighth chapter, turning her attention to the pages and focusing on reading each line. Arden sets his own drink down on the desk and then heads into the kitchen. A few minutes later, he returns to the study with a full glass of wine for his beautiful company.

He sets the glass down next to Lilly and then sits down in his own seat, grabbing his glass of bourbon and taking a sip. Lilly's attention is still focused on the book, quickly flipping through each page as she finishes it. Arden sits back and watches. He breathes in her beauty with his eyes and admires the intensity with which she devours each page of the chapter. He sits patiently and watches her, waiting for her to finish. Once she finishes the chapter, she closes the book and sets it back down on the table. She picks up her own glass and takes a quick drink.

"I can see why your books are popular. You have a gift for making the reader feel like they are the ones in the place of your characters."

He watches as she takes another sip of her wine.

Lilly nods towards his fourth novel on the table. "Well, looks like we'll have to watch the news closely for a while to see if any of those deaths get reported."

Arden smiles. "We?"

Lilly looks from the books on the table to Arden. "Well

yes, we. You let me in on your little mystery. As a writer myself, I love a good mystery, and what is better than a real-life mystery?"

Arden averts his eyes from hers. "One that doesn't result in innocent people dying." He sighs deeply. "In all seriousness, Lilly, if these are not just coincidences, I might not be the safest person to be around right now."

Lilly leans forward and puts her left hand on his right leg. "I can take care of myself Arden. I might be little, but I'm fierce. It comes with being a redhead."

Arden laughs and looks back into her eyes. Her green eyes exude a fire behind the sparkle he hasn't seen yet. He nods. "I believe you. I just don't want to see you get hurt."

Lilly smiles. "So I can confidently tell myself you won't be chaining me up to a tree outside for ritualistic torture now?"

Her response makes him laugh. "No, not just yet."

Still looking into her eyes, Arden sets his bourbon down on the table and reaches out with his right hand and touches the left side of her face. "Thank you for being so understanding," he softly says while he lightly traces her jawline with his fingers, slowly running them from below her ear to her chin.

Lilly closes her eyes while his fingers trace across her skin and then opens them as his fingers pull away. As he pulls his right hand away and lowers it down to his leg to lie upon the top of her left hand still resting there, she sets her wine glass down on the table and slides forward on her chair. She reaches forward with her right hand and grabs the front of his shirt, forcefully pulling him towards her.

His heart almost pounding out of his chest and butterflies suddenly making themselves known in his stomach, Arden doesn't resist and allows himself to be pulled forward towards Lilly until their lips touch.

Once her soft lips press against his own, Arden feels as though an electric current explodes from the contact and proceeds to travel down from his lips and through his entire body, racing over his arms and legs all the way to the tips of his fingertips and toes. He allows himself to melt into their connection, the passion in their kisses slowly escalating. He feels her right hand leave his shirt and tangle itself in his hair on the back of his head while her left hand tightens its grip on his right leg.

He leaves his right hand resting on the top of hers while his left hand finds the right side of her face, holding it softly while their tongues dance with each other, exploring the soft, wet warmth of each other's mouth. Arden isn't sure what is affecting him more, the electric current from their connection or the passionate, sweet taste of Lilly's kisses.

They continue to kiss, unable to get enough of each other, until Arden feels Lilly's hand leave his hair and start to press against his chest, pushing him lightly back from her. He pulls himself away and leans back in his chair, letting his hand fall away from the side of her face.

"I'm so sorry..." he stammers, immediately thinking he might have been too forward, too needy once his lips were upon hers. Lilly smiles as she looks into his eyes and shakes her head no.

"No, don't apologize. I've wanted to kiss you since the first time I saw you. I just know where this will lead if we keep going, and I'd like at least a couple more dates before I let you in my pants."

Arden nervously laughs and feels his face turning bright red. He tries to pretend he doesn't feel the heat radiating from his face with her statement about getting into her pants. *I'm blushing like a schoolgirl right now. Way to show my manly side,* he thinks.

As if she could hear his thoughts, Lilly giggles and pulls her left hand away from his leg. "C'mon, Romeo. Let's get back to the popcorn and find a good movie to watch. We can continue this at a later time."

Arden nods and stands up from his chair, grabbing his glass of bourbon in the process. Lilly follows suit, standing up with her wine glass in hand. They both head out of the study and into the living room, resuming their previous positions on the couch. Lilly once again grabs the remote and turns the volume of the television up to a normal level. She brings up the guide, flipping through the channels one additional time to find a movie for them to watch. Arden grabs a handful of popcorn from the bag still sitting on the couch and takes a few bites, watching as Lilly scrolls through the available channels. Stopping the channel search on a recently released comedy that started a few minutes ago, Lilly sets the remote back down on the table and leans back into the couch cushions. Arden takes a sip of his bourbon and settles into watch the movie.

The minutes quickly pass, filled with smiles and laughter, until the credits begin to roll on the screen.

Arden steals a glance at Lilly and catches her in the middle of a yawn. "Oh no, the yawn!" he jokes.

Lilly covers her mouth with her right hand as she finishes the yawn and giggles. "Yeah, I fear I might not be awake too much longer. And no, that's not a hint that I'm staying the night."

Arden exaggerates a depressed sigh with as much drama as he can muster and nods. "I would not dare to offend the lords and ladies of etiquette by presuming I might be able to convince you to stay the night and possibly take off all your clothes in the process."

Lilly continues to giggle and gets up from her spot on the couch. She extends her left hand out to him. "C'mon and walk me out." Arden accepts her hand and stands up in front of her. Still holding her hand, he turns towards the front door and pulls her along behind him. Lilly does a quick detour to the kitchen counter where her purse and phone are sitting so she can grab them and then returns to Arden, who is holding the door open for her to step outside. He walks with her to the passenger's side door of her vehicle and waits while she puts the items from her hands into the center console and onto the passenger seat. They both walk to the driver's side and stop next to the door.

As she turns back around to face him, Arden reaches out

and takes both her hands in his own. "Thank you."

Lilly smiles, entwining her fingers with his and stepping closer to him. "For what?"

"For being amazing. For not running away, screaming for the hills, thinking I'm insane. For not seeing the shackles and chain attached to the tree out back next to the fire pit."

Lilly laughs, lowering her head a moment and giving it a quick shake before looking back into his eyes. "Oh I noticed the shackles and chain. I was just planning on pulling a plot twist. Instead of you drugging me one night, I was going to drug you instead and you would be the one who wakes up chained to the tree."

Arden laughs and nods. "Fair enough," he responds as he leans towards her, lightly putting his lips against hers. Lilly responds, pressing back with her lips harder in return, tightening her grip on his hands. He feels her body move against his own as their kisses grow in intensity, their tongues once again dancing with each other. The electric tingling from earlier once again races from his lips and throughout his body.

Seconds turn into minutes and Arden is lost in his connection with Lilly, not wanting it to ever come to an end. With their bodies pressed close together, he begins to feel a stirring in his pants which he immediately realizes that Lilly notices as she stops kissing him and chuckles a bit.

"It appears I may have woken someone up," she says, motioning with her head down towards his pants.

Arden feels his face turning bright red again and tries to

mask it the best he can. "Well, he was getting jealous that he wasn't getting any attention so he decided to say hi."

Lilly laughs and pulls her body away from his, letting go of his hands in the process. She looks down towards his pants. "Sorry buddy, not going to happen tonight. You're going to have to work…harder…than that." She looks back up at Arden with a smirk and winks at him. He tries to keep a straight face and respond but is unable to do so, busting out laughing. Lilly joins him in his laughter and turns to open up the driver's side door of her vehicle.

"Well played, beautiful, well played. It's not too often I'm stunned into silence," he tells her as she gets in behind the wheel. He walks over to where she is sitting and leans slightly forward to see if he can steal one last kiss before she leaves.

In response, Lilly reaches out with her left hand and puts her index finger against his lips. "As much as I would like to, I fear another set of kisses might end up with me giving into staying the night. And it's a bit early for that." Arden smiles and nods, stepping back from the vehicle and grabbing the car door.

"Be safe driving and please let me know when you get home," he tells her. Lilly nods and blows him a kiss, starting up the vehicle and turning on the headlights. Arden closes the door and steps back, watching as she puts the vehicle into gear and backs away, turning around in his driveway and aiming the vehicle to head down the road. Arden waves as she pulls away and watches her taillights until he can't see them anymore. He turns and heads back into the house, closing and locking the door behind him. After taking a few minutes to clean up the remaining popcorn and two empty glasses from the living room, he heads back into the study and checks his phone.

Four missed calls, all within the last hour, from a restricted number.

Arden frowns, reminding himself again he probably should change his phone number. As he is carrying the phone into the kitchen to place it on the charger, he notices the screen is suddenly lit up with an incoming call. From a restricted number.

Irritated, Arden swipes to answer the call and finally find out who keeps calling. "Hello? Who is this?" he demands.

Arden is greeted by silence on the other end of the line for a few moments until a deep, guttural voice speaks three words and then disconnects the call.

"Soon, Arden. Soon."

Chapter 8

RESONATION

A squawk from the radio pulls Officer James Collview away from his brief nap and back to reality. He reaches forward and grabs the mic.

"Go for Collview," he says.

The voice on the other end of the radio comes back at him. "Jim, remember that reclusive author who lives out near Ben's place? The one who had a trespasser issue a few years back?"

Jim furrows his brow a moment in thought. "Oh yeah, the guy who had the crazy fan that was in hanging out in his driveway, right? Had a weird name? Arlo, or Argon, or something along those lines?"

Dispatch responds. "That's the one. Apparently, he's been getting harassing phone calls and was just threatened over the phone. Mind heading out that way and speaking with him?"

Jim hesitates as he checks the clock on the dashboard. It would be about an hour there and back, and that's not counting how long he would spend talking to the guy. "Is this something that can wait until tomorrow? My shift ends in half an hour and I would rather spend the rest of the night with my family than with someone complaining about some phone calls that made them feel uncomfortable."

The radio squawks once again. "Negative, Jim. Apparently, there is also something about deaths in the news mimicking things he wrote about and he's worried more might happen."

Officer Collview sighs. "Affirmative, dispatch, I'll head out there. Although I want it noted that I'm not a fan of dealing with someone with an overactive imagination when I'm supposed to be getting off shift."

Dispatch doesn't respond while he replaces the mic in its holder next to the radio.

Jim frowns and reaches forward, starting the cruiser. He turns on the headlights and stretches a bit, chasing away the lingering remnants of his nap. The spot he's currently parked is quiet, and usually is at this time of the evening. During the day it can be a different story, since the main road in front of him is one of the larger thoroughfares in and out of town. The spot is located just outside the north side of town, in a little clearing between two trees, and most of the locals know the police use this location all the time as a spot to catch speeders; however, unwary truckers and out of towners will often be going twenty or so miles per hour beyond the speed limit by the time they reach this point. Jim, who has the early evening shift, will often park out here to encourage drivers to slow down.

And they often do, because as soon as they see the black and white of the front of the cruiser just barely sticking out between the trees as they race on by, they instantly hit their brakes. Jim rarely pulls anyone over though, even if they are speeding past. The sight of their brake lights immediately lighting up as soon as they pass to slow down their vehicle is satisfaction enough.

Putting the cruiser in drive, he pulls from the small clearing and onto the road. He yawns as the car speeds up and the miles begin to pass, trying to remember what the guy was like the last time he was out there. If Jim remembers correctly, the guy is somewhat quiet, almost as though he is always taking notes about what is going on. *Hopefully this will just be a quick report and I don't have to spend an hour standing there listening to some weird story this guy has invented.* He glances at the clock on the dashboard. *Better call Hollie and let her know I'll be late tonight.*

He reaches down and grabs his cellphone, quickly unlocking it and hitting the icon to call home. He puts the phone on speaker and sets it back down on the center console, listening to the rings. His wife picks up on the fourth ring. The voices of both their boys can be heard screaming in the background.

"You going to be home soon? The kids are having a meltdown right now because I won't let them paint on the wall with their ice cream."

Jim chuckles a bit and responds, "No baby, sorry. I was actually calling to let you know I was going to be late tonight. Dispatch has me doing a call on the outskirts of town that might take a couple hours."

He can hear Hollie audibly sigh, even over all the crying in the background. He listens as she tells the boys to stop crying, or she will take the ice cream away immediately and send them to bed. "Well, your wife might just be drunk and passed out by the time you get home because these two have been a handful all day today, and I'm about to gag them and duct tape them to the wall."

"I know, baby, and you are the best mother and wife ever for putting up with both of them and me," he says while smiling, "I will be home as soon as I can, I just wanted to make sure you didn't worry. Give the boys my love, and I love you, babydoll."

"Yeah, yeah, whatever. Be safe, and make sure you come home to us. I love you too," she says in response as she once again tells the crying children in the background to stop crying. The inside of the cruiser goes silent as she disconnects the line.

Still smiling, knowing his wife has her hands full right now, Jim recognizes the turnoff to Ben's place as he drives past it and begins to slow the car down, looking for the entrance of the writer's driveway, which should be approaching pretty quickly on the right side of the road. A few moments later, the car's headlights fall upon the driveway.

Jim slows the cruiser down and makes the right turn onto the lightly rutted dirt road. He gets about thirty feet down the driveway when suddenly his headlights illuminate a dark figure standing in the middle of the road, which causes him to bring the car to a complete stop. *What the hell?* he thinks, surprised by the sudden appearance of someone in front of him.

A feeling of apprehension washes over him, and he glances around the outside of the cruiser that he can see from where he is sitting, trying to see if there are any other figures around him. There are no streetlights out this far, and the cloud cover overhead has stripped away any of the usual light from the moon. The figure, still standing in the middle of the road, maintains their position at the far edge of where the headlights can reach. Jim reaches forward with his left hand and turns on the switch for the cruiser's spotlight, mounted on the driver side of the car.

Instead of the spotlight immediately bathing the area in bright white light, it remains off. He turns the switch off and on a couple times with no response from the light.

A slight wave of fear races through him.

This light worked just fine earlier this evening, he thinks. *It picked a damn fine time to stop working.* He takes a deep breath. *Ok, think logically, Jim. So maybe this is just the author who was coming out to meet me and doesn't realize who I am. Maybe he's thinking I'm whoever was threatening him on the phone and is afraid to move.*

Jim nods to himself in agreement that what he thinks might be happening makes sense. *Better let him know I'm the good guy here.* He reaches forward and flips the switch that turns on the red and blue lights on top of the cruiser.

Instead of seeing the surrounding area bathed in alternating blue and red light, the dark maintains its control. He flips the switch a couple times with no response from the light bar on the other side of the roof above him.

Another wave of fear washes over him. *What the fuck is going on?* he asks himself. The figure in the road still hasn't moved yet, but it almost appears as though the portion of the headlights that fall upon the figure is getting dimmer. As if the darkness of the figure is growing.

Jim frowns and reaches forward to grab the mic, anxious to request backup and notify dispatch of what is happening, both outside of the car and with the car.

In the couple of seconds it takes his hand to reach the mic, several things happen. In the first second, when he initially begins to reach for the mic, the cruiser's headlights flicker and momentarily dim. In the next second, when his hand reaches the mic, the vehicle's lights shut off and the world around Jim is plunged into complete darkness. The cruiser's engine also turns off and suddenly the world is overtaken by absolute silence.

It takes Jim a few seconds to register just what happened. His hand moves from the mic to the keys in the ignition and tries to turn the vehicle back on. The car is unresponsive. Letting go of the ignition key, he fumbles for the mic and grabs it from the dash, hitting the talk button. "Dispatch, come in." The speaker is silent in response. He tries the walkie attached to his vest. "Dispatch, this is Collview; come in. Over." Still nothing.

He reaches to his right and feels around for his cellphone, quickly finding it. He pushes all the possible buttons to turn it on, only to find that it is not responding either.

A flood of fear surges through his system, and he can feel the release of adrenaline coursing through his body. Something inside him screams to run, but his training refuses to let him listen.

Taking a deep breath to steady his nerves, Jim grabs the door handle and opens the door, quickly getting out of the driver's seat. The crunch of the dirt road underneath his boots seems to echo off the trees on either side of the driveway. In the same fluid motion, he pulls his flashlight from his belt with his left hand and releases the safety clasp on his service revolver with his right.

He presses the switch for the flashlight, praying it will turn on. The beam quickly lights up the area in front of the cruiser and allows a brief wave of relief to wash over him. That relief is quickly replaced by another rush of fear, as the figure is now gone from the spot they were standing before the world went dark. With his right hand, he tries the mic attached to his vest on more time. No response at all. His hand lets go of the mic and quickly goes to the butt of his revolver and rests on it, ready to draw if needed.

"This is the police! Identify and show yourself!"

He pans the flashlight's beam around the dirt road, which extends in front of the cruiser. Empty. He turns to his left and right and waves the beam through the trees on either side of the car. Still no sign of the figure. Before he has a chance to turn around to check the back of the car, he hears a voice right behind him.

A raspy, guttural voice. One that sounds like it is only inches away from him. One that makes every cell in Jim's body flush with terror.

"You're next, Jim."

With every fiber of his body screaming for him to run, Officer Collview ignores the urge and once more relies on his training. In one quick move, he pulls his service revolver from the holster and steps forward, spinning on his front foot to face whoever is behind him while raising his weapon to the ready position so he can fire it if needed.

He never has a chance to pull the trigger.

He barely has a chance to acknowledge what happens before he is lying on his back on the ground, staring wide eyed into the darkness above him.

Unable to speak. Unable to breathe.

A searing pain from his neck, just below his chin, radiates throughout his entire body.

The flashlight is now on the ground, several feet away, and the beam is aimed towards him. With the light, he can see the open door of the cruiser is only a few inches away from the top of his head. He tries to take a breath but it's like his lungs are no longer responding to his requests for oxygen. He can feel his heartbeat match every surge of pain tearing through him. His right hand fumbles around on the ground to find his revolver but the only thing he finds is the cold, hard dirt underneath him. He tries to sit up but his body doesn't respond to his attempt.

Thoughts are scattered through his mind. *What the hell just happened? Where's my weapon? Why can't I move?*

The pain grows in intensity the longer he goes without breathing, and Jim begins to realize this might be it. His thoughts turn to his family. *Am I never going to see my family again? Did I tell them I love them earlier? What is going to happen to them if I'm gone?*

Jim tries to speak, but like breathing, he is unable to do so. *Why can't I breathe or speak?*

As if in response to his thoughts, a dark hand appears in view above him, silhouetted by the light from the flashlight. A mass of bloody flesh with the shredded end of what appears to be a tube hanging out of it is surrounded by the five fingers of a hand. At the end of each of those fingers is a sharp, pointed claw. Like the claws of a tiger or a bear. Wet with a dark red liquid and glistening in the beam of the light.

The mangled mass is still dripping blood and Jim can feel a few of the drops fall on his face. He stares at this mass and tries to figure out exactly what it is he is looking at. *That can't be my throat, can it?*

The pain slowly starts to subside, and he can feel his heartbeat beginning to slow. The thoughts in his mind are pure panic now, as his brain tries to make sense of what is happening and why parts of his body are no longer responding to its commands. He tries to think of his wife and his kids, and how he wishes he could hold them and kiss them just one last time, but the panic overrides these thoughts and forces them away as fast as they form. The beam from the flashlight starts to dim, and the darkness beyond the light quickly begins to take over. He watches as the hand above him pulls the mass away and disappears from his fading field of vision.

Just before the pain finally stops and just before his heart beats its last beat, the panic ravaging through his thoughts abates and allows Jim a few fleeting seconds of peace.

In those last couple of seconds, he wonders if Hollie and his boys will miss him.

*

The sound of an approaching siren pulls Arden from his slumber, and he opens his eyes. The ceiling of his bedroom comes into view. He yawns and stretches his arms and legs while the siren appears to be getting closer.

Arden furrows his brow. *Why am I hearing a siren?* He sits up in bed and listens to the siren until it abruptly cuts off. *It can't be that far away. Maybe something happened at Ben and Cassie's?*

He gets up and heads towards the kitchen to grab his phone to check on them, as well as make a morning cup of coffee and to see if the police department called him back. After Lilly left and he spoke with the police last night, he waited up for a few hours for the officer that they told him they were sending out, but the officer never showed up. Arden figured they had more pressing matters to deal with and would get back in touch with him today, so he went to sleep.

Glancing out his front living room window to make sure

there were no squad cars parked out front, he proceeds into the kitchen and grabs his phone. No missed calls. *Well, that's a good sign then*, he thinks, his curiosity piqued by the siren. He lives far enough out of town that it's very rare to hear anything beyond the normal sounds of the forest, and the few sirens he has heard over the last couple years have kept on going until they completely faded away.

He sets his phone back down on the counter and proceeds to make a cup of coffee, stifling a morning yawn. He leans back against the counter and enjoys the hot beverage, partially daydreaming about seeing Lilly again and how much more he can get done on the next chapter. Halfway through his first cup, the phone rings.

Arden reaches over and picks it up, looking at who is calling. Ben.

He swipes the answer button to the left and puts the phone to his ear. "Hey Ben, everything ok?"

Ben's voice loudly greets him on the other end of the line. Yes, everything is fine and he was actually calling to make sure Arden is ok, since he heard the sirens coming from his direction. Arden assures him he's fine and isn't sure what the sirens were about. Ben makes sure Arden promises to give him a call if he finds out what is going on and Ben states he will do the same. Before Arden can gracefully exit the call, Ben begins to chit chat a bit more about his plans today with Cassie and prods Arden a little bit about how it's going with Lilly. He assures Ben it is going well and a true gentleman does not kiss and tell.

Another sound, beyond Ben's laughter on the other end of the phone line, catches Arden's attention. The crunch of dirt and rocks underneath the tires of an approaching vehicle.

"Hey Ben, don't mean to interrupt you but someone just arrived at the house. Can I call you back later?"

Ben voices his agreement and again says to keep him posted if it's related to the siren. Arden agrees and disconnects the line. Setting the phone back down on the counter, he walks over to the front door and looks out the window.

A police cruiser is now parked next to his Jeep.

Arden takes another sip of his coffee and opens the door just as the door to the squad car opens up. "Good morning, officer," he says while a rather large man in a dark blue uniform slowly extricates himself out of the car. Arden momentarily wonders how the man even fit in there to begin with.

The officer nods at Arden and smiles as he closes the car door behind him. "Good morning. I apologize for coming by at such an early hour but I was wondering if you had some time to talk."

The uneasy feeling from the last couple of days briefly returns. The officer's tone of voice and the fact that his statement was more of an order than a question is not how Arden expected this conversation to start. Especially one that merely involves harassing and threatening phone calls.

Arden nods hesitantly. "Sure thing officer, would you like to come in?" The man in uniform nods at him and crosses the distance between the squad car and front door. Arden steps back, holding the door open. Once his unexpected guest is inside his house, Arden points at the mug in his hand. "Coffee?"

The officer nods, "Yes please, if that's ok."

Arden closes the door after the officer is inside and heads over to the coffee machine. He nods at the chairs lined up along the breakfast bar. "You want to sit down?"

"I'll stand for now; thank you, though," the officer states in response. "I'm Officer Holden. I don't want to take too much of your time so I will get right to the point. I wanted to ask you a few questions about last night."

Arden nods while the cup of coffee finishes brewing. The uneasy feeling briefly washes over him once again. He grabs the cup when it finishes and turns to the officer. "Sugar or cream?" The man shakes his head no. As Arden hands the coffee to him, he remarks, "So I have a feeling this isn't about the harassment complaint I made last night, is it?"

Officer Holden takes a sip of his coffee and shakes his head. "No sir. What can you tell me about last night after you called and filed the complaint?"

Arden finishes off his own coffee and shrugs. "Not much, really. I waited a couple hours for the officer that I was told would come by, but they never showed up, so I went to sleep." He watches as his guest takes a sip of their coffee and nods.

"Did you hear anything out of the ordinary? See anything?"

Arden shakes his head no in response. "No, nothing beyond the calls I have been getting."

The officer continues his line of questioning. "Did you leave the house any time between last night when you made the call and this morning when I arrived?"

The uneasy feeling comes back in full force. Something definitely happened, and nearby. Arden is almost afraid to find out. "No, I went to sleep and the sound of a siren woke me up."

The man nods, watching Arden as he responds. "What about animals in the area? Any predators, such as bears or wolves?"

Arden thinks for a moment before he answers. "I had a problem with some raccoons getting into my trash about six months ago. Other than that, only the occasional deer or rabbit comes by. If there are any bears or wolves, I haven't seen any." Arden hesitates a moment and then asks, "May I ask what this is about?"

The officer takes another sip of his coffee before responding. "There was an incident last night near the end of your driveway involving an officer who was responding to your complaint call."

The uneasy feeling is replaced by a surge of fear. *That explains why the siren from earlier sounded so close,* Arden thinks. "Are they ok?" he asks.

The officer standing in front of him sets the coffee down on the counter and shakes his head no. "We believe it was an attack by a large animal. Are you sure you didn't hear or see anything unusual last night after you called?"

Arden again shakes his head no. The officer starts questioning him about the phone calls he has been getting and the threat that was made last night; however, Arden is now only half paying attention to the conversation, his responses on autopilot. Instead of being focused on the officer, Arden is now focused on trying to remember the deaths from his fourth novel. *One was a police officer wasn't it? How did they die?* he wonders. The urge to excuse himself from the conversation and race into his study to grab the book setting on his desk and scour the chapter for details is growing stronger. *Sure, Arden, that wouldn't be suspicious at all. Gee, officer, this is real fun, but please excuse me so I can go read a book for a while and feed a sanity-questioning paranoia that I have been nurturing for a couple days now.*

"Sir? Are you ok?"

The officer's voice cuts through Arden's thoughts and pulls him out of autopilot. "Yes, I'm ok. Just worried about the phone calls and now with what you told me happened last night on my own property…" he lets his voice trail off as he refocuses his attention on the cop. The man nods at him.

"I can understand your concern. Unfortunately, there isn't anything we can do about someone calling your phone repeatedly. If you get any more of the calls where a threat is made, please contact us, but the best way to deter someone from harassing you by phone is to just not answer any numbers you don't recognize. I also recommend you call your service provider and change your phone number."

Arden nods. *Of course, common sense. I shouldn't have picked up the phone last night in the first place and I probably should have changed my number days ago like I was planning to,* he thinks.

The officer continues. "We will have Wildlife Services out here later today to check for signs of any territorial predators, so for the time being I recommended you stay close to your house if you do go outside, and don't go wandering around the woods at night. I also ask that you please refrain from leaving the house until the Wildlife officer comes to see you later, as we still have an active investigation at the end of your driveway. If you are going to need anything between now and then, please let me know and I will see what we can do."

Arden nods in agreement and tells the officer he won't need anything and will stay inside until the Wildlife officer shows up. The officer hands him a business card with his contact info on it and hands the now-empty coffee mug back to Arden. "Thank you for your time and the coffee."

Forcing a smile while he shows the officer to the door, Arden's thoughts quickly return to his fourth novel and the deaths from the eighth chapter. *At least, I'm pretty sure one of them was a police officer, right?* he asks himself, while internally chastising himself for not remembering his own creations better or paying closer attention when he was discussing the chapter with Lilly. *Isn't that the typical downfall of a man? Failure to pay attention to what is happening around him because he's focused on the woman instead of the task?* He waits at the door while the officer maneuvers himself back into his cruiser and starts up the car, reversing it from its current position, and then finally pulling away down the driveway.

Closing the door, Arden swiftly crosses the distance to his

writing room. He grabs the book from his desk and hastily opens it to the dog-eared page marking Chapter 8.

It doesn't take him long to find what he is looking for. The death of a police officer, several pages in. He focuses on the details. The officer in his book was terrorized by his monster, and ultimately had his throat ripped out on an isolated stretch of highway.

The police determined it was merely an animal attack.

A massive wave of fear washes over him and Arden lets the book fall from his hand. The sound of it hitting the floor seems to echo off the walls of the enclosed room.

His thoughts suddenly jumbled, he tries to think of what to do. This is more than just a coincidence. It's just not possible, especially now, that this is all happenstance. Someone is recreating the deaths from his books and clearly wants him to figure it out. Arden thinks about the call last night. He bends down and picks up the book from the floor, adding it back to the pile on the desk.

Soon, the voice had told him. *Soon what?* he asks himself while trying to make sense of it all. He thinks about the pattern he and Lilly identified when it came to the order of the deaths. He grabs his fifth novel from the shelf and frantically flips through the book until he reaches Chapter 10. He scans the chapter for any deaths and finds there are three in the chapter.

A general contractor, a homeless man, and an agent for an author.

The hair on Arden's neck rises and a cold chill tears through his body as he rereads the portion of the chapter with the third death in it.

An agent for an author.

Saphina.

Arden sets the book down on the table and stares at it, unmoving, his heart now racing.

No, whoever is doing this wouldn't kill Saphina, he tells himself, *It's too obvious. It would attract too much attention.*

Arden pulls himself away from staring at the cover of his fifth novel and turns towards the kitchen, willing himself to race to his phone, pick it up, and call to warn his agent. His thoughts stop him from moving.

Whoever is doing this doesn't care about too much attention. They killed a high-level executive and an actress already. Whoever is doing this wants the attention. Wants his attention. And what would Saphina say if he tells her he thinks she is next? Probably laugh at him, tell him he has finally gone crazy, and have him committed to a mental hospital.

Arden takes a deep breath and tries to calm his nerves. He tries to push the fear away. He tries to push the uneasy feeling away. Neither one of the feelings abate. He needs to tell someone, to make sure that he isn't crazy or imagining things.

Lilly.

Pushing himself into motion, Arden heads into the kitchen and grabs his cellphone from the counter. Before he has a chance to unlock it and dial Lilly's number, the phone rings in his hand.

The caller ID states the number is restricted.

Arden swipes the screen and sends the call to his voicemail.

A second later, the phone rings again. Restricted number is displayed on the screen one more time. Arden swipes and sends the call to voicemail.

Before he has a chance to dial Lilly, the phone rings a third time, once more displaying restricted number as the ID of the call. Arden angrily swipes the call to voicemail and slams the phone face down on his counter.

Immediately regretting his decision, he hopes he didn't shatter the screen.

The phone rings a fourth time.

Taunting him. Daring him to answer the call like he did last night.

A rage begins to form in his core, its volcanic heat quickly expanding from deep inside. It pushes against the frozen tendrils of fear that have their icy grip wrapped completely around him. Arden grabs the phone from the counter and flips it over. Only partially registering that the screen is thankfully not shattered, he swipes the answer button and puts the phone to his ear.

He yells at his tormentor on the other line.

"Why are you doing this to me!?"

Chapter 9

RETREAT

Arden waves at the Wildlife officer as they pull away and steps back inside his house. The officer confirmed the information Arden was told previously about what happened to the cop at the end of his driveway. According to the police, the man was attacked by a large animal and died from his wounds.

The Wildlife officer didn't find any of the typical territorial markings of a large predator, but that doesn't mean one didn't recently stake claim to this area. The officer advised that the Wildlife Service has retained a trapper to lay several traps in the surrounding forest and warned Arden to avoid taking any walks in the woods for the time being. He was also advised that if he heard anything while he was out back of his house, or anywhere around the outside of the house for that matter, to pay attention and be ready to run for safety if needed and then call them immediately.

The officer also confirmed the scene investigation had been

wrapped up and Arden was free to leave as needed.

Back at his kitchen counter, Arden grabs his phone to call Lilly and let her know it's ok to come over now. When he answered the phone earlier this morning, he was expecting to confront whoever was harassing him. Instead of a rough, guttural voice on the other end of the line, the voice of a very confused Lilly greeted him. Several apologies later, and after a brief explanation of what happened last night, Lilly insisted that he contact her the moment she could come over so they can talk about it.

She picks up on the second ring and after confirming she can come by, lets him know she will be on her way shortly.

While Arden waits for her to show up, he takes the opportunity to get a shower and clean himself up a bit. After stripping out of his pajamas, which consist of T-shirt and sweatpants, he tosses them in the hamper and grabs some fresh clothes from his closet. A few steps later and he is in his bathroom, turning on the handle for the shower and adjusting the temperature to somewhere between bright pink skin and skin melting off.

The almost scalding water of the shower helps wash some of his fear away and relaxes him, allowing him to temporarily forget the uneasy feeling while the steam from the hot water fills the shower enclosure and overflows into the rest of the bathroom. Some soap, shampoo, and conditioner later, Arden turns off the water and grabs the towel draped over the top of one of the glass shower walls. He quickly dries off and then hangs the towel on the rack along the wall.

Stepping out of the shower, he grabs his clothes stacked on the back of the toilet and puts them on. He combs his hair back and out of his eyes and quickly styles his beard. He splashes on a small amount of cologne and takes a look at his reflection in the mirror, content with the reflection he sees staring back at him.

A quick brushing of his teeth later, Arden is back in his study. He stacks and organizes his novels on the table and then pours himself a small glass of bourbon and proceeds to the kitchen, pausing momentarily in the living room to turn on the television, flipping the channel to the local news channel. The news anchor's voice fills the room, talking about the weather forecast and the rain that will be coming through the area later this evening.

Arden half listens to see if the anchor talks about what happened last night as he heads into the kitchen.

He checks his phone to see if he missed any calls while in the shower and sees a couple texts from Ben asking Arden to give him a call and tell him all about what happened in the driveway.

Well, that answers the question of whether it was reported on the news, he thinks.

Arden sighs as the now-familiar, uneasy feeling makes itself known, clawing its way back into his mind and skittering across his skin.

Against his better judgment, Arden opens his contacts and

scrolls through the names; once he finds the name he is looking for, he hits the call button and puts the phone to his ear.

While the line rings, he takes a sip of his bourbon to try to steady his nerves.

Saphina answers on the fifth ring.

The first thing Arden tells her is to please keep an open mind while he talks, which of course is greeted with her usual skepticism and sarcasm. He explains what has happened since the last time he talked to her and how he thinks she might be in danger.

As expected, Saphina asks him to put his imagination to work on his novels and not his reality and that if he is looking to spend some time in a mental institution to just ask her outright and she can arrange something that won't be permanent.

Arden presses the issue a bit more and asks her to just be careful and watch for anything out of the ordinary. She finally gives in and agrees to keep her eyes open and then asks for status on his manuscript. Arden cringes. *Shit, I haven't gotten any work done recently*, he thinks.

Promising he will throw himself into writing later this evening and hopefully will have it wrapped up within a few more days, Arden reiterates that he wants Saphina to be careful. She tells him to stop being paranoid and to get the manuscript done, and hangs up the line. He sets the phone down on the counter and takes a few steps forward towards the living room so he can see if the news anchor is reporting anything about last night. A reporter, smartly dressed in a blazer and tie, is talking about the upcoming yearly pumpkin festival and where you can buy your tickets early.

He glances at the clock on the wall to see how much longer he has before Lilly shows up when his phone rings.

A small surge of fear races through his body as he turns back to the counter and reaches for the phone, hesitant to see if the caller ID reads restricted number.

His fear subsides when he sees Lilly's name on the screen. He swipes to answer the phone.

"Hey there beautiful, everything ok?" he asks. Lilly affirms everything is fine but she is going to be running a lot later than expected. Cassie needs some help with something and begged Lilly for her assistance.

Arden laughs. "That's fine, take your time. This will give me a chance to try to get some more work done on the manuscript anyways, since I'm already well behind schedule."

Lilly thanks him for understanding and promises she will be over as soon as she can.

"I can't wait to see you, so don't let Cassie hold you hostage, for too long."

Lilly's light laugh reaches his ears, and she tells him she misses him too before she disconnects the line.

He sets the phone back down on the counter and, after grabbing his glass of bourbon, heads towards his study to hopefully get some work done on Chapter 15. As he is walking through the living room, the news anchor launches into the day's current news stories and begins to talk about a recent animal attack that took the life of a local police officer.

Arden stops dead in his tracks and turns towards the television.

According to the news anchor, the officer was killed by a large animal, presumably a bear, just outside his squad car on the far outskirts of town. The officer, a ten-year veteran of the local police force, leaves behind a wife and two young boys. Wildlife Services is searching the area for the predator and officers hope to catch it soon. The news anchor continues on and asks the viewers that if they see any large predatory animals to call Wildlife Services immediately and not to approach the animal. The anchor then launches into their next story and begins to talk about an upcoming tax-free weekend for the purchase of school supplies.

Arden tries to ignore the uneasy feeling as it races through his body, now entwined with tendrils of fear, and continues on his way into his writing room.

After a quick refresh of his bourbon, he sits down at the desk and turns on his laptop. While he waits for the computer to come out of sleep mode, he stares at the stack of books currently sitting on the right side of his desk, in order from his first novel on the bottom of the stack to his fifth novel resting on the top.

He gazes at the cover of the top book, thinking about what is written within it, letting the fear inside him build that someone else is going to die soon at the hands of some murderer recreating deaths from his novels. He continues to stare at the book's cover, unable to pull his eyes away, trying to make sense of it all, trying to will this nightmare out of existence. Trying to make himself believe that all these deaths are truly coincidences.

A beep from the laptop pulls him from his thoughts, notifying him that the computer is ready to go. He pulls up the manuscript and stares at the screen in front of him.

Chapter 15.

The cursor blinks its steady blink, waiting for his input. The chapter patiently waiting to be completed once again.

Arden grabs his notebook from the desk and flips through it until he reaches his notes about the chapter. He quickly skims through what he wrote down, refreshing his mind on the plot line yet again. He smiles. He may not be able to do anything just yet about the monster in his reality, but he can definitely do something about the monster in his novels. He puts his hands to the keys of the keyboard, takes a deep breath, and begins to type.

Line after line begins to form on the bright white of the screen in front of him.

Lines slowly turn into full pages while Arden is transported back to the world he has created over these last several years. Enmeshed in the lives of the characters he built. Enveloped in recreating the scene where the protagonist finally realizes they can beat the monster that ended the lives of so many of his other characters.

Focused on his work, Arden stops only to take the occasional sip of his drink or research something on the internet to ensure he is describing it accurately.

As he reaches the part in the manuscript where the protagonist learns how they will be victorious, he stops writing and sits back in his chair, staring at the screen. He grabs his now-empty glass of bourbon and absentmindedly takes a sip of nothing but air from the glass.

Arden looks at the glass, momentarily surprised it is empty, and then laughs, setting it down on the desk.

He looks back at the screen and smiles. *This is it. This is where you write the main culmination, the climax, the key turning point. This is where the monster's downfall begins*, he thinks, partly anxious to get it back down in writing and partly nervous as well. *Get ahold of yourself. You already wrote this once before*, he tells himself.

Nodding in agreement with his thoughts, Arden grabs the empty glass and stands up from the chair, stretching his legs and back. He walks over to the decanter and pours some more of the amber liquid into his cup. He looks out the window as he takes a sip, realizing how late it must be getting as the setting sun in the back of the house must be low in the sky on its journey to the horizon, since tints of orange and pink are beginning to streak across the growing cloud cover rolling in. Lilly enters his thoughts, and he wonders if he missed any calls or texts from her since he clearly lost track of time.

Turning from the small window and walking back to his laptop, he sits back down and takes a moment to save the manuscript to both the saved file on the laptop as well as the backup file on his thumb drive. *Not going to lose the work this time*, he thinks, smiling.

Resisting the strong urge to continue writing and once again develop the monster's downfall, Arden remembers how long it took him to write it the first time. Almost bittersweet, like saying that final emotional goodbye to a longtime friend when you know their end is swiftly approaching.

He will need to be able to give it all of his focus, which is something he won't be able to do tonight with Lilly coming over. Nonetheless, Arden is happy with how much work he was able to accomplish today. He may not be back on schedule yet, but he is much closer now than he was this morning when he talked to Saphina.

Saphina. The thought of her name causes a quick rush of worry and Arden wonders if he should check in on her to make sure she is ok. *Sure Arden, that's exactly what every agent needs. A worrisome author who has convinced themselves that their agent is in danger and needs constant reassurance that their agent is still alive.*

"Yeah, it does sound silly now that I think about it that way," he states to the quiet room.

He gets up from his chair with glass in hand and heads towards the kitchen to check his phone. Sometime over the last couple hours, the television had automatically turned off and the shadows are growing in the house as the setting sun dips lower, the increasing cloud cover racing to block out the rest of the sky. He turns on a couple of lamps in the living room and glances out the large window behind the couch, confirming he doesn't have any visitors yet.

None he can see, anyway.

Reaching the kitchen, he turns on the recessed overhead lights and grabs his phone. One missed call with no voicemail and six missed text messages. The missed call and four of the missed texts were from Lilly. The messages were asking him if he was hungry, that she was hungry and picking up a pizza, what would he like on the pizza, and then the last one was her telling him he's stuck with her favorite toppings since he isn't responding and she will be there shortly.

Arden laughs and checks the two remaining texts, both from Ben, asking him why he told Lilly what happened but not his favorite neighbor, and why his favorite neighbor had to find out about the animal attack from the news and why didn't he at least call to warn Ben there might be a killer bear roaming around their area. The second message from Ben continues; however, Arden doesn't feel like scrolling through the message that far and instead sets the phone back down on the counter. He looks around the kitchen at the two coffee cups from this morning still sitting in the sink and realizes he should probably clean up a bit before Lilly arrives.

*

Arden is able to get most of the kitchen and living room cleaned up before a set of headlights can be seen winding down his driveway towards his house. Lilly's now-familiar black SUV pulls up next to Arden's Jeep and the headlights lights turn off. He meets her at the front door, holding it open while she steps through the doorway, pizza box in one hand and two books in the other, her purse hanging over her right shoulder. She heads to the kitchen to set everything down while Arden pushes the door closed behind her and turns on the outside porch lamps.

"My, look at what a gentleman you are. Holding the door for me but not willing to take anything out of my hands. Where did I ever find a catch like you?" she says as she sets everything down on the kitchen counter and takes her purse off her shoulder.

Arden laughs. "That's the kind of high-end quality you get when you go fishing in mud puddles instead of the ocean, my dear." Lilly joins him in laughter and walks up to him before he can step away from the front door, throwing her arms around him and giving him a quick kiss on the cheek.

"You ok? I see you haven't started boarding up the windows or running around with guns strapped to your body. Safe to say what happened last night wasn't in your last novel?"

Arden sighs and pulls himself away from her embrace. "Quite the opposite, actually. It was in the novel, in that chapter. And with a large number of similarities. Here, let me show you," he says as he turns towards his writing room to grab his fourth novel from the desk. Lilly stops him by grabbing his arm.

"Not so fast creepy killer. Your date is hungry and after a day spent with Ben and Cassie, I need food and I need a drink. Mostly, the drink."

Laughing, Arden takes her hand and leads her back into the kitchen. Letting go of her hand, he opens up the cabinet in front of him, grabs a wine glass and hands it to her. He retrieves the wine from the fridge and pours a good amount into her glass until she says stop.

As he is getting two plates from another cabinet, he stops just before he hands her a plate and looks back and forth between her and the pizza box, trying to do his best impression of being wary. "Now remember, beautiful, I trust you and I hope you trust me. I would never do anything to betray that trust so I'm only going to ask this once." Arden smiles and pauses for dramatic effect.

"What's in the box?"

Lilly fights back a smile and looks at Arden as seriously as she can. "Anchovies. Artichokes. Pineapple. Sardines. Wrapped in aged goat cheese and layered over a robust but unseasoned tomato paste resting upon a soft sourdough crust. It's the envy of all the competing pizza joints."

Arden tries not to laugh and slowly turns back towards the cabinets to put the plates away. "I'm sorry but you lost me at tomato. Just no, I can't eat that. Nor will I allow you to. Tomato is a gateway food and then the next thing you know you are going to be experimenting with onions. Or even worse, bell peppers. Bell peppers ruin lives, I read about it on the internet. And if it's on the internet, you know it's true."

Unable to keep a straight face anymore, Lilly busts out laughing. Arden follows close behind with his own laughter, and turns back around, handing her a plate. As she takes a sip of her wine, Arden opens the top to the pizza box. A half pepperoni and half cheese pizza greets him. Lilly's voice reaches him.

"Disappointed it wasn't what I said it was earlier?" she asks, still giggling.

"Not at all. I'm a pepperoni, chicken, and bacon kinda guy so you'll get no complaints from me. Although I'm a sucker for a good white garlic pizza as well."

Lilly sets her wine glass down on the counter and steps forward, reaching in to grab a slice from the cheese side of the pizza. "I actually thought about bringing over a white garlic pizza because I love cheese and garlic but then anything heavy on garlic for a date isn't the best decision for a food choice."

Arden chuckles and nods, "True story there. Well thank you very much for bringing over the pizza. You would've been stuck with pot pies again, or maybe some frozen dino nuggies for dinner if you left it up to me with what I have here at the house."

Lilly stops her hand in midair, her pizza slice suspended over her plate. "Wait just a second. You have dino nuggies stashed away and you had the nerve to feed me a pot pie for our first meal? Clearly, I see now how much you like me."

Arden sticks his tongue out at her and reaches forward for a slice of the pepperoni pizza. "I was going to save them for a special occasion, you know, like when we have our massive seven-day anniversary celebration."

Lilly giggles some more and sets her pizza down on her

plate. "Seven days, huh? Dare to dream sir, because that is a long, long way off and I still don't know if I like you yet."

Arden blows her a kiss and places his own slice on his plate.

Lilly nods towards the living room. "Let's go find something to watch while we eat, then we can talk about last night and your book." Arden nods in agreement and they both head into the living room and take a seat. With his plate balanced on his lap, Arden reaches forward and grabs the remote, turning on the television. As he leans back into the couch, Lilly reaches over and grabs the remote from his hand.

"That is my remote, handsome, thank you very much," she tells him.

Arden chuckles and nods, turning his attention to the still-warm slice of pizza on the plate. Lilly scrolls through the channels until she finds something to watch and then sets the remote down, digging into her own pizza.

They eat their dinner in silence, occasionally laughing together at something funny on the television. One trip to the kitchen to grab the pizza box so it can be placed on the coffee table in the living room for easier access and several slices of the pie later, both Arden and Lilly have had their fill.

Arden sets his plate down on the now-empty pizza box and leans back in his seat on the couch. "Now that I have reached my maximum fatness level, I shall try to extricate myself from the couch and clean up a bit in an effort to lose the newfound weight."

Lilly smiles and sets her empty plate on top of his. "Weakling.

I could have eaten at least another three slices."

Arden leans forward and turns his head towards Lilly, looking her petite frame up and down in an exaggerated motion. "Well, that at least explains why your butt is that big." he says, immediately curling back into a defensive ball and raising his arms in front of him to protect himself from the probable incoming attack.

Lilly looks at him with wide eyes, slaps at him with her left hand, and then leans back and crosses her arms. "Wow. Just wow. See, I knew you were sizing me up to wear me as a skin suit down the road. Is my ass acceptable to your standards? Will it make a pretty hat for you?"

Arden lowers his arms and cautiously looks at Lilly, who is currently somehow both pouting and smirking at him. "Did you just call me an asshat?"

Lilly snickers and uncrosses her arms. "If the hat fits…"

Arden laughs and gets up from his spot on the couch, reaching down and grabbing both plates and the empty pizza box. He turns towards the kitchen and takes a couple steps before he pauses and looks back at Lilly. "For the record, I think you have a spectacular ass."

Lilly laughs and sticks her tongue out at him. "Stop picking on it and maybe one day I'll let you touch it."

Arden chuckles. "Once again, I dare to dream." Lilly's laughter follows him into the kitchen as he places both plates in the sink and tosses the empty pizza box in the trash. "How's your wine?" he asks her.

Lilly's response makes him chuckle. "Currently empty, so a good step towards being allowed to touch my ass would be for you to refill it."

Arden looks over at Lilly to make sure she is watching him, then he pulls out his imaginary notebook and once again pretends to write in it. "Note to self, get Lilly drunk and you can touch her butt."

Lilly rolls her eyes and holds up her empty wine glass. "You have a long way before you get me drunk, so the longer to you take to refill my glass, the less chance you'll have."

Arden nods and quickly makes his way over to Lilly and her awaiting glass. He grabs her glass and returns to the kitchen, hastily refilling it and then delivering it to her still outstretched and waiting hand.

"Took you long enough," she tells him. Arden crinkles his nose at her and grabs his own empty glass so he can get a refill as well.

"I apologize for my lack of haste, my lady. I shall return in just a moment," he tells her as he heads into his writing room to refresh his bourbon. A moment later, he is on his way back to the living room couch. As he passes his desk, he grabs the top two books from the stack of five on his desk and carries them with him into the living room, sitting back down in his seat next to Lilly. He hands her both of the books and waits for her response.

"Eighth chapter from the fourth book, right?" she asks, as she turns the volume down on the television.

Arden nods and watches as Lilly scans the pages until she reaches the part with the police officer. She reads the section several times before she closes the book and sets it down on the coffee table. Grabbing her wine, she takes a sip and sits quietly for a few moments. She sets her wine back down and then grabs the fifth novel and flips through the pages until she reaches the part she is looking for. She reads through several pages and then sets the book down next to the other one. With wine glass now back in hand, she looks over at Arden. It's a couple minutes before she speaks.

"Your agent. Did you talk to them? Warn them? Tell them why you think they might be in danger?"

Arden lowers his eyes and nods. "Saphina. Her name is Saphina. And yes, I did. She told me to stop being paranoid and to put my imagination into my writing and not my real life."

Lilly takes another sip of her wine. "You know any home improvement contractors at all? Any homeless people?" she asks.

He shakes his head no in response. "None. I tend to do all my own home improvements and haven't encountered anyone who is homeless in years, which is why I immediately thought Saphina might be in danger."

Lilly sits in thought for a few moments before she responds. "But you didn't know any of the other people who died, did you?"

Arden shakes his head no. "If I did meet any of them, I don't remember them. See, I thought about that too, which is why I was so hesitant to tell Saphina anything."

Lilly nods, still in thought.

"So these deaths seem to be getting closer to your home, right? And if what happened last night is actually part of some insane person killing people the same way they're dying in your books, then they might try something with you. Maybe in their head you're a contractor because you do your own work on your house. Both the agent and the contractor die by fire so we just have to make sure some crazy person doesn't try to burn your house down."

Arden hesitates before he responds. He didn't think of that. *What if this psycho does consider me a contractor in some weird way? Maybe it's not Saphina at all. Maybe it's me.* Arden thinks about what Lilly just said. *The deaths do seem to be getting closer and closer to me. How did I not realize that?*

Lost in his thoughts, he doesn't notice Lilly's hand reach out or feel it when she rests it upon his right knee. It even takes a moment or two before her voice breaks through his jumbled thoughts and pulls Arden back to the present. "Hey, you ok?"

Arden looks up at her and into her eyes. "I can't believe I didn't think of it that way or figure out that the location of the deaths is getting closer to me. You'd think I would have figured that out." Noticing Lilly's hand on his knee, he takes his free hand and rests it on top of hers. "Thank you for not thinking I'm crazy and running out the door screaming. Although I did wonder if you were going to do that the last time you were here as well."

Lilly smiles warmly at him, her eyes sparking as she does. "Oh trust me, I thought about it. I figure I'm probably quicker than you are so I could get pretty far away without you ever catching up to me."

Arden laughs in spite of his grim thoughts.

Lilly continues to smile. "So I hope this doesn't seem too forward, but maybe I should stay here tonight just in case. You know, in case you need saving." Arden looks at her with one eyebrow raised.

"Is this some coy way of telling me you want me to touch your butt?" he asks.

Lilly immediately blushes and looks away with a suddenly shy smile replacing the one Arden is used to seeing. She waits a moment before responding and then looks back at him. Thunder rumbles outside, announcing the rain is almost here.

"It's not something that's off the table just yet."

Chapter 10

RECKONING

A loud, distant beeping pierces through his dreams and he slowly opens up his eyes. Long red hair cascades down the pillow in front of him. His left arm is extended out underneath that same pillow and his right arm is resting on the side of the woman lying next to him.

He moves his right arm slightly and she grabs his right hand and pulls it down so he will wrap his arm around her more. "Sorry, alarm on my phone, it will turn off in a moment," she mumbles as she scoots backward, moving her body closer towards his in the bed and pushing herself against him.

Still groggy but waking up, and now with his right arm fully around her, Arden can feel Lilly's breasts against his arm and her backside pushing against his groin. He pulls her closer with his right arm and breathes in the smell of her hair, feels the softness of her skin against his own. He kisses the back of her neck and she softly moans a little, ever so slightly gyrating her butt against him and causing him to get hard.

"Mmmm. Someone is awake," she says, still half asleep, as she pulls his right hand towards her face and places a few kisses on it. She pushes herself harder against him. "Don't start something you can't finish," she says.

Arden kisses her neck a few more times and then whispers in her right ear as she turns her head toward him. "It's only fair if we both finish, right?"

Lilly nods in agreement and reaches down with her right hand, carefully finding him and then guiding him inside her while she arches her back and pushes her hips towards him.

Their lovemaking is slow. Deliberate. Every second wanted and enjoyed. Arden pays attention to how Lilly reacts as he pulls himself out and then slowly slides back into her. He listens to her moans and obeys when she tells him what she likes. She moves her hips in opposition to his own, slowly at first and then faster, her right hand guiding his own hand over her breasts and onto her neck where he lightly applies pressure to the sides. Her back arches more and she pushes her hips harder against him. Faster against him. And just before he can't hold back anymore, he feels her release. He feels her clench onto him and feels her body shake against his own.

And at that moment, that very same moment, Arden's vision explodes into fireworks. The heated rush of his own orgasm races through his body and for just a moment, the only two things that exist in the world is him and Lilly and how they are joined together as one.

While the exhilaration of release abates, Arden holds Lilly close, the heat and sweat of their bodies mingling together in the early morning light pouring in from the bedroom window. The rain from the night before didn't last long and had passed before they both went to sleep.

"Well, that's one way to wake a girl up," Lilly states as she rolls around in bed to face him. "Good morning to you too, handsome," she says.

Arden smiles and kisses the tip of Lilly's nose. "I couldn't help it. In my defense, you did wiggle your butt against me. Although had you been facing me, with that morning breath, I may not have been able to perform."

Lilly slaps his right shoulder with her left hand. "Your breath is not any better; I was just nice enough to not say anything about it."

Arden laughs and tries not to breathe into her face. "Touché, my dear. Interested in some breakfast, now that we had dessert already?" he asks.

Lilly giggles and snuggles closer to him, wrapping her left leg over his own legs. "Dessert was perfect. If you really want to woo me, you'll be willing to make that breakfast you just offered while I get a quick shower."

He kisses her forehead and runs his right hand through her hair a bit. "Who said I was trying to woo you? I just needed some great sex and you seemed like the most logical option. It was either you, or Ben."

She laughs, still pressed against him. "Well, you succeeded

there, as I currently have several million little Arden's swimming around inside me from last night and now this morning. Big Arden better be happy I'm on really good birth control or he might be holding on to more than he can handle right now."

Arden pulls away from Lilly a bit and looks into her eyes. "This might be a good time to tell you. I'm not Arden. I'm Steve. I'm actually just house sitting for Arden while he's on vacation and I'm pretending to be him."

Lilly looks shocked and nods. "I think I knew that. You look nothing like the photos of Arden in the back of his books. Then it's only fair to tell you I'm actually not on birth control and I'm extremely fertile. I'm pretty sure I'm already pregnant and you're going to be a father. Of triplets." She briefly feels her breasts with her left hand. "Yeah, definitely already pregnant. Definitely more than two babies."

Laughing, Arden leans forward and gives her a quick kiss, still trying not to breathe in her face. "Well then, beautiful, you take your cute little baby-filled self into the shower and I'll whip up something for breakfast for us. You can find the towels in the small cabinet next to the bathroom door. Sorry I don't have a better selection of soap or shampoo."

Lilly untangles her left leg from his own and rolls away from him, sliding off the bed and pausing a moment while she picks up her underwear off the floor and puts them back on. Arden watches her as she does. "Enjoying the show?" she asks him as she glances at him and sees he is staring.

Arden nods and gives her a thumbs up with his right hand

just before he gets up and out of the bed himself. Throwing on a pair of boxers and sweatpants, he stretches his arms and then his legs and yawns, sleepy again from their morning activity. "I am pretty sure I could go back to sleep if I wanted to right now," he tells her as he hears her rummaging around in the towel closet. He steps from the bedroom and into the living room.

Lilly, now with a towel in hand and standing in the bathroom doorway, looks at him. "No sir, you promised me breakfast, so I expect breakfast when I come out of this bathroom."

Arden nods and does a quick bow while Lilly closes the bathroom door behind her. He heads into the kitchen and briefly checks his phone. Three missed calls.

All from the restricted number.

Arden clears the call history and sets the phone back down, ignoring the fear creeping its way back into his mind. *I really need to remember to change my number today*, he thinks as he opens up the fridge to see what he has available for breakfast. Content with what he has available, Arden grabs several eggs, a few slices of cheese, and a few slices of deli ham. He cracks open the eggs and after adding two eggs each to two small bowls, whisks the eggs together. He dices up the slices of cheese and ham and adds them to the bowls in even amounts. A bit of salt and pepper later and Arden is ready to cook up the omelets. While the pan is heating up, he can hear the shower in the bathroom turn off. He will need to get one himself after breakfast.

While the eggs are cooking, Arden grabs the bread and

tosses a couple slices into the toaster. *Ham and cheese egg sandwiches? Yes please!* he thinks.

It only takes a few more moments for Arden to toast the bread and finish cooking the omelets. Carefully stacking and bringing his sandwich creations together, he sets both plates on the breakfast bar, along with two freshly brewed cups of coffee. Lilly, fresh out of the shower and dressed, crosses the living room and sits down on one of the stools, eyeballing the plate and coffee mug in front of her. She sighs.

"I see we pulled out all the stops and went with black coffee and an omelet sandwich. I'll have you know that I only eat fresh eggs that were laid the same day that I eat them by organically raised, free-range chickens that get weekly massages and pedicures, and are allowed to date whoever they want and not just one single rooster for their lifetime. I also see there might be some cheese and possibly ham in this omelet. I only eat cheese made from the milk of happy animals that have never been under any stress and ones that have fulfilling social lives so I am going to need the social and life history of any animal that contributed to this meal. In addition, I only drink locally sourced coffee from a fifty-mile radius. And I don't see any sugar or cream available for my coffee."

Arden, still standing on the opposite side of the breakfast bar, looks from Lilly to the plate and then back to Lilly with his eyes wide, a surprisingly serious look on her face as she stares back at him.

He reaches forward very slowly and grabs both her coffee

and her plate and begins to take them away from her. Lilly quickly reaches out and grabs his hands.

"I'm kidding. Don't you dare take this deliciousness away from me. I'm hungry and it smells fantastic!" she says, her eyes lighting up as she smiles and laughs at him.

Arden, in an exaggerated motion, pulls out his imaginary notebook and pretends to scribble. "Note to self, Lilly is scary when she looks serious."

Her light laughter reaches his ears and as he is about to head around the counter to sit next to her, she holds her coffee cup up.

"I wasn't kidding about the sugar and creamer though; I really would like some."

Arden chuckles and nods, quickly retrieving both requested items and setting them down on the counter in front of their plates. Taking a seat next to her, they both eat their breakfast in silence, just enjoying each other's proximity and company. Once they are done, Arden gets up and grabs both of their plates and begins to clean up the kitchen.

After he finishes the dishes, Lilly requests a second cup of coffee which Arden makes for her. "So what are your plans today, beautiful?" he asks.

Lilly takes a quick sip of her coffee and smiles. "I promised Cassie I would go into town with her for manicures and pedicures. And I need to do a bit of grocery shopping myself. What about you? Besides the fact you will probably miss me nonstop until we see each other again."

Arden nods and winks at her. "You are correct there, I'll miss you. Your day sounds more exciting than mine. I'm going to shower and then probably try to finish the rewrite on Chapter 15. And try not to think about the fact that myself or my agent might be next on some murderer's killing spree."

Lilly nods and points at his cellphone sitting on the counter. "If anything happens or if you think something is not right, you need to call me. I might be little but I'm very fierce."

He laughs and nods. "Yes ma'am, I remember you telling me that. I promise to call you if anything happens."

Smiling, Lilly gets up from her chair and quickly gathers her things. Setting them on the table next to the door, she walks into the kitchen and grabs the two books still on the counter that she brought in last night.

"Here, these are my last two poetry compilations. I know you are busy with your own work, but if you want to check them out, please do and let me know what you think."

Arden takes the two books from her and looks at the covers, briefly flipping each one over to read the back. "I'd love to, thank you," he tells her, smiling.

"Now listen here, creepy killer, I'm not some famous popular writer like you are, so be gentle with the criticism please," she asks as she steps in closer to him.

Arden sets the books down on the counter and wraps his arms around her, pulling her close to him. "I'm anything but famous and popular. And I'm looking forward to reading your writing." He leans forward and gives her a quick kiss. In response, Lilly puts her arms around him and pulls herself tightly against him for a moment before letting go and pulling herself away.

"Ok handsome, I have to get going. I still need to get home and change clothes before I go see Cassie. Talk to you in a bit?" she asks.

Arden nods, "Of course. C'mon, I'll walk you out." He heads toward the front door, stopping to grab her belongings from the table first before he opens the door, waiting for Lilly to lead the way out. He follows her through the door and to her car where he waits for her to unlock the vehicle before he hands her all her belongings to put everything inside.

A long embrace and lingering kiss later, Lilly is behind the wheel of her SUV and backing away from where Arden is standing. He blows her an exaggerated air kiss as she pulls away and heads back inside the house, the sound of vehicle tires crunching on dirt getting fainter behind him.

Once back inside, he finishes cleaning up the kitchen and takes a shower of his own. A fresh change of clothes later and Arden is again standing inside his writing room, a freshly poured glass of bourbon in his hand, while he stares at the black screen of his laptop. He sits down in his chair and sets his bourbon on the desk. He wakes the computer up from sleep mode and the blinking cursor comes on the screen, welcoming him back.

Beckoning him back to the world he created. To the world he has to bring to an end.

Might as well get started, he thinks. He puts his fingers to the keyboard and starts typing.

Focused on his work, the hours pass quickly and before Arden realizes it, the sun is low in the sky and shadows are beginning to take over inside the room. He types one more sentence and slowly, intentionally, hits the period button. He sits back in his chair and sighs, feeling exhausted.

Chapter 15 is done once again.

*

Cole looks at his watch and frowns. Eight-thirty in the evening. His crew wrapped up their day a couple hours ago but he needed to swing by to see the status of this job before he went home. His wife is going to be pissed with how late he's going to be getting in the door.

He surveys the room in front of him and what still needs to be done. Upper cabinets still need hardware mounted on them. The cabinet crown molding still needs to be measured and cut. Backsplash still needs to be completed. Counters still need to be installed. Water line for the fridge and gas line for the stove, as well as the electrical wiring for one of the overhead kitchen lights, still needs to be completed and covered up. Currently, he's looking at exposed electrical wiring not capped off or taped up, as well as both a water line and gas line capped off with rubber stoppers and not the proper shutoff valves.

He shakes his head in disappointment. This kitchen is a mess, as well as a massive code violation, and nowhere near where it should be to be completed on time. Cole furrows his brow and contemplates firing his entire crew and replacing them with people who actually want their jobs. "How fucking hard is it to do a kitchen remodel?" he asks the empty room.

He sighs. This job is going to cost him more money than he is going to make if he doesn't get it completed on time. It's bad enough the homeowner keeps making random, unannounced visits to see the progress and then immediately calls him to complain and demands a lower price when there hasn't been any progress. He can only fend the owner off for so long before he has to admit his crew has fucked up and give the client a lower cost on the entire project.

Still irritated, Cole turns from the kitchen and heads towards the master bathroom to see the progress there. As he steps through the doorframe, he nods. *At least there is one fucking room they are on schedule to complete in time*, he thinks.

He takes a look around at the completed work, closely inspecting it to make sure it is up to his standards. New tile fully installed and grouted. New shower enclosure completed and sealed. The dual sinks are done and scratch free and the large mirror above them is attached to the wall with no issues. A couple new light fixtures and a bit of polishing up, and this room will be complete.

Satisfied with the quality of the work, he turns from the bathroom to head back to the kitchen when his cellphone rings.

Digging the phone out of his pocket, he answers the phone and puts it to his ear, "Cole Pacet Contracting, Cole speaking."

A gruff voice on the other end of the line greets him,

immediately asking how long it would take him to demo and redesign a kitchen.

Cole grimaces. *Well, sir, with my current crew's daily output and work effort, you can expect it to be done a month or two past the date we agree upon, and then I'll be eating a large chunk of my costs and profit to make you happy*, he thinks.

Instead of telling the man on the other end of the phone what he really thinks, Cole spouts off the average time it takes for a kitchen remodel, as well as the average costs, not including whether the client wants to upgrade appliances or features. The two men chat a bit longer about what the project would entail and what the client would like to get done. Before they disconnect the call, Cole agrees to meet the man for a quote tomorrow afternoon.

As he hangs up the phone and puts it back in his pocket, he hears a loud crash come from the kitchen. *What the fuck was that?* he asks himself.

He quickly navigates through the house towards the kitchen when movement from the encroaching darkness in the far corner of the dining room causes him to pause in his steps and glance in that direction. The corner of the room is bathed in dark shadow but nothing seems out of the ordinary. Nothing is moving. A strange wave of fear rushes through Cole's body. He resumes his steps and heads into the kitchen to see what the noise was.

As he enters the room, he processes what he sees and immediately thinks, *are you fucking kidding me?*

The cabinets above the locations for the fridge and stove have fallen down off the wall and crashed onto the floor. In the process, they knocked the rubber stopper off the water line for the fridge and currently the line is spraying water all over the floor and the remaining lower cabinetry.

"Fuck!" he exclaims, immediately looking around for the rubber stopper for the water line. Not seeing it on the floor or anywhere nearby, Cole turns from the kitchen and races down the hall towards the back door and outside, where his work truck is parked, so he can get a clamp from his toolbox to stop the water and to hopefully prevent any water damage to the cabinetry or the floors. *Why didn't those idiots turn off the main water valve or install a shutoff valve when they installed the new line?* he asks himself.

Now outside and halfway to his truck, Cole stops in his tracks, realizing it would be faster just to turn the water valve off to the house instead of digging through his toolboxes for the right size clamp and allowing more water to spray all over the kitchen while he is trying to find what he needs. He can always clamp it after he stops the water.

Cole turns to the left side of the house and sprints towards the main valve.

The dark of the evening is growing quickly, obscuring areas that were exposed by light only a short while ago. Cole has to strain to see where the valve assembly is sticking out of the ground and going into the house.

He reaches the main valve and grabs it, hastily turning it to the off position. As he does so, in one of those now obscured areas, near a dark recess of the house, Cole's peripheral vision picks up movement. As though the darkness itself is moving, reaching for him.

Startled by the movement, Cole jumps back from the side of the house and looks in the direction of the darkness, his heart now pounding in his chest. His vision, still straining to see anything in the failing light, sees nothing but black enshrouding that portion of the house. He stares for a bit but sees no movement.

Taking a couple of steps back, and still warily looking in that direction, Cole finally turns and rapidly heads back towards the house to confirm the water has stopped.

Before he heads inside, he swings by his work truck and opens up the back gate. He digs through the closest toolbox and pulls out a large flashlight, turning it on to ensure the batteries are working. Bright, white light floods the back of his truck and he swiftly turns the beam of light towards the corner of the house wrapped in darkness where he thought he saw movement. The beam illuminates the area and chases all the shadows away, showing just an empty corner of the house. Cole takes a deep breath and tries to calm his nerves. *This project has you so stressed out you're imagining shit moving in the dark,* he thinks, laughing to himself and forcing the growing fear away. *Get a fucking grip, Cole, and focus on the clusterfuck you now have to fix.*

Satisfied, he turns the flashlight's beam away from the house and back to his work truck. He locates two small squeeze clamps; one for the water line and one for the gas line, as well as a clamp tool to pinch the lines shut and hold them while he installs the clamps. Not to code, but a lot better than the rubber stoppers. He also grabs two wire twist connector caps to cap off the exposed wires for the recessed overhead light. He puts all the items in his pocket and then grabs a couple large work towels from the stack in the corner to help clean up the water already sprayed in the kitchen. He turns from the back of his truck and towards the rear door of the house. As he does, the front of the house is briefly silhouetted in light as a vehicle pulls in the front driveway.

Fuck, please tell me that isn't the client stopping by for an inspection. I do not need that bullshit right now.

Cole sighs, dreading how the conversation is going to go if this is the homeowner, the fear from a moment ago forgotten. He heads toward the back door carrying the towels and flashlight and wonders how late he will be here trying to clean up his crew's mess.

He steps through the door and into the back hallway, following it towards the kitchen. As he gets closer to the kitchen, he begins to smell something in the air. A familiar smell, one of sulfur and rotten eggs. It takes a few more steps and a moment longer for Cole to be able to place the smell.

The smell of natural gas.

A chill immediately runs up his spine and his thoughts race. *The cabinets must have knocked the cap for the gas line off as well as the water line. Why the hell didn't they turn the gas line off to the house?*

Before Cole can take another step, he hears the front door open up and the front entryway light turns on, bathing the surrounding area in warm yellow light and chasing the shadows away. Some of that light reaches into the hallway in front of Cole and for a moment he can see tendrils of darkness quickly retract, as if they were reaching for him but the light has forced them to pull back. As the shadowy tendrils retract, two small red plastic caps are revealed lying next to each other on the floor of the hallway, just in front of the back kitchen entryway. They were not there when Cole came through here a moment ago.

A surge of fear intermingles with his panic and he hears a voice from the entryway complaining about how messy the floor is.

He recognizes the voice. The client.

He hears their footsteps crossing the grand entryway and approaching the kitchen.

It takes a second longer for Cole to realize the entryway light is on. Which means his crew may not have turned the circuit breaker off to the kitchen and the power is still live. And a couple of the overhead light wires are currently exposed.

He hears the owner's voice again as their footsteps stop upon reaching the kitchen. "Why the hell is the floor soaking wet, and what the hell is that smell?!"

Not taking another second to try to remember if the exposed

electrical wires are touching each other or not, Cole drops the towels and races to cross the last four feet towards the back entryway into the kitchen. He screams out, hoping to stop what he knows is going to happen next, "Don't turn on the lights!"

The moment he reaches the entryway and looks in the kitchen, he sees the homeowner framed from behind by the entryway light. He also sees them reach over and flip on the light switch for the overhead lights.

In response, the lights come on, as well as a bright spark from the one recessed light socket with the exposed wires. One brief thought crosses his mind, *well, that answers the question on if the wires were touching or not.*

What happens next seems to initially move in slow motion.

As if by magic, Cole watches as a small fireball forms below the spark and grows bigger and bigger towards him. He closes his eyes just before it reaches where he is standing. Once it has filled the kitchen, it releases its energy in a large outward explosion, throwing Cole violently backward and down the hall, into the dining room. Immediate pain erupts from his ears and the front of his body, as well as his right arm. The smell of burnt flesh and hair assaults his nostrils, fighting for dominance over an extreme heat. He opens his eyes and blinks several times, trying to remove the sudden gumminess coating his eyes.

Cole sits up and looks around to see where he is, momentarily disoriented by the blast. He finds that he is lying against the back wall of the dining room, about forty feet away from where he was standing when the explosion happened. The back wall of the kitchen has collapsed and is blocking the back hallway with debris and flames. He looks down at himself. The front of his shirt, and most of his pants, has been burned off and almost all of the skin he can see on his body is charred and bubbled up. He forces himself to stand up, to try to get out of the house in case there is another explosion. The heat around him is immense as the fire begins to eat its way through more of the furnishings. He carefully places his steps, the ringing in his ears finally abating, as he makes his way from the dining room and to the grand entryway in search of escape from the growing inferno and heavy smoke. As he makes his way into the entryway, the thick smoke clouds his vision and fills his lungs, causing him to fall to his knees while trying to find his way to clean air and freedom.

Cole continues to crawl in the direction of the front door, the flames behind him quickly gaining on him and working their way through the large room on either side of him, trying to cut off his escape.

Fear, panic, and adrenaline surges through his body, keeping the pain he knows is coming at bay as he crawls.

As he reaches the front door, his outstretched left-hand hits something hard in front of him. Something charred, something that once was a living person, the heat of fire still upon it.

It only takes a moment for Cole to realize it's the client's body, burned to a crisp and now completely unrecognizable.

Pushing the body to the left and away from the front of the

door, Cole reaches up and turns the door handle, pulling the door towards him and allowing a new direction for the thick, choking, black smoke to go.

He crawls out the front door and rolls his body down the front steps and across the lawn, ignoring the molten pain caused by his seared skin touching the cold, hard concrete and ground.

Unable to roll or crawl any farther, Cole lies on his back in the cool grass of the yard and stares up into the dark night sky, his eyes still sticky and blurry. The burning house to his left illuminates everything around him. He watches the black smoke billow upwards and the light of the firetrucks and ambulances reflect off the thick plumes as they arrive. He doesn't hear what the paramedics are saying to him, but he can understand them when they tell him he is going to live, that he will make it, and for him to just keep holding on.

As they lift him into the back of the ambulance, he tries to speak, but his lips feel as though they have been fused together. As the back door closes and the ambulance starts to move, he is able to peel his lips apart and speak to the two paramedics administering aid to him.

"There were two other people in the house with me. Saphina, the client I'm working for, and someone who said, '*You're next, Saphina*,' just before the explosion."

Chapter 11

REFUGE

After Arden finished up Chapter 15, he took a moment to step away from the computer and get another glass of bourbon. He hadn't expected it to take as much of an emotional toll as it did the first time he completed the chapter, but this time seemed just as hard as the first. *I guess getting ready to say goodbye to something that has been a part of your life for so long is hard no matter how many times you do it*, he told himself.

Now standing in the kitchen, almost two hours later, with a drink still nearby, Arden takes a deep breath and nods.

Now the fun part. Allowing the protagonist to finally claim victory over the monster and to put this series to bed forever, he thinks, as he finishes reading the notes he wrote on Chapter 16. He sets his notebook down on the counter next to a plate holding the last remaining crumbs of a couple of frozen hamburgers he cooked up for dinner.

Glancing at the clock in the living room, Arden is surprised at the time. Already ten in the evening. He wonders if it's too late to check to make sure Saphina is ok.

Lilly had called him while he was eating to let him know she wouldn't make it back tonight, but he should keep his schedule open for tomorrow evening. He happily agreed, although it wasn't like he had any plans anyway.

Stifling a yawn, Arden cleans up the mess he made in the kitchen and puts his notebook back in his writing room, next to his laptop. After a quick refresh of his bourbon, he finds himself sitting on the couch and turning on the television. He takes a look at the drink he's holding. *You know, if anyone was to write a book about your life, they would think you are an alcoholic with the amount of time you have a drink in your hand.* The thought makes him half smile.

He stretches out while he pulls up the guide and flips to the nearest news channel. Half listening to the reporter on the screen, he yawns again and takes a sip of his bourbon before leaning forward and setting the glass down on the coffee table. He leans back and sinks deeply into the couch cushions. Arden tries to pay attention to what the reporter is talking about, but he feels his eyelids getting heavier and heavier.

The ringing of his phone jolts him out of his half-slumber. *Who the hell is calling me at this hour?* he thinks, groggily glancing over at the clock and blinking his eyes a few times to focus as the living room seems much brighter than it did a moment ago. The clock on the wall reads eleven.

It takes a few moments before Arden realizes the television

has turned off and that the room is much brighter due to the sunlight pouring in from the large window behind him.

So, definitely not eleven at night, he deduces, frowning. *Probably not good when you sleep that many hours and feel like you didn't sleep at all.*

As he stands up from the couch, his phone stops ringing. A stiffness laced with pain radiates from his neck and back, reminding him that he's not in his thirties anymore. "No more falling asleep on the couch," he tells himself, his voice loud in comparison to the silence of the room. He tries to stretch the stiffness out of his neck and back to no avail.

Sighing, Arden heads into the bathroom and grabs a bottle of aspirin from the medicine cabinet. Removing the cap, he shakes two of the little white pills into his left hand and recaps the small plastic container. After returning the bottle to the cabinet, he takes the aspirin with him into the kitchen and gets himself a glass of water to wash them down. *Getting old is an adventure, they said,* he tells himself while smiling. *What they don't tell you is if you sleep wrong, just once, then you are in pain for a week afterwards.*

Setting the now-empty glass in the sink, he turns to the counter and grabs his phone to see who called him a moment ago. A brief flash of fear that the screen might display restricted number races through his body. He sighs in relief when he sees a number displayed, although he doesn't recognize it. They didn't leave him a voicemail so Arden surmises it must not have been very important.

Better check on Saphina, he thinks. Before he dials her number, he sends a good morning text to Lilly and tells her that he is looking forward to seeing her later today. He then locates Saphina's number in his contacts and hits the call button. The phone rings multiple times before her voicemail picks up. He leaves a brief message asking for her to give him a call back and then disconnects the line, setting the phone back down on the counter. He turns to the cabinets above the counter and grabs a coffee mug. It only takes a couple of minutes before he has a hot cup of coffee in hand while he heads into his writing room to get his laptop ready to go.

Time to get some work on Chapter 16 done, he surmises, *so I can let Saphina know I should be wrapped up and ready to go within the next couple days. That should make her happy and less convinced I've gone mental.*

Before he has a chance to start working, he hears his cellphone ringing in the kitchen. Expecting the call to be from Saphina, Arden grabs his coffee and makes his way to where his phone is setting. He picks up the phone and pauses when he sees the screen.

A restricted number.

Fighting back the sudden rush of fear, he swipes the call to voicemail and sets the phone down. The phone immediately starts ringing again, restricted number displayed once more on the screen. Arden watches it ring until the voicemail picks up, refusing to answer.

Afraid to answer, the icy grip of fear holding on tightly.

Time to change my number, he tells himself, *right now.* Grabbing his phone from the counter, and still holding his cup of coffee, Arden heads into the writing room and sits down in his chair. He places the phone down with his coffee and wakes his laptop up. It only takes a couple of minutes for Arden to pull up the website to his phone service provider and log into his account. A few clicks later and he is one step away from confirming his number change. He pauses before he hits enter to process the request.

Leaning back in his chair, he grabs his phone and gets ready to send all of his saved contacts a text message letting them know he's going to be changing his number. Before he does, a new thought comes into his mind.

What if this is someone I know that's doing all this? Making the calls and harassing me? As part of some sick joke they think would be funny?

Arden frowns. It isn't too far-fetched of an idea. At the release party for his fourth novel, one of his friends hired an actor to dress up like his monster and jump out at him as he walked to his vehicle. He doesn't stay in constant contact with a lot of people in his life, but they are still part of it. The more he thinks about it, the more it makes sense that it might just be someone he knows messing with him since most, if not all of them, know he is currently working on wrapping up his last novel in the series. *But that doesn't explain the deaths*, he thinks, *they can't be mere coincidences, can they?*

Arden sighs and looks at his phone. "Well, only one way to

find out I guess," he tells the black rectangle in his hand.

He sets the phone back down on the desk, leans forward, and hits enter on the keyboard. The screen displays a confirmation and lets him know his new number will be active within fifteen minutes and he will need to restart his phone for the changes to take effect.

Grabbing his coffee, he relaxes back into his chair, takes a drink and sighs. *Well, that is that*, he thinks. Arden makes a mental note to call Lilly and Saphina in a couple hours to let them know the new number. He makes a note to also call Ben as well. Everyone else in his contact list can wait for a few days, just so he can make sure the calls have stopped.

He has no reason to suspect it could be Saphina, Ben, or Lilly making the calls. Or even Cassie for that matter. Saphina might be sarcastic and a pain in the ass at times, but she isn't the type to do something like this to one of her authors. Neither was Ben, who can be a pain in the ass in his own way with his regular need for interaction with someone other than Cassie.

And Lilly? Arden is pretty sure the calls started before he even met Lilly, so it wouldn't make any sense that it would be her doing. Especially after the last couple of days that they have been together.

He continues to absentmindedly stare at his phone while he drinks his coffee, still deep in thought about what has happened the last several days, both the good and bad. As he finishes his coffee, he glances at the time on his laptop. The necessary fifteen minutes has passed.

Setting his cup down on the desk, he grabs his phone and holds down the button to restart it. It only takes a couple of minutes before the phone has completed the power cycle and is up and running again. Arden checks the settings and confirms the phone is registering his new number as the number programmed to the phone.

Satisfied, he gets up and walks into the kitchen to make another cup of coffee before he throws himself into rewriting Chapter 16. As the machine rumbles to heat up the water, Arden wonders if he should grab some breakfast before he starts to write. A noise from his stomach answers the question for him.

Fifteen minutes and two over easy eggs later, Arden's stomach is content and quiet. Having finished his second cup of coffee during breakfast, he takes a few more minutes to wash the dishes, as well as his mug, and sets them on the drying mat next to the sink. Out of habit, he glances at the clock. Ten minutes after noon. He should probably try Saphina again, as well as let Lilly and Ben know his new number. Before he has a chance to step away from the kitchen counter and towards the study, a sound causes him to freeze. A sound that causes a spike of fear to rip through his body and allow the uneasy feeling from the last couple days to come flooding back in.

His cellphone is ringing.

That's not possible, he thinks, *that can't be possible*. Arden tries to get a grip over the sudden fear clouding his thoughts. *Most cellphone companies recycle numbers, right? How long does a number have to be out of use before they reuse it? Did they give me one that was recently disconnected?* He tries to rationalize why the phone might be getting a call when the ringing stops. Silence fills the void left by the departing sound of the phone's ringtone until that silence is quickly chased away by the phone ringing once more.

Arden is afraid to move from where he is standing but he knows he needs to see what is displayed on the phone. He can feel his heart beginning to race and the trembling return to his hands.

The terror building inside him tells him he already knows who is calling. That he can't get away from what is happening so easily. That there is more yet to come.

The rational part of his mind fights back, telling him that it's just someone calling his new number and looking for the prior owner. Maybe it's a concerned parent looking for a child they haven't heard from in a few months. An angry ex-lover looking to yell at the person who broke their heart. A pushy debt collector anxious to demand payment for an overdue bill. It might even be the service provider doing a test call on the number to make sure it works.

Arden laughs nervously. *Ten points for me and my extremely overactive imagination,* he tells himself. He pulls himself away from where he is standing and slowly walks towards his study. The phone, silent again, remains that way as he approaches the desk upon which it sets.

Fuck, I need a drink for this, he thinks, as he reaches the doorway to his writing room. As he walks through the doorway, he turns to his right and to the table with his decanter on it. A small pour later and he is sitting down in his chair, the phone only a couple feet away from him, lying face down on the desk. He takes a small sip of his bourbon and sets the glass down to the right of the phone.

He takes a deep breath and grabs the phone with his right hand. A quick flash back to the morning after the lightning storm, when he was shocked by his laptop, crosses his mind.

The uneasy feeling that has been plaguing him recently makes itself known in full force as he turns the phone over in his hand so he can see the screen.

His hand shaking, Arden hits the button to unlock the phone to see what is displayed.

To see who, or what, just called him.

*

Seven in the evening.

He sets the phone down on the cinder block next to him and stares at the flames as they dance in the air above the glowing coals of the wood below, releasing the occasional small burning ember into the sky. The sounds of the early night forest mingle with the popping and crackling of the wood fire, a familiar and soothing sound, and one much needed today.

Lilly should be here any moment.

After Arden saw what was displayed on the screen of his phone when he checked it after changing his number, he had no interest in writing anything. He wasn't able to focus on anything but what he saw. On anything but the absolute fear inside him.

Because that screen, when he unlocked the phone, displayed restricted number.

It just wasn't possible, he kept telling himself. But he knew, deep down inside. He knew that whoever is terrorizing him knew the moment he changed his number. He should have known that changing his number wasn't going to do anything at all.

And he was right.

And whoever is terrorizing him made sure he knew it.

Once he was able to regain his composure, Arden texted almost all his contacts and let them know of his new number. He also left Lilly and Saphina voicemails, letting them know about the change. Lilly called him back within a few minutes and he explained how the morning went. She confirmed she was still coming over later so they could talk about it more and for him not to worry. *Easier said than done*, he remembers thinking. Ben also received a text message, merely because Arden didn't want to spend twenty minutes on the phone trying to explain to Ben why he changed his number, nor did he want to hear about Ben and Cassie's latest adventure.

Although in retrospect, their latest adventure might have been a good distraction.

Once he was done notifying everyone in his phonebook about the change, he went into his bedroom and dug out a lockbox stored in the back of his bedroom closet. He punched in the four-digit code and opened the box, revealing a subcompact 9-millimeter handgun.

Arden had purchased the gun shortly after the stalker issue and after familiarizing himself with how to operate and fire it, stored it away and almost forgot he owned it.

Currently, it's loaded and tucked into a small holster attached to his belt in the small of his back.

He takes a sip of the bourbon in his hand and continues to watch the flames in front of him. The upper parts of the trees on the other side of the fire pit, on the back side of his backyard, are briefly illuminated in white light, which gets brighter until it abruptly disappears. The treetops are plunged back into the dark, only the flickering light of the fire to light them once more.

Lilly must be here.

Arden doesn't move from his seat next to the fire. He hears a car door shut and a few moments later, Lilly's voice from the back door of his house reaches his ears.

"You ok?"

Arden looks over his left shoulder and back towards the sound. "Yeah, I'm ok. Just needed to get my mind of stuff a bit and this was the only thing I could think of."

"Is it working?" she inquires.

"Nope, not at all, but I'm glad you are here. Want to join me?" he asks her.

"Depends. Are there any chains with leg clamps anywhere near you that might also be conveniently attached to a large tree nearby?"

Arden laughs, still looking back at her, despite how he feels inside right now. "Do you think I would tell you if there was?"

Lilly giggles and he watches as she disappears back inside a moment. He turns his attention back to the fire and takes another sip of his drink.

It only takes her a couple more minutes before she is crossing the backyard to where he sits, glass of wine in hand. She pauses next to him and leans down, giving him a quick kiss on his cheek, before she continues on and sits down on the cinder block seat to his right. "Want to talk about it?" she asks.

"Might as well, since I haven't been able to think about much else today," he says as he takes another small sip of his bourbon, still staring into the flames of the fire. "So I changed my number this morning, hopefully to get the harassing calls to stop. It didn't work. I ended up getting two calls shortly after the change, when no one had my new number."

Lilly nods, watching him from her seat, the light from the fire accenting her red hair and her delicate features.

Arden continues on. "What bothers me even more is that I haven't heard back from Saphina since yesterday afternoon. It's not like her to not return my calls or messages. Especially when I am almost over deadline on a manuscript. I left a message with her assistant earlier today to see if they have been in touch with her but they haven't called me back yet."

Taking a sip of her wine and moving her gaze from Arden to the fire, Lilly waits a moment before she speaks. "Are you sure it wasn't just a coincidence that those calls came in after you changed your number? Have they called anymore today?"

Arden looks over at her and shakes his head no, "No, no more calls yet. But something inside me just knew. I just knew it was whoever has been harassing me. I don't know how to explain it. Just a gut feeling, I suppose."

She looks back over at him. "Hmm. Anyone ever tell you that you might have an overactive imagination?"

Arden chuckles. "Yeah, me, literally earlier this morning." His response causes a laugh from her.

"As long as you can admit it, Mr. Creepy Killer," she says, still smiling, "I know you are worried about your agent and with all the stuff happening in the news lately, and especially with what happened in your own…"

Her voice trails off, causing him to look back over at her. He watches as she quickly glances all around her and scans the tree line along the edges of the backyard.

"Are we ok to be outside if there might be a large, man-eating predator running around?"

Arden hesitates a moment before he responds, not sure if he wants to tell Lilly about the pistol. "Well, I figure the fire would keep them away but…," letting his own voice trail off.

Lilly quickly speaks up, "But what?"

"But what the FUCK is THAT?!" he almost yells as he swiftly stands up and points to the far back corner of the yard, currently shrouded in darkness.

Lilly, barely glancing in the direction he is pointing, immediately jumps up from her seat, drops her wine glass on the ground, and bolts towards the back door of the house.

Unable to keep a straight face, Arden bursts out in laughter.

He's still laughing when Lilly's voice reaches him from his back door. "You are not funny, sir. I have no interest in being a snack in some flesh-eating Yogi Bear's picnic."

Her response causes Arden to laugh harder, almost spilling his own drink in the process.

"Yeah, keep laughing, funny man, and see who doesn't get laid tonight. We'll see who is laughing then. And you made me lose my wine, and I'm pretty sure I may have peed myself a little bit."

Arden, still unable to keep a straight face, walks over and picks up Lilly's wine glass from the ground in front of where she was sitting. He walks the glass back to her and hands it over while she waits in the doorway of the back door, not willing to move from her spot or meet him halfway.

Handing her the glass, he leans forward and kisses her forehead. "I'm sorry, beautiful, but you did set yourself up for that one." She sticks her tongue out at him and turns back into the house and towards the sink to rinse her glass off.

"Nice butt," he says as he watches her walk away and stop at the sink.

Lilly smiles. "One apology and one compliment about my ass does not get you off the hook just yet, mister. You have more making up to do."

"Yes ma'am," he says as he turns from the doorway and back towards the fire pit. He grabs a couple pieces of firewood from the stack on the porch and carries them with him as he returns to his seat. Setting his bourbon down, he adds the two pieces to the fire so they will help rekindle the fire. The dying flames briefly flare up as they explore the surface of the newly added logs. Satisfied, Arden picks his drink up and sits back down, watching a couple of small embers drift upwards until their light dies out against the night sky.

As he watches the fire and waits for Lilly to come back outside, his phone rings. An instant sense of dread overtakes him and for a second, Arden is afraid to pick up the phone. *Get ahold of yourself. It's just a fucking phone*, he thinks as he tries to force the fear away. He reaches over and picks the phone up, quickly looking at the caller ID on the screen.

Saphina's assistant.

Arden's relief is almost palpable when he sees what is displayed on the screen. Although it's unusually late for her assistant to be calling, he still quickly swipes to answer the phone and puts it to his ear, anxious to make sure Saphina is ok. "Hey Angie, thanks for the call back. How's Saphina doing?"

As she begins to speak, the terror from earlier welcomes him back with open arms. Unable to respond, unable to move, Arden just listens until she is done talking. When she finishes, he is able to break through his stupor and thanks her for the call and disconnects the line, not giving her a chance to say anything else. He sets both his drink and the phone down on the chair next to him.

It takes a couple minutes more for Angie's words to really sink in.

Saphina died at her house last night in a fire. Some accident with her house renovations that caused an explosion in the gas line and set her house ablaze. The agency will be in touch in a couple of days with his new agent's information, and he can call if he has any questions or if he needs any assistance.

Arden stares at the fire in front of him in disbelief. In shock. In fear.

The deaths are not coincidences. Someone is killing people in the same manner that they die in his books. There is no question about it now.

A hand falls upon Arden's left shoulder and he jumps, almost reaching for the pistol resting against the small of his lower back.

Lilly's voice stops him before he does. "Whoa! Hey, it's just me. You really sure you're ok?"

Arden turns towards her, still sitting down, and wraps his arms around her, pulling her close, his head resting against her left shoulder.

"Saphina's dead. She was killed in a fire that they are calling an accident."

Lilly tosses her wine glass to the right, allowing it to disappear into the darkness of the yard and wraps both her arms tightly around him, resting her left side against his. "I am so sorry, Arden."

Unable to hold it in any longer, Arden starts to sob, clinging to Lilly as though she is the anchor keeping him from being swept away to sea. His tears are not because someone else might be hurt next. His tears are not in fear that he might be in danger himself.

His tears are because he just lost one of his closest friends.

Minutes pass while Arden lets his grief out. Allows it to abate. Unsure of how long he spent holding Lilly, his face buried in her left shoulder, he slowly pulls himself away. As he lets go of her with his right arm so he can wipe the tears from his face, she stops him.

"I'm here. You're safe. You're with me," she says softly as she takes her left hand and places it under his chin, tilting his face upwards towards hers. He closes his eyes while she takes the same hand and tenderly wipes the tear tracks away from either side of his face. When she is done, she leans forward and gently kisses him.

After her lips pull away from his own, Arden lowers his head and sighs, his eyes still closed. "What am I going to do? What am I supposed to do?"

Lilly puts both of her hands on either side of his face and leans forward, kissing his forehead. "Whatever you decide, you'll have me with you. You won't be alone."

Arden raises his head, looks into her eyes, and nods, releasing her from his embrace and grabbing her hands with his own, pulling them down from his face to his chest and entwining his fingers with hers. "If Saphina was the death from the fifth book, and the sixth book I am writing isn't even done yet, then I don't know what to…"

His voice trails off as he realizes that he sent Saphina a recent copy of his current manuscript. If someone actually killed Saphina, then there is a good chance they may have that copy. And if they do, according to the pattern, then the next death will be copied from Chapter 12.

"Chapter Twelve."

Lilly hesitates a moment before she responds to him. "Chapter Twelve?"

Arden nods. "The next death should be in Chapter Twelve of my current manuscript." He lets go of her hands and reaches over to where his phone sets, picking it up and putting it into his pocket. After grabbing his glass, he gets up off the chair. "I have to see who it might be."

Lilly nods and watches as Arden picks up a bucket of water and dumps it over the fire, extinguishing the dying coals as well as the new flames of the recently added logs, plunging the area around them into almost complete darkness only broken up by the light pouring out from the windows of the house. Grabbing her hand, Arden leads Lilly towards the back door, intent on reviewing Chapter 12.

The two walk across the yard, through the back porch, and into the house. They close the back door behind them and from the two windows on this side of the house, they can be seen walking through the kitchen towards the study from the kitchen window. Then, for a brief moment through the bedroom window, they can be seeing walking across the living room and into the study.

Even if they had stopped in their path, just to look out the windows, they still wouldn't have seen the set of eyes that has been watching them for the last couple of hours. Watching them both, intently, from the back end of the yard, hidden just inside the tree line and outside the reach of the light from the fire.

Chapter 12

RUMINATION

Watching patiently, the eyes in the tree line look across the backyard and through the two windows that allow them visual access to Arden's home.

Windows that allow them to see what he is doing. To see what the woman keeping him company is doing.

These same eyes watched them both a couple nights ago. Watched them laugh and eat and entertain themselves with the television. Watched them talk back and forth about subjects the owner of the eyes could not hear.

These are the same eyes that dared to approach the house as the sun was beginning to rise and look in the bedroom window. The same eyes that watched them make love that morning.

Now, from their new vantage point near the bedroom window, they are watching Arden and his female friend talk in the living room. Arden has his laptop on the couch between him and his company and he's pointing at the screen. The female companion has a glass of wine in her hand and she is also occasionally pointing at the screen. Unsure what the two are talking about, the eyes just watch. Like they have been for the last few days.

In the dark, just outside the reach of the light from the bedroom window, they smile. *Tonight,* they think, *Tonight is the night, Arden. Tonight you get to learn what you have created with your writing. You get to learn I exist. That I am real.*

They continue to wait and watch. They watch as Arden and his female friend talk about what is on the laptop screen. As the two exchange playful touches and smiles. As Arden gets up several times to refill his glass from the room he likes to write in, or to refill the glass of his companion from the wine in the kitchen. They wonder what the couple is talking about. What they are laughing about. Smiling about. Frowning about.

They consider going around to the front of the house and near the large living room window so they can hear the conversation, but they know from experience that Arden looks out that window a lot and that, one night, he almost saw them there.

Almost saw them behind his Jeep, watching him. Observing him while he ate dinner in the kitchen and worked on his writing in the room with all the books. Thankfully, a rabbit had appeared at the edge of the driveway and pulled Arden's attention from where they were hiding.

Where they were waiting for him to go to sleep so they could watch him as he slumbered.

But tonight is the night. Their time has finally arrived after all their waiting. After all their watching and observing.

They are looking forward to seeing how Arden reacts. To what he does when he realizes they are here. They wonder how his female companion will react. She's a new addition to his schedule, to his life.

Not that they are complaining. She allowed them to see a side of Arden they have not seen yet. His intimate side. Plus, the female might be useful for what they have in store for him.

They continue to watch through the bedroom window, as Arden closes the laptop and returns it to the room he spends so many hours in. As Arden and his female companion get close on the couch, showing intimacy towards each other, they smile, knowing what is to come.

Shortly after Arden returns the laptop to his writing room, the lights go off, one by one, until he and his company end up in the bedroom.

They move closer to the window, the dark of the night provided by the cloud cover overhead their comfort. Their concealment. Their home. They watch through the glass as Arden and his female companion remove their clothes, faintly illuminated by the light from a digital clock on the nightstand.

They are used to the dark though. Used to seeing in the dark. They wouldn't need any light to see what Arden and his companion are doing. They continue to watch, their breathing increasing as the passion between the two people on the other side of the glass grows. Grows until it reaches a final peak and then both Arden and his female friend curl up together, exhausted, allowing sleep to pull them away from the events of the day.

They continue to wait and watch, the darkness swirling around them, making them feel comfortable. Making them feel safe. Minutes slowly turn into an hour. Into two hours.

Confident Arden and his companion are fully asleep, they move into action. They have to be tactful. Careful. So they are not seen.

Not yet, anyway.

Moving from their spot next to the bedroom window, they quietly move around the back of the house to the side, watching the bathroom window to ensure Arden or his friend do not get up to use the bathroom and are now looking out the window. They move past the window and down the rest of the side of the house until they reach the corner that leads to the front. To where all the light is.

They hesitate a moment and carefully look around the corner to make sure the way is clear. Moving as quietly as they can, taking meticulous care to not break any branches or knock over any décor, they move across the front of the house.

They pause as they reach the small window to the writing room, reminiscing on how many times they watched Arden standing at that window and looking out. Not seeing them. Not acknowledging their existence.

That will change tonight.

They continue along the front of the house, avoiding the

light from the porch lamps and staying in the shadows cast by Arden's Jeep and his company's SUV. They take extra care once they are able to be seen from the large living room window, pausing and watching to see if there is any movement on the other side of the glass.

The interior of the house remains still. Dark. Quiet. Just like they want it to be.

For now.

The first task will be difficult. After confirming neither Arden nor his companion is awake and staring out the window, they move back to the safety of the darkness at the corner of the house. They plan their route to get to the two bright porch lamps illuminating most of the front of the house. Staying low, they slowly move forward toward the lights, braving the possible exposure by the light to the two individuals inside the house. They remain as low as they can, trying to avoid being visible through the living room window, until they are just below the first of the two porch lamps. The bright lights above them have chased off their shroud of darkness, and they hesitate a moment, feeling fully exposed. *You waited long enough*, they think.

Staying pressed against the side of the house, they carefully reach up and into the glass enclosure of the first lamp. They slowly unscrew the light, oblivious to the heat of the bulb, until it goes out and allows darkness to overtake some more of the front of the house. *One more to go.*

Taking the bulb with them, they carefully move to the

other lamp, stopping underneath it. They repeat the process of reaching up and unscrewing the light until the second bulb goes out, allowing the comforting darkness to completely reign where there was once nothing but light.

They smile, welcoming back the black veil that keeps them company.

They look down at the two light bulbs in their hands, now cool to the touch. They set them both down on the concrete stoop below them. Smothering the noise the best they can, they crush both the bulbs, taking care to smash all the large pieces into small pieces.

Now that their first task is complete, it's time for the second. Confident they will not be as easily seen from the windows as they would have been with the porch lamps still casting their hateful light, they move towards the two vehicles in the driveway, pausing only to make sure there is not the visage of Arden or his female friend looking at them from the large living room window.

They continue around the back of the two vehicles until they reach the passenger side of Arden's Jeep. Once they get to the front of the passenger side, they carefully begin to create four gouge marks in the paint, starting at the front fender and dragging them the length of his vehicle, ending at the rear fender. They take their time, staying as quiet as possible while leaving the deep scratch marks. Thankfully, Arden does not lock or set the alarm on his Jeep, so they have no fear of the vehicle alerting Arden to their presence or current activity.

Once they finish the lines, they carefully carve one word in the paint under the long symmetrical gouges. A word Arden used throughout all his novels as a warning to the next victims, indicating they were now marked. *SOON.*

Their second task now complete, they move back slightly and admire their work. *Soon indeed*, they think, smiling, their facial expression lost to the darkness that cloaks them.

Looking back at the house, they decide it's time. They leave their position at the back of the Jeep and return to their prior position at the bedroom window. A quick glance inside confirms that both Arden and his company are still asleep.

Putting their right hand at the top of the glass of the window, they drag their sharp, pointed nails down the length of the glass. The noise, although not as piercing as they hoped, is still loud enough to make Arden and his company stir on the other side of the glass. They repeat the process, pressing harder this time, the noise increasing slightly as scratch marks appear in the glass from the pressure. As their nails continue down the window, they say one word, loud enough to be heard by the people lying in the bed, their voice raspy as it cuts through the soft sounds of the night forest.

"Arden."

This time, they get the response they are expecting. They watch as Arden groggily sits up in bed and looks at the window behind the headboard. They watch as he sees their clawed hand pressed against the glass and listens to him as he screams in response, his voice loud and abrupt as it echoes through the inside of his house. Before they pull their hand back to disappear into the dark beyond for the next step, they watch as Arden scrambles backward away from the window and off the bed, his female companion now sitting up and intently watching him. Reaching out for him. Asking him what's wrong.

They pull their hand away and step back from the window, still watching as Arden points in their direction, directing the eyes of his companion, who quickly looks at the window, a confused look on her face.

Confident that they cannot be seen where they are standing, encased by the black of the night all around them, they turn from the window and head back to the side of the house where the bathroom is located. As they reach the corner of the house, bright light floods out of the bedroom window as the light inside is turned on, piercing the darkness for several feet into the backyard.

They smile again and continue onward until they are located by the bathroom window, where they patiently wait. They can hear Arden arguing with his companion inside the house. They can hear him swearing it was real and that it wasn't a human hand at the window. They can hear his companion telling him it was just a dream and that they didn't see anything.

That's right Arden, just a dream, they think, *A dream you are about to realize is a nightmare. Your nightmare. The one you created.*

The arguing inside the house slowly settles down. They continue to wait patiently next to the bathroom window.

Their patience is rewarded when the bathroom light comes on. They glance in the window, at the very edge of the light escaping from the vanity bulbs above the bathroom mirror. Arden is standing at the counter, looking at himself in the mirror, his hands placed on either side of the sink. As he turns on the water and bends down to splash some on his face, they put their hand on the window and begin to drag their sharp nails down the glass, once again repeating that one word in their raspy voice.

"Arden."

They stand in the darkness at the edge of the window, their hand the only thing visible in the light from the bathroom. They continue to scrape their nails down the glass until they hear the desired reaction from the man inside the house.

Another scream, immediately followed by a loud crashing noise.

They pull their hand back and quickly move from their position next to the bathroom window and back to the edge of the yard, plunging into the black void of the currently lightless forest. Staying in the tree line along the edge of Arden's home, they move around to the front of the house and select a vantage point where they can easily see into the large living room window.

They watch as all the lights inside the house quickly turn on.

They watch as Arden locates and turns on a large flashlight and begins to shine it out of the various windows on either side of the house, the beam reaching beyond the light from the windows and dancing across the ground and trees as he waves the light around. Searching for them.

They continue to watch, satisfied with what they have accomplished tonight and filled with excitement about what tomorrow night may bring.

Knowing that daylight will soon be upon them, they turn from their victim's home and proceed into the dark of the forest, carefully maneuvering around the trees and through the underbrush. They need to find a safe place to rest and will need to be a good distance away from Arden's house to do it so they are not discovered by any police searching the area. They won't be able to stay at their usual spot just behind his house this time. They continue on into the forest, the dark beckoning them to go farther.

Content with what they have done tonight, they begin to smile as they move along until they step down on something hard.

Something out of place on the forest floor.

Something that clicks loudly as their weight is placed upon it.

✳

Arden glances at the clock for the third time in five minutes, wondering when the officer will arrive. His handgun tucked in the back of his waistband once more, he paces around the house with a cup of coffee in hand, looking out every window he walks by.

Looking for anyone out of the ordinary. Any*thing* out of the ordinary.

Unable to go to sleep after seeing the clawed hand at both his bedroom and bathroom windows last night, and hearing that voice utter his name twice, Arden spent the remainder of the night looking out his windows with all the lights on. Trying to see who, or what, was outside his house. Trying to see who, or what, owned the hand and the voice he just heard.

Lilly, who didn't see or hear anything, kept trying to tell him he might have just dreamt it, but he knew what he saw. It wasn't merely a dream.

Still, she stayed awake with him, making coffee for them both and cleaning up the broken water glass in the bathroom, until daylight came and she let him know she needed to go home for a bit. As he was stepping out the door to walk her to her car, that's when he discovered that the outside lights had been shattered all over his front stoop.

After Lilly left, he cleaned up all the broken glass from out front and replaced the two empty light sockets with new bulbs. He then went inside and called the police to report the incident. They told him they would send a deputy out to talk to him.

That was almost an hour ago.

Still pacing around the house, Arden has to force himself to think about anything else beyond that hand he saw and the voice he heard. The raspy, almost otherworldly voice that said his name. The misshapen hand with the sharp claws that glinted in the light as though they were made of metal.

It was the hand and voice of his monster. The monster he created in his books. There was no other explanation. Somehow, his monster has come to life and has been killing people like it did in the books. Slowly working its way to him.

But why? he wonders, *If, somehow, I'm the protagonist in this nightmare of a reality, then I would triumph over the monster, right? That's how this story ends. When Lilly and I looked at Chapter 12 of my latest manuscript, there were no deaths in it. The chapter is about the monster terrorizing its next victim…,* Arden's thoughts trail off and go silent as the realization kicks in. *I am the victim. I am the one being terrorized now.*

Arden continues to pace, thinking about last night and the events of the last few days while he finishes his coffee. Pausing in his circuit around his house, he takes the coffee mug to the kitchen and places it in the sink next to Lilly's cup from earlier. Trying to keep his mind occupied, he washes both of the mugs and dries them off before returning them to their spots in the cupboard above the coffee machine. He also washes the wine glass and bourbon glass they used last night. Using the same paper towel to dry the glasses as he did for the coffee mugs, he places the wine glass back on the rack.

Bourbon glass in hand, Arden heads into the study and stops at the decanter to pour himself a drink in an effort to calm his nerves a bit. As he takes a sip, he looks out the small window in front of him. His eyes survey the parking area in front of his house that he can see, looking for any movement. Anything unusual. Satisfied there is nothing there that normally is not, he begins to turn and head back into the living room. Briefly glancing at his Jeep as he goes, he's already two steps away towards the living room by the time his mind registers what he just saw.

Cautiously turning and walking back to the window, Arden looks out the glass once more and at the passenger side of his Jeep. What he sees chills him to the core, allowing the fear and unease from the last several days to wash over him like a tsunami.

Four large, deep scratch marks run the entire length of the passenger side of his vehicle. Underneath those marks is one word, carved into the paint.

SOON.

Arden steps back from the window and blinks his eyes a few times, as though blinking his eyes will make what he just saw go away. Stepping forward again and looking at his vehicle once more, the marks and word remain.

Taking a deep breath, he reaches back with his right hand and confirms his handgun is still there. Unsure if the weapon will protect him from who or what did that to his Jeep, the coldness of the steel still offers some comfort. Still makes Arden feel like he has a way to defend himself. Forcing the fear and unease as far away as he can, he determines that he needs to check out the rest of the exterior of the house to see if there is any other damage.

Any other warnings. Any other signs that his monster is now somehow real.

Heading towards the front door, he briefly stops to put on his shoes. The officer should be here any moment, and Arden is not going to allow this fear, this terrorization, to keep him prisoner inside his home. He steps outside, the morning sun warming his face, and looks around the front of his house. This once common and familiar sight now feels foreign to him, as though there is something evil hiding behind every shrub or tree.

Arden walks over to the passenger side of his Jeep and surveys the damage, the fear and uneasy feelings becoming omnipresent. He tries to slow his pounding heart as it now feels as though it might pound right out of his chest. The gouges are deep, through the clear coat and paint, down to the bare metal. He wonders how this could have been done last night without him hearing it. Without Lilly hearing it.

He runs his hand across the gouges and over the letters, every hair on his arms and his neck raised as though the vehicle is electrified. He tries to swallow but his mouth is completely dry. Pulling his hand away from the marks in the cold metal, he turns from the Wrangler and looks around the property again. Looking for watching eyes but only finding the normal activity and sounds of the surrounding forest in the morning. Not sure who, or what, he expects to see as he scans the area, he continues on his trek to check the rest of the house's exterior. Reaching the bathroom window, he looks in. Whoever, or whatever, was out here last night could have easily seen everything in the bathroom from their vantage point.

Arden reaches out and touches the glass where he saw the clawed hand. The surface of the glass is scratched from top to bottom several times in four almost even lines, similar to his vehicle.

Even with the morning sun shining on him and the warm air around him, Arden shivers. *There is no way a human hand could do this*, he thinks, *Is there?*

Stepping away from the bathroom window, he continues around the corner of the house to the backyard, looking around to ensure he is still alone. He repeats the process with the bedroom window, feeling the scratch marks in the glass with his own hand, tracing the path the sharp claws created. He wonders if the monster watched him and Lilly make love last night, shivering again at the thought of it standing here, right here, and staring at them through the window. He clenches his hands into fists to stop them from shaking and in an effort to rekindle the rage from before. He narrows his eyes and grits his teeth as he ruminates on the image in his head of the monster, his own creation, standing right here and feeding on his fear. The anger springs back to life within him.

Arden forces the thought out of his head and pulls himself away from the glass separating him from his bedroom. He completes his walk around the house, not finding any other scratches or additional notes carved into anything. As he is about to head back inside, the sound of an approaching vehicle catches his attention.

A local police cruiser is approaching, carefully navigating the various ruts and dips in his dirt driveway. Arden waits by the front door as the car approaches and pulls up next to his

Jeep on the driver's side. The car's engine shuts off and the door opens. The same officer as the other day works his way out of the car and onto his feet. Officer Holden.

The two men exchange pleasantries and after a few questions, Arden explains what happened last night. He shows the officer the two windows and the passenger side of his Jeep. He also tells the officer about the restricted calls right after he changed his phone number. One thing he doesn't tell the officer is that he thinks this is the work of a monster he created in his novels. Of course, he didn't tell Lilly that's what he thinks either. Not yet anyway.

The officer is patient and takes thorough notes. He even takes photos of the bedroom and bathroom windows as well as the side of Arden's Jeep. He confirms Arden has a way to protect himself and recommends that Arden gets blinds or curtains to cover his windows at night as well as either a security camera system, motion sensor lights, or both. The officer also takes the time to dust the windows and the side of the Jeep for prints, pulling a few clear prints from each location. Arden willingly allows himself to be fingerprinted as well, so they can confirm if the prints are his or not. The officer wraps up his investigation and reminds Arden to be careful and to call them immediately if anything else happens.

As he watches the cruiser's taillights disappear down the driveway, he hears his cellphone ringing from inside the house. He proceeds back inside and to the counter, grabbing his phone and glancing at the screen.

Restricted number.

Arden hits the button to silence the ring, then sets the phone down screen first on the counter.

It knows. It knows I spoke with the police and it wants me to know it's aware. That it's watching. The fear building inside him erases any feeling of bravado he had while the officer was here. Arden continues to stare at the back of the phone, lost in his thoughts, when it begins to ring again. He doesn't attempt to silence it this time. He doesn't even attempt to look at the screen.

He already knows who it is. What it is. He just doesn't know why yet.

Frustration mingles with his fear and unease and Arden grabs the glass of bourbon from the counter he left behind when he went outside to walk around the house. He finishes the glass in one quick drink and then heads into the writing room to get some more. Before he gets to the decanter, he stops at the end of his desk and stares at the laptop sitting on it. Waiting for him to wake it up and continue his work. With what has happened over the last two days, Arden isn't sure if he has the motivation to start to rebuild Chapter 16. If he even wants to finish the manuscript at all anymore.

He sets the empty glass down on the desk and walks over to his chair, sitting down into it, continuing to stare at the laptop.

His thoughts remain scattered. He wonders who his new agent will be if he does finish it? Will they understand him like Saphina did? And poor Saphina, rest her soul. Can he even do this without her support? Without her pushing him to make sure it's all done?

And what if he doesn't finish it? What happens then? Does he just start in a new direction like he planned before and leave this part of his life to just fade off into history without closure?

A new thought, one that slowly rekindles the fire of courage within him, begins to fight its way through the chaos and to the forefront of his mind.

What if putting Chapter 16 back down in writing, and killing the monster in my manuscript, will also be the death of the monster in my life?

Arden lets the thought roll around in his head, pushing all the others away. The more he thinks about it, the more it makes sense. The more it's a possibility. Kill the monster in the manuscript to kill the monster in real life.

He sits back in the chair and repeats the thought out loud, as though he needs to hear it outside the confines of his head. "Kill the monster in the book to kill the monster in my life."

Arden cringes at how it sounds in the quiet of the small room, spoken into existence.

He continues to talk. "Yeah, that's right. I sound completely off my rocker right now. I'm convincing myself that I can write things into reality. And on top of it all, I'm now having conversations with myself."

Arden sighs and shakes his head in disbelief. Saying it out loud made it sound ridiculous. How could he even entertain the idea that he can write things into existence? His monster is not real. His monster wasn't magically brought into this world. He's being terrorized by some unstable fan that read his books and is now trying to scare him, and a series of deaths that coincidentally occurred the way the deaths in his books have happened to add to this paranoid fantasy he is now trying to convince himself is true.

Nodding to himself in agreement, he tries to ignore all the hypotheses he has come up with the last several days and push the fear-laced, uneasy feeling away. He reiterates to himself several times that yes, the deaths are just freak coincidences and that if he was to go online and research deaths that recently happened like those in his novels that he might find ten of each with similarities.

And the phone calls? he asks himself. Most of them were probably his unstable fan that was nice enough to scratch up his windows and carve into the paint of his Wrangler. The others that he didn't answer might just be wrong numbers. Telemarketers. Determined fans looking for signed copies of his novels who somehow came across his number. Angry ex-girlfriends looking for some sort of revenge or closure.

The last thought makes Arden chuckle a bit. *Probably isn't some angry ex-girlfriend,* he thinks, *as there are not very many of those and none of them are angry at me that I know of.*

Pushing himself up and out of the chair, he grabs his glass and walks over to the decanter, pouring a small amount. He takes a sip while he looks out the window, wondering if his monster, this unhinged fan, is out there right now looking back at him. He furrows his brow in frustration, allowing his anger, his rage, to override the terror he has been allowing himself to succumb to.

A rage again starts deep in his core and grows like an explosion, pushing outward until it reaches his skin. He can feel the heat begin to radiate from his body.

"No more of this bullshit," he announces to the quiet house. "I am done being a pawn in this stupid fucking game you are playing."

As if in response to his statement, his cellphone starts ringing.

Chapter 13

REPENTANCE

After half-heartedly convincing himself that everything that happened in the last week is just a series of bad-timed events coinciding with one mentally unstable fan trying to torment him, Arden made the determination that he would not avoid the restricted calls and instead answer them to find out exactly who is calling.

Because of this, when his phone rang earlier this morning, he marched into the kitchen to answer it, expecting to confront his harasser head on. Instead, he ended up talking to Ben for over an hour, discussing everything from the possible large predator roaming around the area where they live to the current status of his relationship with Lilly. Then, in typical Ben fashion, Arden got the pleasure of learning about Ben and Cassie's latest adventure where they attempted to grow some marijuana plants, which actually turned out to be kenaf plants instead.

Once Arden was released from his aural captivity, he made some breakfast and called the insurance carrier for his Jeep, explaining the vandalism and confirming when the company could send an adjuster out to look at the vehicle. He then looked up and called a couple of glass repair companies for quotes on repairing or replacing the windows in the bedroom and bathroom.

His primary to-do list completed, Arden turned his attention to getting the windows of his house covered up so his late-night visitor couldn't have the pleasure of staring at him through the windows anymore.

After a short drive to the main part of town, he currently finds himself in the local hardware store, standing in front of a large display of curtain rods and accessories. He digs through the various sizes and designs until he finds a design he likes, adding several of the rods as well as their mounting brackets to his shopping cart. A few aisles later and Arden has added several curtains to his cart to go with the rods.

While in the store, he picks up some additional supplies that were beginning to run low in the house, such as light bulbs and a couple of jugs containing cleaning solution. Taking the officer's advice, he also picks up three solar-powered motion sensor flood lights, with the intention of placing one on either side of the house and one on the back side of the house. After a brief chat with an employee, he grabs some abrasive paste designed to remove scratches from glass. Arden figures he can try to fix the scratches himself, and if he only makes them worse, he can still hire one of the glass repair businesses he talked to earlier this morning.

Satisfied with all his selections, Arden heads to the checkout line and pays for his purchases. As he's crossing the parking lot to where his vehicle is located, he notices several people gathered near the passenger side of his Jeep, taking photos with their cellphones.

Great. A fan club. I knew I should've taped something over that side, he thinks.

Arden looks around at the faces of the people gathered as he approaches, watching as they all turn to look at him one by one, inquisitive, as though they are all expecting an explanation.

He goes with the first thing that comes to his mind.

"It's a promo in anticipation of a book I'm about to publish," he tells everyone as he stops the cart at the back of the Jeep and begins to open the rear gate. The gathered group, clearly disappointed that there's not a more dramatic explanation, nods and wishes him best of luck, and quickly disperses.

Arden unloads the contents of the cart into his Jeep as fast as he can, closing the rear of the vehicle back up and pushing the cart to the cart return stall. A minute later and he is behind the wheel, on his way out of the parking lot and back on the road, heading home. Before he leaves town though, he swings by the local liquor store to grab a couple of bottles of wine to replace the ones that he and Lilly drank, as well as to grab a bottle or two of his favorite bourbon to ensure he is well stocked. He also stops at the fast-food restaurant right next to the liquor store and grabs a couple of bacon cheeseburgers off their value menu for a late lunch.

Once again behind the wheel, Arden leaves the small town in his rearview mirror and drives home in silence, the sound of the tires on the road and his chewing as he eats his burgers keeping him company. He thinks about what he plans to do when he gets home. There is enough time left in the day that he should be able to get all three of the motion sensor lights installed and hopefully fully charged before dark. He should also have enough time to attempt to fix the scratches on the two windows and get the curtain rods mounted with the accompanying curtains attached.

He finishes both of the burgers before he reaches his driveway, their cellophane wrappers crumpled up and returned to the bag the sandwiches came in. As he pulls onto the familiar dirt road, he brings the vehicle to a stop, leaving the engine running. Hopping out of the Jeep, Arden walks over to his mailbox and collects the last few days' worth of mail that have been accumulating, flipping through the various sealed envelopes to see if there is anything of interest. Electric bill, internet and television service bill, various fliers and junk mail, and, shockingly, another bill. Inside the Jeep again, Arden tosses the stack of envelopes on the passenger seat next to the fast-food restaurant's bag. He navigates the rest of the way down his driveway and parks in his usual spot in front of the living room window, setting his mind to the tasks at hand.

It doesn't take Arden long to unload the vehicle, and as

he is carrying the last couple bags inside, his cellphone rings, the sound muffled as it escapes the confines of his right front pocket. He sets the two bags down on the kitchen counter and pulls the phone out of his pocket, letting a warm flash of the anger from this morning rush over him, reminding himself that he is going to get the answers he deserves from whoever is behind the restricted calls.

He looks at the screen and to his relief, Lilly's name is displayed. He swipes to answer the call and puts the phone to his ear, happy to be able to hear her voice. The call is brief, with Arden filling her in on the events of the day and confirming that she will be over later tonight. He lets her know he picked up a couple more bottles of wine and has a special dinner planned so she better bring her appetite. They say their goodbyes and the line is disconnected. Smiling as he stares at the now-black screen, Arden sets the phone down on the counter and proceeds to put the wine and bourbon away, one of the wine bottles going into the fridge to chill for tonight. He separates the curtain rods, hardware, and curtains for their respective rooms and stores the light bulbs and cleaning solution in their usual locations.

Satisfied, he grabs the bag with the motion sensor lights and heads out the back door and onto his back porch. He digs through his tool chest and pulls out a drill. With the drill and the bag in one hand, he props open the back porch screen door. Grabbing the stepladder next to the tool chest with his free hand, Arden heads out the back door and to his left, towards the side of the house where he keeps his trash can. Setting everything down on the ground, he moves the can out of the way and sets up the small ladder. He eyeballs what he thinks would be an appropriate distance and location to mount the sensor and after tearing open one of the packages, he climbs the ladder with the light and drill in hand. A couple minutes later and the first light of the three is mounted on the house.

Arden steps back several feet and admires his handiwork. The light is mounted relatively level and at the right height to illuminate the entire area should anything set the light off. As the lights are LED lights in hard plastic housings, he doesn't expect his unwelcome visitor to be able to remove these or break them as they did with his porch lamps. He smiles, content with how quick and easy it was to install. He returns the garbage can to its usual location and gathers everything else up, proceeding to the back of the house.

He pauses in the backyard, looking at the back of the house and figuring the best spot to put the light. Mounting it in the center of the house, on his porch, would result in it being set off anytime he walked out to the fire pit. Deciding it would be best suited above his bedroom window, he walks over to that side of the house and sets up the ladder. It only takes him a couple of minutes to get the second light installed above the window, and again he admires his work and the location where he mounted it. *One more to go*, he thinks. A quick repeat of the process with the ladder, and the third light is swiftly mounted on the side of the house that provides a wall for the bathroom and his writing room.

As Arden returns the ladder to where he keeps it on the back porch and puts the empty boxes for the lights in the garbage can, he realizes he probably should have done this a long time ago. *Hindsight is twenty-twenty, right?* he asks himself.

He returns to the inside of the house, drill still in hand, and kicks his shoes off. Intent on getting the curtains hung up, Arden starts in the living room. The mounting brackets are easy to install, just a couple of screws for each metal hanger. Hoping he installed the brackets as level as possible, he attaches the curtains to the rod and extends it out to what he estimates is the proper length. He places the rod on the hanger and adjusts the length of the rod until it's just the right distance for the hangers, as he initially slightly overestimated how long it needed to be.

Not bad, sir, not bad at all. They look perfectly level, he thinks as he mentally pats himself on the back for a job well done.

Closing the curtains fully, Arden is surprised at how much light they block out. *Well, if I ever want to go full hermit and become a dark dweller, this is definitely a step in the right direction.*

He slides the curtains open, allowing the remaining late afternoon daylight to chase the sudden darkness inside the house away. Twenty minutes later and Arden has installed the remaining curtains in his bedroom, the study, and the bathroom.

Well, no one is going to be playing creepy Peeping Tom at night here anymore, he thinks as he checks to ensure the curtains offer complete coverage for each of their respective windows.

As he walks into the kitchen to grab one of the clean hand towels he keeps under the sink, as well as the abrasive paste for the glass, he wonders if he should've purchased curtains for the front and back doors, as well as the front-facing window in the dining room. He makes a mental note to pick up another rod and set of curtains for the dining room window, although it doesn't offer much of a view into the house beyond his normally unused kitchen table, part of the kitchen, and the door to the back porch.

He only has a couple more hours before the light of the day is gone and Lilly will be here, so with the paste and towel in hand, he heads out the door and across the backyard to his bedroom window. Before he applies any of the paste to the glass, he pauses. Lilly will be here in a little bit and it might be a good idea for her to see these. To show her that he isn't crazy. Plus, he should probably clean the glass thoroughly before he tries to fix the scratches anyway.

Nodding in agreement with his thoughts, Arden turns and goes back inside, setting the towel and container of paste on the kitchen table for use tomorrow. He should probably clean up before his company arrives anyway.

It doesn't take him long to shower and brush his teeth. After a quick change of clothes into a fresh pair of jeans and a black V-neck T-shirt, and a splash of his favorite cologne, Arden feels like he is brand new.

Now, with a small glass of bourbon in hand, standing on his back porch, Arden watches as the last remnants of the dying light from the setting sun fight to maintain control of the sky. Shades of orange and red clash against the approaching black, slowly retreating with the sun as it dips farther below the horizon, allowing the dark of night to claim dominion over the land. He takes a sip of his bourbon and pulls himself from the sunset, turning his attention towards making sure the newly installed curtains are closed in both his bedroom and his bathroom. He heads back inside and after closing the curtains for both rooms, he focuses on the ones now hanging in front of the large living room window. As he slides them closed to block off any view into his house from the outside, two bright lights can be seen approaching through the trees.

Lilly's here, he thinks, a warm smile making its way to his face.

He finishes his task and grabs his bourbon from the coffee table, heading towards the front door and turning on the newly replaced outside porch lamps in the process. Arden opens the door and steps out onto his front stoop, watching as the lights approach down his driveway until the vehicle is close enough that he easily recognizes Lilly's SUV.

As she brings the vehicle to a stop next to the driver's side of his Wrangler, he walks over to her door, excited to see her again.

Excited to be able to hold her and kiss her and tell her about what has happened.

Excited because, despite everything going on, he thinks he might be falling in love with her.

*

The oven chimes, letting Arden know it has reached the desired temperature. He puts the sheet pan in with tonight's dinner and sets the oven timer to the required cooking time.

"You burn dinner and I'm going to be a very unhappy date," Lilly chimes in from her seat on the living room couch. "I still don't know why you won't tell me or let me see what you are making for dinner."

Arden lifts his head up and looks at her over the breakfast bar. "Because I wanted to surprise you with an elegant dinner that I'm confident you will love. Then, while you are distracted by the amazing food, I'll drug your wine and you'll wake up tomorrow chained up to a tree out back. Oh, wait, I mean…I just wanted to give you a really nice dinner."

Lilly giggles and takes a sip of her wine. "Well, sir, the joke is on you, because if this meal is as good as you say it will be, I was planning on chaining myself to the tree anyways. This way you will be stuck with me indefinitely."

Putting his right hand to his chin, Arden strokes his beard in thought. "And where is the negative in all of that again?"

Lilly sticks her tongue out at him and scrunches up her nose. "How long until dinner is done, creepy killer?"

Arden checks the timer on the stove. "Eighteen minutes. Just enough time for some quick lovin on the couch."

Lilly attempts to raise one of her eyebrows in a quizzical

manner at him. "You planning on lovin yourself? Because these legs are staying closed until the owner gets the dinner they were promised."

Arden laughs and grabs his glass of bourbon from the counter, making his way into the living room and to a seat on the couch next to her, turning his attention to the show on the television that Lilly selected when she sat down.

When she arrived earlier this evening, he showed her the side of his Jeep and the scratches in the two windows. Clearly equally concerned and uneasy, she was relieved when she learned the police had come out and that he had installed the motion lights and curtains. They talked for a bit about who it might be, and why, and Lilly agreed she would stay the night tonight to keep him company. He also confided in her about his handgun and was mildly surprised when she told him she was familiar with guns and knew how to use one, pulling her own small caliber pistol out of her handbag to show him. She reassured him he wouldn't have to deal with this alone and her resolve helped fuel his bravado, reinforcing in his mind that he will face this head on and bring it to an end so he can continue his life without this unnecessary fear.

The actor's voices on the television pull him from his thoughts and he looks over at Lilly, who is laughing at the screen, wine glass in hand. He smiles, absorbing her beauty with his eyes, the warmth in his heart when he is with her quickly forcing the worries of the day away.

"Ok, creepy killer, you can stop staring at me like I'm the

one on the menu," she says without taking her eyes off the television.

Arden chuckles. "Do you think you would taste better slow cooked at three hundred and fifty degrees or broiled at five hundred?"

She looks at him and smiles coyly. "I taste good at all temperatures. But if I don't eat, you won't eat, so is this surprise dinner done yet?"

As if in response to her question, the timer on the stove goes off, announcing that the contents of the oven should be fully cooked now. Arden winks at her. "Saved by the bell," he tells her as he gets up off the couch and proceeds into the kitchen, locating his oven mitts. Turning off the timer, he pulls the sheet pan out of the oven and puts it on top of the stove, confirming the food is done. He puts the mitts away and turns off the oven. After retrieving two plates from the cabinet above the stove, he looks over at Lilly and beckons her to come forward. "Dinner is served, my lady."

Lilly gets up from the couch and walks towards him. "So let's see what this surprise dinner is," she says as she takes a seat at the breakfast bar, opposite the sink. Arden waves his hands in a flourish over the sheet pan, as if displaying the food in a royal manner.

"Feast your eyes, and then your gullet, upon the oven-baked mastery of the evening. Of course, only the finest pure aluminum, mined and smelted with the utmost care, was used in the making of the pan upon which this meal was created. As you gaze upon the meal, please observe the elegantly carved shapes, created by master crafters. The perfectly molded forms, made to evoke your wildest dreams. The succulent taste and texture of the highest quality meat. The crisp crunch of the breaded shell, specifically designed to tantalize your taste buds with a dance of desire. And tonight, for tonight only, it's paired with an expert blend of premium ingredients into a savory sauce that is the envy of barbeque masters all over the world."

As he finishes his presentation, Lilly giggles and shakes her head in disbelief. "I'll never look at dino nuggies and barbeque sauce the same way ever again."

"I know, I know. I outdid myself, what can I say? Only the very best for you, beautiful," he says in response.

Lilly points at one of the plates and then at the chicken nuggets. "Sir, less talky talky and more feedy feedy. Your date is hungry and she's going to need a lot of those nuggets to stop her from being hangry."

Arden obliges her direction and puts a dozen of the nuggets on one of the plates, setting it down in front of her with a paper towel for a napkin. He also sets the bottle of barbeque sauce on the counter in front of her.

"And, garçon, although I'm sure the five-star chefs who created this barbeque sauce are at the top of their craft, I'd prefer some ketchup. Did they happen to create a bottle just for you that's hiding in your fridge?"

Arden laughs and nods, grabbing the barbeque sauce and

returning it to the fridge. In its stead on the counter, he places a bottle of ketchup.

Lilly smiles. "Now you are speaking my language."

He fills his own plate with the small dinosaur-shaped chicken nuggets and then walks around the counter and takes a seat next to Lilly. They quietly eat their dinner until there are only a couple left on each plate.

Arden pauses before he puts one of the last two nuggets still on his plate in his mouth and sets it down on the plate, holding it so it appears to be standing up. He reaches forward with his other hand and grabs the other nugget, standing it up as well so it's facing the first nugget. Lilly looks over at him with her eyebrows arched, glancing between his plate and his face.

Arden begins to mimic a conversation between the two dinosaur nuggets, moving each one as it talks. "Why, hello there you sexy dinosaur, how are you?" "Why, I'm great, thank you for asking." "So what brings you here today?" "Oh, you know, I heard about this great ketchup pool just begging for some dinosaur love." "Oh, me too! Not here for the pool, but definitely begging for some dinosaur love." "Why, you naughty dinosaur! Rawr!"

He then proceeds to simulate dinosaur chicken nugget sex with the two nuggets.

Lilly laughs and then looks at him with a serious look. "You have a lot more problems than you initially let on, you know that?"

Arden sets the nuggets down and turns to face her, trying

to keep a straight face. "Today's episode of a day in the life of a dinosaur nugget is brought to you by the letters A and L."

Unable to keep the serious look on her face anymore, Lilly busts out into laughter with Arden doing the same right after her.

"Dinner and a show. Tonight's been quite the treat," she says between laughs.

Arden nods in response. "Just wait until you see what I have in store for dessert. Rawr indeed," he says as he looks her up and down as she sits in the chair next to him.

Lilly, still laughing, rolls her eyes at him. "Don't count your chickens before they hatch, sir. I'm going to need more than an elegant dinner and show before I'm the one on the menu."

Getting up from his seat and grabbing both his plate and her plate, he leans over and plants a quick kiss on her left cheek. "Yes ma'am, I wouldn't expect anything less. At least, until the drugs kick in and I have to carry you into the backyard to chain you to the tree."

Lilly holds up the almost empty wine glass in front of her and inspects the remaining liquid. "I don't see any residue from any dissolved powder in my glass though." Setting her glass back down on the counter, she reaches over and picks up his bourbon glass. "Oh my," she says as she inspects the glass, "Now your glass has some of the telltale residue. You sure you spiked the right drink?"

Setting the two now-clean plates on the drying mat next to the sink, Arden pauses and tilts his head as though in deep thought. "Oh shit, that's right, you drink the wine. I drink the bourbon." He puts both his hands down on the counter in front of him and leans forward on them. "Why is the room starting to spin? I'm so sleepy all of a sudden."

Lilly giggles and sets his glass back down on the counter, next to hers. "Before you pass out, would you kindly refill my wine for me? I'd like to enjoy another glass before I have to drag your limp body somewhere."

Arden nods, smiling, and grabs her glass. He refills it from the half-empty wine bottle from the fridge and sets the glass back down in front of her. "So what shall we do now, gorgeous?" he asks her.

She reaches forward and grabs her glass, taking a sip of her wine before she responds. "How about some cuddling on the couch and we can see where it goes from there?"

Reaching for his own glass, Arden nods. "Sounds like the perfect plan to me," he says as he finishes off the last of the bourbon in his glass. "Let me refresh this really quick and I'll meet you there."

Turning from the counter, he heads into his writing room while Lilly gets up from her seat at the counter, following him as she makes her way to the couch to sit down. As he approaches the small table where his decanter sets, he glances at the black screen of his laptop, making a mental note that he really should attempt to do some work on the manuscript tomorrow, regardless of whether he feels ready or not. He also makes a mental note to write a dedication to Saphina at the beginning, thanking her for pushing him to become the author he is now and that he will forever miss her. He pauses before he picks up the decanter and looks out the small window in front of him, the recently installed curtain still open. The dark of the night has taken over most of the view, fighting against the light from the porch lamps to lay claim to the front of the house. A brief flash of fear races across his skin at the thought that his tormentor may be out there right now, looking at him from beyond the reach of the light. He quickly pours himself a drink and slides the curtain closed across the window in front of him. He heads to the bathroom and then the bedroom, quickly peeking past the curtains to see if any of the motion sensor lights are on. Lilly's voice reaches him from the living room, asking him if everything is ok. He nods at her and smiles as he exits the bedroom and heads towards the kitchen to take a quick look out the back door. As he reaches the back door, he realizes he didn't test any of the lights to see if they worked or not.

Slipping a pair of shoes on, he lets Lilly know he is going to step outside a moment and check to make sure the new lights work. Focused on the television, she nods and tells him to be careful.

He sets his glass down on the kitchen table before he heads out the back door, checking to make sure he can easily access the handgun still tucked away in the small of his back if he needs to. A moment later and he is in his backyard, rounding the corner to the side of the house where he keeps his trash can. As he clears the corner, the darkness surrounding him is quickly chased away by the motion sensor light turning on, bathing the surrounding area in white light. Surprised by how bright the little LED lights are, Arden steps back around the corner to the back of the house and waits to see how long it takes before the light turns off.

About thirty seconds, he thinks, as the light turns off and allows the darkness to regain control. He turns towards the other side of the house and walks in that direction until the light above his bedroom window picks up his movement and turns on. The welcoming light fills a good portion of the backyard, pushing back the black shroud of the night.

Arden smiles as he continues on to the side of the house with the bathroom window, happy to see how well the lights are working. As he expects, the moment he rounds the corner, the third motion sensor light turns on, illuminating the area around him. He continues walking, not stopping to time how long it takes the light to turn off, and soon he is in front of his house and almost at the front door. As he was checking the lights, he was also seeing how well the curtains worked at keeping him from seeing inside the house.

As he reaches the door and grabs the handle, he nods to himself and sighs in relief. The new motion lights should keep his unwelcome visitor at bay, and they won't be able to watch him through his windows anymore either. Before he steps inside, he turns to the darkness behind him, beyond the reach of the light from his porch lamps, and speaks to whoever may be watching and listening.

"The show is now officially over. Go find something else to do with your time and leave me the fuck alone."

Chapter 14

RESCUE

Trapper Tony Piercet scratches his left arm and sighs. This is the fourth trap this morning that has turned up empty.

He frowns. Normally he would find one or two of the traps set off, usually by small game that escaped getting caught up in the large metal jaws, or by fallen tree branches that happen to fall at the right angle to hit the pressure plate.

Shrugging, he continues onward, making his way through the trees and underbrush towards the fifth trap. *A trap not set off is one less trap I have to take the time to reset*, he thinks.

Hired by the local Wildlife Service to trap and catch a large, dangerous animal of an unknown type, he only found out this morning that this animal attacked and killed a local police officer just outside his squad car. The Wildlife Service officer reassured him that the nearby residents were warned not to go wandering around the woods for the next few weeks until the animal could be captured and killed. Although he was advised to catch the animal humanely, Tony wasn't taking any chances using a rubber jaw trap or a snare and merely pissing off some animal that has already tasted human flesh. If the Wildlife Service wants to humanely catch a maneater, they can just do it themselves.

He set up twelve large, not exactly legal, steel jaw traps in a five-mile radius around the location where the animal was last presumed to be, but when he was setting up the traps, he didn't find any of the typical markings from a territorial predator. He wasn't expecting to catch much, if anything.

Pausing to look at his map and make sure he was heading in the right direction, he resumes his walk through the forest, enjoying the early morning sounds and the smell of the trees. He has always loved being outside, and having grown up in a family of hunters, it felt right when the opportunity to go into business as a trapper presented itself. It took him quite a few years to make a name for himself, but now he is known across most of the state as the one trapper that can always get the job done.

This one was a peculiar one, though. Predators large enough to be able to overpower or catch a human off guard and kill them don't do it for fun. They do it to eat or to protect their territory, or sometimes both.

But Tony hasn't seen any territorial markers at all, beyond a couple buck rubs. No droppings from a large animal either, or any carcasses of smaller animals that became an unfortunate snack.

Then there is the fact the Wildlife Service officer was extremely vague when they hired him, calling it just a large animal attack, and not divulging many other details beyond that. Thankfully, the local news station isn't as tight lipped as the Wildlife Service and told the whole state this morning that a local officer was killed by a large, dangerous predator and a tracker has been hired to catch it. And since the news didn't say the officer was eaten by that same predator, then Tony can only presume it was protecting its territory. The same territory that he's currently walking around in.

And that's why we used the steel traps when our gut said something was a bit fishy, he thinks to himself, content with his trap choice.

As he makes his way around some thick underbrush and approaches the fifth trap, Tony isn't worried if he does stumble into his prey. With his .357 Magnum strapped to his side, he's the apex predator in these woods now, and he has full confidence he can draw the weapon and empty all six rounds into whatever comes after him before it reaches him.

He smiles, thinking about the conversation he had with his wife this morning after they watched the news. She was all in a panic because this animal killed a trained police officer and here he was going to walk around those same woods again looking for it. Tony reminded her several times that the officer was probably caught off guard at night and didn't know how to react, but that her loving husband, Tony Piercet, best trapper in the state, has stared down a three-hundred-pound black bear as well as handled an entire pack of wolves before. The same Tony Piercet that tracked and killed both a thirteen-foot-long crocodile and a full-grown lion in Africa. And even though she rolled her eyes at him when he told her that he is the apex predator, as she always does when he says that, she stopped her fussing and told him to just be careful.

Still smiling, the fifth trap now in sight, he confirms it is still set and in place. He checks the map again and the chalk arrow mark he left on a nearby tree when he initially set out the traps. He sets off in the direction of trap number six while once again getting lost in his thoughts, thinking about what might be for dinner tonight and if the new scope he ordered for his favorite hunting rifle will come in today.

Once Tony is a few hundred feet away from the sixth trap, a loud noise about sixty feet to his right causes him to come to a complete stop and put his hand on the butt of his revolver, ready to draw. He remains motionless, next to a large tree, staring in the direction of the sound, watching for even the slightest movement. The noise repeats itself, confirming to Tony that something bigger than the average forest creature is out there, moving around. With the thick underbrush in that direction, he can't determine what is making the noise, but he is ready.

He waits, unmoving, as the noise continues to approach his location.

Forty feet. Thirty feet.

Staying as quiet as he can, Tony unsnaps the small strap retaining his weapon in the holster and slowly draws the gun, aiming it in the direction of the noise. The thick, entangled underbrush starts about fifteen feet away from him, and the noise continues to draw closer as it moves towards where he is standing.

He listens intently. Listens to the occasional crunch of a leaf or dried twig underfoot. The rustle of the low branches being moved as the maker of the noise draws ever closer.

Twenty feet away.

Whatever it is, it doesn't walk with a heavy step like a bear, he thinks, *but it's definitely not very small either.*

He watches as the heavy underbrush in front of him begins to move as the approaching creature pushes its way through.

His finger on the trigger, he prepares to fire if necessary.

With a loud rustle, the brush parts and the antlers and head of a buck exits from the undergrowth, the rest of the body appearing shortly afterwards.

Tony remains motionless, waiting for the buck to notice him standing there. He must be downwind, or the buck would have picked up his scent long before it reached him. He keeps his finger on the trigger. A spooked buck, in this proximity and near the yearly rut, might attack, and Tony isn't planning on getting gored by antlers or pummeled by a set of hooves today.

It's only a brief moment more before the buck sees Tony standing next to the tree and startles, snorting loudly and immediately turning to its left and bounding off into the forest.

He waits a moment longer just in case any does are following and then lowers his gun, breathing a sigh of relief. He places the pistol back in its holster and re-snaps it in place.

"Well, that was fun," he tells the surrounding trees. "Guess who's coming back out here during deer season and bagging himself that buck? That's right, Mr. Tony Piercet."

Tony chuckles and continues on his trek to the next trap, finally pulling away from where he rooted himself when he first heard the approaching sounds. The sixth trap, upon reaching it, is still set and in place like the five others before it.

Another check of the map and a quick verification of the arrow he marked on the nearby tree and Tony is on his way to the seventh trap.

He continues to move with care through the forest, navigating around the dense underbrush locations and being wary of the placement of his feet. Ensuring the noise he creates is minimal, Tony confidently works his way among the trees, headed for his next destination.

As he approaches the next stop on his forest tour, he senses something is off. When he's about eighty feet away from the trap, he pauses, studying the terrain around him. The ground shows a clear disturbance, as though someone or something was shuffling or dragging their feet as they walked. Several twigs on a shrub nearby have been recently broken off, the white center of the branch still fresh. *Someone else has been through here since I was here last*, he thinks, *and didn't do a good job of covering their tracks*. Tony kneels down and inspects the disturbed ground. *Definitely not something with four legs, but two. And they were not moving with any sort of care at all, as though they were fumbling around trying to find their way.*

Tony stands back up and follows the direction of disturbed forest floor with his eyes. Towards where the next trap was waiting.

He waits a moment before proceeding forward, lost in thought. *Well, either I'm looking at the path of a human or a Sasquatch. Although it's possible a medium-sized bear did this, they don't tend to stay on their hind legs for very long when walking.* Frowning, he begins to move forward again. There isn't supposed to be anyone wandering around the forest, or so he was told. Hopefully, some rookie hunter or ignorant local didn't decide they wanted to go for a midnight stroll in the woods and came across one of the traps.

As he draws closer to the seventh device, following the recently created haphazard trail, Tony realizes that whatever was making this journey through the forest has found the trap, and not in a good way. The metallic smell of iron floats heavily on the air, indicating a large amount of blood has been lost nearby. As he takes one step after another, he once again unsnaps the strap to his revolver, listening closely for any noise. Anything indicating labored breathing, as though in pain.

The sounds of the morning forest remain normal as Tony clears the last ten feet between himself and his destination. As he steps around the last tree that separates his view from the trap, he comes to an abrupt stop at what he sees in front of him.

The large steel jaws of the trap are closed, the steel of the teeth covered in dried blood. Below the clenched jaws is the lower part of a leg, the tissue and muscle shredded, the jagged edges of two bones exposed.

It takes a few moments for Tony to realize that at the end of that mangled leg, doused in blood, is a shoe.

He blinks a couple times as it sets in that he's looking at the lower half of a human leg.

"Fuck me," he says out loud, "That's not good."

Tony looks around the small clearing for any signs of the owner to the grisly sight in front of him. A wide swath of ground is disturbed, leading away from the tightly closed steel jaws, a dark trail of blood soaked into the ground behind it.

"Hello?" he calls out, hoping to get a reply in return. No response reaches his ears. Although Tony has seen a good share of animal legs mangled and sometimes removed by one of his traps, it has never been a human leg. The result is unsettling and a rush of fear hits him. *If this person is dead, am I going to end up in jail?* he wonders as he starts to follow the blood-soaked path leading out of the clearing.

He doesn't have to follow the trail long until he finds the owner of the leg left behind. His thoughts of how he can avoid jail time are quickly replaced by confusion at what he sees on the ground before him.

"What the flying fuck?" he asks out loud, his brows furrowed as he steps forward to see if the leg's owner is still alive.

On the ground in front of him is the body of a human being, lying on their stomach, the bloodied and mangled stump of their right leg clearly indicating they are the one who found the trap. Their arms are stretched out in front of them, as though they're still trying to drag themselves away. A belt is wrapped around their right leg, just below the knee, a few inches above the shredded mess. They are dressed in an odd sort of homemade ghillie suit from top to bottom, and both of their hands are covered in some kind of metal gloves with sharp claws at the end of each finger.

Tony hesitantly approaches the body, unsure if he wants to get close or not.

"Hello? Still with us?" he asks as he takes a couple steps towards the outstretched body. The body remains motionless. Unresponsive.

With his hand on his pistol, he takes the last couple steps separating him from the figure and kneels down next to its left side. He reaches out with his left hand and pushes on the shoulder of the figure next to him, shaking it. "Hey, I'm going to get you some help, ok?"

The body remains silent, unmoving.

Taking his right palm off the pistol, he reaches forward with both hands and rolls the figure onto their back. Their face is covered by a black shroud, which Tony pulls up and off their head.

He wasn't prepared for what he sees under that shroud.

Unable to take his eyes off the person's face in front of him, Tony fumbles for the long-range walkie attached to his belt, finally locating it and putting it in front of his mouth.

He hits the transmit button, hoping the Ranger's Office on

the other end of the programmed frequency can hear him. "Uhh, this is Trapper Piercet out at trap site seven. I have a dead body out here that you need see. You're gonna want to bring the police with you."

✳

The timer on the stove goes off, letting Arden know the bacon in the oven should be done. He removes the sheet pan and sets it on the top of the stove, quickly and carefully transferring the hot bacon slices to a paper towel-lined plate. As soon as he is done, he turns his attention to the pan on the stove with an omelet in it, quickly grabbing the spatula to flip the eggs so they don't burn on one side.

"You burn my brunch and you're going to have to drive into town to buy the ingredients to make me a replacement meal," Lilly tells him as she points to the now-empty egg carton setting on the counter, "Since you decided to use up all the breakfast supplies this morning."

Arden chuckles and nods, "Yes ma'am, read you loud and clear. One mega crispy omelet coming right up with some ultra-crunchy charred bacon."

Lilly rolls her eyes. "You keep that up and see what happens."

Smiling, he flips the omelet one more time to make sure it's evenly cooked and then transfers it to the plate in front of Lilly. He adds several slices of bacon to the plate next to the omelet and winks at her. "Breakfast is served, my lady."

Arden starts cooking his own omelet while Lilly waits for

him. "You're going to be eating a cold omelet if you wait for me to finish making mine," he tells her.

"I wouldn't have to wait if you knew how to cook two omelets at the same time, sir."

Visibly cringing, he keeps his attention on his own omelet as he folds it over and then looks up at Lilly, who is smiling at him with a devilishly cute grin on her face. "You know, I don't see your highness over here cooking, so a little appreciation for the cook would be nice," he tells her in response, winking at her with his left eye.

Lilly giggles and nods. "Yes, sir," she says in response as she picks up the fork next to her plate and begins to carve her omelet up into bite-sized pieces. Arden continues to monitor the pan in front of him, grabbing a piece of bacon from the stack on the paper towel to munch on while his eggs cook through. A quick flip and it's only a few minutes more before he is transferring his own meal to the empty plate next to Lilly, who has already eaten half of her omelet and most of her bacon. He transfers a couple more pieces of bacon from the stack to her plate and then proceeds around the counter to the seat next to her at the breakfast bar. They finish their breakfast in silence and once they are done, Arden gets ready to stand up and clean up the mess. Lilly puts her left hand on his shoulder and pushes him back down into his seat.

"No sir, my turn to clean up. You stay right there and relax. I'll even get you another cup of coffee," she tells him.

"Ohh, spoiling me now I see," he tells her as she makes her

way around the counter and to the spot in front of the sink, "Someone must feel guilty for giving me grief earlier." Lilly sticks her tongue out at him and at the same time, hands him the rest of the bacon from the paper towel. Happily accepting the remaining slices, Arden eats them while watching Lilly as she washes the dishes in the sink and stacks them, one by one, on the drying mat.

"See, isn't this a better show than watching me struggle while I'm chained to a tree outside?" she asks him.

Arden smiles and shrugs, allowing her to take the empty plate from in front of him. "I don't know. For me to give you an objective opinion I'd need to experience both situations and so far I only have this one."

Lilly pauses while washing his plate and looks at him suspiciously, both her eyes narrowed. "So far?" she asks.

"Well yeah, and I have to say the experience was great until about a minute ago when you stopped just to glare at me," he says in response, lightly chuckling. "And where is this other cup of coffee I was promised?"

Lilly sighs loudly and returns to washing and rinsing off the last plate in silence. After drying her hands, she grabs his coffee cup and proceeds to make him another cup of coffee. As they both wait for the machine to finishing brewing the cup, she speaks, her voice laced with sarcasm. "See, Lilly, this is what you get when you don't bother reading the warning label or looking for red flags before hopping into bed with some random guy. They go from sweet, creepy killer to ultra-demanding prima donna who can't even make their own cup of coffee or wash their own damn dishes."

Leaning back in his chair, Arden folds his arms across his chest and nods, a big smile on his face. "Lilly didn't tell me she had multiple personalities. Which one are you?"

Lilly laughs in response and hands him his freshly brewed cup of coffee. "That was good," she says, "Although I was half a second away from saying you haven't seen the half of them yet."

He smiles as he takes a sip of his coffee, "Thanks, I try. And I hope over time I get to see them all." Lilly blushes a bit and blows him a kiss.

"We'll see about that mister, as long as you keep playing your cards right."

Arden smiles, gets up from the chair, and stretches, taking a quick look at the clock as he does. Almost eleven-thirty. Lilly, still wearing only a T-shirt, excuses herself to clean up and change clothes while he sits down on the couch and turns on the television. He switches the channel to the local news, only partially paying attention to the latest stories, while he sips on his coffee and waits for Lilly to finish up in the bathroom so he can hop in there himself. It doesn't take her very long, and once she is done, Arden takes the opportunity to shower and clean up as well.

After his shower and a quick trip to the bedroom to put on clean clothes, he exits the room and sees Lilly sitting on the couch, her overnight bag packed back up and setting next to her as she rummages through it.

"Lose something?" he asks as he sits down next to her.

"Just making sure I don't leave a pair of panties or a sock behind. Wouldn't want all your other women to get jealous."

He laughs and before he has a chance to retort, the sound of an approaching vehicle cuts into their conversation, causing both Arden and Lilly to turn to look out the living room window, the curtains open from when they got up earlier this morning.

A local squad car can be seen approaching and comes to a stop next to Lilly's SUV.

Arden and Lilly look at each other momentarily and Arden shrugs. "I have no idea. I haven't had any other incidents since the last time they were here. Maybe they are here for you this time?"

Lilly playfully swats at him with her right hand. "Clearly you didn't hide the bodies well enough and now they're here for us both."

He chuckles and looks back out the window as the same officer from the last two visits extricates himself from the patrol car. "They probably should've sent more police then, because we're about to go full Bonnie and Clyde up in here. Should we warn Officer Holden out there first, or just surprise him?"

Lilly glances out the window at the robust man and then back at Arden. "Forget his surprise. What about my surprise that you know his name? Is this a set up? Did you rat me out? Did you bargain for a plea deal?"

Arden stays quiet as he gets up from the couch and in a

dramatic fashion, slowly backs away from Lilly and towards the front door. "Why no, gorgeous, I would…uhh…never do that. You just sit there nice and quiet and I'll talk to this police officer who I've never met before in my entire life." He looks over at the clock on the wall. Almost two in the afternoon.

Lilly is still giggling as Arden opens up the door and greets the officer now standing on his stoop.

"Good afternoon Officer Holden. What brings you out here today?"

The officer exchanges pleasantries and asks if he can come inside. Arden obliges his request and introduces the policeman to Lilly, who is now getting off the couch to join the two men at the breakfast bar. After confirming it's alright that Lilly is present for what he has to tell Arden, Officer Holden is quick and to the point.

He tells Arden about the body that was discovered a couple miles away from his house earlier this morning by a trapper who was hired to catch the large predator presumed to have been involved in the animal attack a couple days ago.

He tells Arden about how the person was dressed. About their homemade metal gloves and sharp claws at the end of each finger. He also tells Arden about what they found on the body. Five photos of Arden, torn from the back page of each of his novels. Several random pages torn from his books describing how the monster would terrorize its victims.

Pages about how it would kill its victims.

The officer also told him about what was carved all over

the person's face, clearly done over a long time, as most of the carvings were fully healed scars. *SOON.*

It takes Arden a few moments for the words to really sink in.

There is no question this person they found is who has been tormenting him the last week or so. Who has been terrorizing him. They also believe this is who may have killed the officer as well, as one of the pages they had on them was about the killing of a police officer in the same manner that it happened the other night. It stands to reason they knew the police were on their way out here if they were watching Arden, and they set up an ambush for the officer in his driveway. Forensics is currently running tests on the homemade metal gloves to confirm the suspicions.

Arden's thoughts race in light of this new information. *But what about the other deaths? Did this person do all those as well? Or is my imagination in overdrive and trying to create a connection when there isn't one?* Another thought forces its way through all the others. A more perverse thought given the situation. *This would make a really good addition to my last novel if I didn't already have it planned out.*

Lilly's hand coming to rest on his upper back pulls Arden from his musings and back to reality. Officer Holden, staring at him, asks him if he's ok.

Nodding, Arden takes a deep breath and releases it. "I'm fine, just processing what you told me. It's a lot to take in, knowing this psycho was recently outside my windows."

He pauses a moment and then asks the officer a question. "How did they die?

The officer looks between Arden and Lilly and sighs. "I shouldn't share this, but you deserve to know and what I'm about to tell you doesn't leave this room. Apparently they stepped on a trap that was set for a large predator and they ended up bleeding to death on the ground."

An odd sense of satisfaction floods through Arden and he nods. "Good," he responds, trying to keep the sound of content out of his voice as he says it.

Both Lilly and the officer remain silent for a moment, and then the officer asks Arden if anything else has happened since the last time they spoke. Arden shakes his head no, suddenly realizing that he hasn't gotten any calls from the restricted number recently either.

The policeman, turning to leave, makes sure Arden doesn't have any other questions and reassures him everything will be ok, and that if anything else does happen, to contact the officer immediately. Arden shows him to the door and stands on the stoop as Officer Holden climbs into the patrol car, backs out of the spot next to Lilly's vehicle, and then drives away.

Once he is back inside the house and the door is closed behind him, Arden heads right for his study and to the small table which holds his decanter. He grabs one of the lowball glasses and pours himself a small shot of bourbon, quickly drinking it down in one swig. He pours himself another and swirls it in the glass a moment, taking a moment to open the curtains and look out the small window in front of him at the sun filled world beyond. Lilly's voice reaches him from the other room.

"You ok?"

Arden quickly drinks the second shot of bourbon and sets the glass down next to the decanter. He turns and heads back to the kitchen where Lilly is now setting at the breakfast bar, watching him with concern. "I'm good, just needed a quick drink. Or two."

Lilly nods. "At least it was good news, right? The bastard got what they deserved. And what kind of person makes homemade metal gloves with claws and carves up their face?"

He sits down next to her and puts his hands over hers. "I agree, but…," he says as his voice trails off.

"But what?" Lilly asks.

Arden holds both of her hands tightly. "I can't shake the feeling that something is still off. That this isn't the end of what's been happening. It just doesn't make sense when I think about all the other deaths, and although I'm telling myself it's just my imagination, I still think there is something else going on. That it's not over."

Lilly squeezes his hands in response. "It's a lot to take in. Some lunatic who quite possibly killed someone in your driveway was looking in your windows for god knows how long. Carrying around photos of you. Watching you. Hell, watching us. It even makes me feel uneasy. But all that is over now."

Arden lifts both of her hands to his lips and kisses them. "I know, and you are probably right," he tells her in response, not sharing his remaining thoughts.

But if you are right, then why is this uneasy feeling that has been bothering me stronger now than it ever has been before?

Chapter 15

REWRITE

The cursor blinks a steady beat on the almost fully blank screen in front of him. The only thing written, marring the otherwise pristine white of the page on the screen, is *Chapter 16* centered two spaces just above the cursor.

The blink of the cursor doesn't falter, as though it's the steady heartbeat of this living document, waiting patiently for the next keystroke.

Arden takes a deep breath and exhales. The final chapter. The chapter where the protagonist finally defeats the monster. The long overdue end of the series.

He's as nervous and excited now as he was when he wrote it the first time, before the lightning storm erased his work.

Damn. That's right. The lightning storm. I almost forgot about that, he thinks, *That seems like it was forever ago with how much has happened since then.*

Arden sits back in his chair and takes a sip of his bourbon, mentally preparing himself for the work ahead. After Lilly left a few hours ago, Arden called Ben and let him know the so-called predator was captured and then patiently listened to Ben tell him all about how Cassie decided she wanted to get into pottery and how their house is now covered in random droplets and smears of clay. Arden patiently listened to Ben as he explained all the steps to make pottery and what steps Cassie decided to skip to speed up the process, all while making mental notes about this new additional content for the book about Ben and Cassie's adventures. *The pottery adventure, Chapter 15,* he remembers thinking while Ben was telling him about how hard it is to get dried clay out of bedsheets. Arden was glad Ben didn't elaborate on that last part as he had no interest in learning why there was clay in their bed.

Once he was finally off the phone with Ben, Arden decided it was time to get back to writing and try to wrap up this series once and for all. And remember to save it this time.

Now, sitting in front of his computer and ready to go, he finds himself hesitating, thinking about the events of the last week. The event from this afternoon and the brief thought that came with it.

What if I don't end the series just yet? What if I change it up? What if I add this twist of someone pretending to be the monster to this last chapter and draw the conclusion out for one more book? Would my readers like that? Would they want to read another book in this series?

He takes another sip of his bourbon while he contemplates

completely changing Chapter 16 from what it had been when he originally finished it.

The cursor patiently waits while Arden is lost in his thoughts, daydreaming about an alternative ending and what direction he could go with another book. He wonders if he even has another book about the monster inside him. Another book about the terror it causes and the death its existence feeds upon.

And what if there are more unhinged fans out there and extending the series inspires them? Inspires them to stand in his driveway at night looking for an autograph or show up at his house wearing metal claws, trying to terrorize him.

He sets his glass down on the desk and sighs. *No, I have to end this series. I have to bring the monster's reign of terror to an end once more,* he tells himself. *It's time to move on with my writing. To try something new. Like a romance maybe. Or even actually write about the adventures of Ben and Cassie instead of always making mental notes about them.*

Arden smiles when he thinks about all the quirky stuff his neighbors have subjected him to over the years. *Definitely a full book's worth of material there,* he thinks.

He leans forward in the chair and puts his fingers on the laptop's keyboard. Hesitating just a moment, Arden nods as if confirming he's ready and begins to type.

The words come slow at first, and he struggles over phrases and content, trying to recall as much as he can from the first time he wrote this chapter. After he pushes through the first couple pages, the words begin to flow and Arden loses track of time, as he normally does. One blank page after another fills with letters, yet again crafting the climactic end for the monster he created so long ago.

As he gets about halfway through the chapter, his cellphone rings from its current position on the kitchen counter. The tone fills the otherwise silent house, overtaking the sound of the laptop keys as he types and interrupting his current train of thought. Arden pulls his eyes away from the screen and looks out the study door and towards the sound. *Must be Lilly checking in*, he thinks. He sits back, the leather of his chair creaking as he does, and stretches his fingers a bit. As usual, his bourbon glass sits empty on the table, finished quite a few pages ago.

The phone in the kitchen continues to ring and Arden gets ready to stand up, pausing just before he does. Not willing to lose his current progress like last time, he leans forward and quickly saves his work to both the laptop's hard drive as well as his back up thumb drive. Satisfied his progress is properly saved this time, he grabs the empty glass and gets up from the chair just as his cellphone goes quiet.

Sorry Lilly, I'll call you back in just a moment, he thinks as he detours to the decanter to refresh his drink. After pouring a small amount, he looks out the window in front of him. The dark of the evening has taken over completely and only a bit of his driveway is visible from the light being cast outside from the warm colored, low wattage bulb above him in the study's ceiling light fixture. He breathes a sigh of relief, happy to know that this time there shouldn't be any eyes looking back at him from the darkness, beyond the occasional forest animal passing by. While he's staring out the window at the black void beyond his driveway, a bright flash of light illuminates the sky and surrounding forest. The deep baritone rumble of thunder quickly follows the lightning, announcing a storm is on its way.

Arden pulls himself from the window, glass in hand, and walks throughout the other rooms of his home, turning on lights and making sure the curtains are drawn across the windows. *Better safe than sorry,* he tells himself, *just in case someone else decides to play some creepy Peeping Tom game.*

The television now on, he pauses in front of the screen while an advertisement for a new chicken sandwich at a local fast-food restaurant plays. *That actually does look pretty good,* he thinks, *might have to give that one a try the next time I head into town.* His stomach growls in agreement, reminding him he has not eaten since breakfast earlier this morning with Lilly.

Finally making his way into the kitchen, he grabs his phone from the counter and hits a button on the side to check to see who called.

Restricted number.

Arden frowns, the uneasy feeling resurging and making itself known. *Relax, Arden, they only called once and you did just change your number.* He sets the phone down and stares at the screen until it goes black again. *This is just a coincidence,* he tells himself, trying to push away the now familiar feeling that has been haunting him for days. *A coincidence. That's all. Right?*

Arden thinks back to the conversation he had with the officer earlier this afternoon. *What did the officer say his tormentor had on them? Some photos of me, I think. Some book pages from my novels. Did he say if they found a phone on the body?* He furrows his brow trying to remember the details of the conversation and if the policeman mentioned a cellphone or not.

Another rumble of thunder reverberates throughout the house and Arden can hear the rain start to beat against the roof above him.

As if in response to his thoughts, the phone on the counter begins to ring again, the noise startling Arden. Almost expecting to see restricted number displayed for a second time, he's relieved when it's Lilly's name that is currently on the screen. He swipes to answer the phone, puts it on speaker, and her voice quickly fills the kitchen. They chat for a bit and she lets him know she would like to see him tomorrow night, but this time he has to come visit her at her place. Arden happily agrees and then asks her if she remembers the conversation with the officer and if they had mentioned anything about finding a cellphone on the body. Lilly confirms she doesn't remember and inquires why he is asking.

Not wanting to worry her, Arden tells her he was just wondering and was trying to remember everything that was found on the body. Lilly confirms she remembers him saying something about Arden's photos and pages from his books, but nothing more.

They chat a bit longer before Lilly says she has to go, and she reminds him to call her if anything happens, which he agrees to do. As he disconnects the call, his stomach growls, reminding him he still needs to eat. It doesn't take him long to make a couple of sandwiches and Arden eats them both while still standing at the counter, anxious to get back to work and see how much more of Chapter 16 he can complete before he is unable to keep his eyes open any longer.

As he finishes the second sandwich, the dining room window lets him know the outside world is filled with bright white yet again, the ominous rumble following immediately afterwards. The rain intensifies its attack on the shingles. *Damn, that storm is close,* Arden thinks, *maybe not the best idea to have the laptop plugged in, considering what happened last time.* He turns from the counter and, after placing his empty plate in the sink, makes a beeline towards the study. Reaching his desk, he unplugs the laptop's cord from the wall outlet and checks to make sure the battery indicator on the screen shows that the computer's charge is full. *No more electric shock incidents this time,* he tells himself, smiling. As he returns to the kitchen, he stops to turn off the television, a strong rumble of thunder letting him know the storm has just begun. *Don't need this getting fried either.*

Once he's back in the kitchen, Arden cleans up the mess from his dinner and puts everything away. Just as he is plugging in his cellphone to charge up the battery, the house is plunged into pitch black and the steady hum of the refrigerator goes silent. *Well isn't that nice,* he thinks. He checks how much battery life is remaining on the phone.

Eight percent.

Of course the power goes out when my phone is about to die. Why wouldn't it? Arden sets the phone down on the counter and opens the nearest drawer in front of him. He fumbles around in the drawer until he finds what he is looking for. A flashlight and a USB charging cable for his phone.

Turning the flashlight on, its bright white beam chasing the sudden darkness away, Arden checks the cable he pulled out of the junk drawer. The cable in his hand is not the USB charging cable for the phone, but a charging cable for an older model phone he had a few years before his current one. *Well, that isn't going to do me any good*, he thinks as the plug for this cable doesn't match his latest phone's receptacle. He tosses the cable into the trash can next to the counter. Returning his focus to the drawer, he resumes his hunt for what he needs. While searching, he comes across and pulls out three candles and a lighter and sets them aside. After a couple more minutes of shifting everything in the drawer around, Arden comes up empty handed.

Arden frowns, unsure where the cable could be if it isn't in this drawer. *Well, that's just fucking dandy. How many times can a man end up with a dead phone because he fails to charge it? Well, class, let's ask Arden the idiot.* Frustrated, he makes a mental note to pick up a replacement charging cord the next time he goes into town, as well as a couple of portable phone charging power banks he can keep stored away in case this happens again.

Closing the drawer, Arden turns his attention to getting the candles in place. A few moments later and he has set up the three candles: one for the bathroom, one for his study, and one for the kitchen.

Satisfied with the candle placement and confident he won't end up burning his house down, he grabs his phone and his glass of bourbon from the kitchen counter and heads into his study. *May as well see what else I can get done tonight and hopefully the phone will last until the power company gets the power back on.*

Reaching his destination, Arden sets everything down on the desk and takes a seat in his chair, ready to dive back into work while there's still life in the laptop's battery. The bright white of the screen lights up the study, the cursor once again beating its steady heartbeat, waiting to be fed. Before he has a chance to put his hands on the keyboard and begin to type, the phone rings. *Seriously?* he thinks in frustration, *The phone is about to die and someone decides to call me. Who the hell is calling this late anyways? Lilly said she was going to sleep. This better not be Ben just confirming my power is out too.*

Irritated, Arden picks the phone up from the desk and looks at the screen.

Restricted number.

A cold chill runs down his spine, dousing the flames of irritation he felt just a moment ago. He hesitates to answer it, the phone in his hand suddenly seeming sinister in the light from the computer monitor with those uncomfortable words displayed on the screen.

Arden grits his teeth and shakes his head. *It's just a damn phone call.*

Swiping to answer the call, he puts the phone to his ear and answers with a less than pleasant tone of voice. "Hello? Who is this and why are you calling me this late?"

The voice on the other end of the line says three words before the line is disconnected. Three words in a voice that Arden has heard over the phone before. A raspy, guttural voice laced with evil.

"Your turn, Arden."

✳

The cold steel in his hand doesn't offer the comfort that it did a couple days ago. Now, it just feels like an impending doom. A useless toy in the face of what he fears is coming.

Arden's thoughts were of chaos and fear after hearing that voice on the phone. After hearing the words it spoke. *Your turn, Arden.*

The resulting flood of panic and terror had washed over him like a tsunami, causing him to drop the phone and race into the bedroom to grab his pistol.

Now, sitting on the floor in the corner, his back pressed firmly against the intersecting walls, he watches the dimly lit doorway to his bedroom. Light from the candle in the bathroom just barely reaches this door, and the constant flickering of the flame casts large moving shadows all over. As the storm outside continues to beat against the house with all its fury, each rumble of thunder now causes him to jump slightly. Each flash of lighting that can be seen from the edges of the bedroom curtains causes his heartbeat to escalate and his hands to shake more than they already are.

Get a grip on yourself, Arden, he thinks while he tries to rationalize what he just heard. *It's just the same person who was messing with you before. That's it. Just like your phone always dying when you conveniently don't have a way to charge it. You're just lucky enough to have two different people terrorizing you at the same time in two different ways.*

But something inside him fights back against his logic, telling him his reasoning is wrong, that the voice he heard really is his monster. His monster that has somehow come to life and has been the one killing all these people, working its way to him.

Just like he thought when all the coincidences seemed too familiar. Too related.

Arden takes a deep breath, trying to steady his nerves, doing his best to keep his finger off the trigger to his weapon. The last thing he needs is to panic and open fire at a shadow, putting a bunch of bullet holes in one of his walls.

Just someone harassing you. That's all.

He repeats this mantra several times to no avail. Deep down he knows this call wasn't from some unstable fan. It isn't some lunatic with gloves and metal claws. It's the monster he created, the evil entity born of nightmares, existing solely for the purpose of terror and death that feeds on the fear of its victims.

And this is why Arden doesn't find comfort in the steel of

his pistol like he did before, because he knows this won't work against his creation. In his books, bullets merely pass through the monster, not even slowing it down. Yet he continues to hold onto the weapon, clinging desperately to the fleeting thought that the call was from a person and not some figment of his imagination that he created with his writing.

Another flash of light forces its way into the room from around the edges of the curtains, accompanied by a deep rumble that makes Arden involuntarily jerk.

Shit, Arden, seriously. It's literally just thunder and lightning. Something you have lived with your entire life, he tells himself while trying to bolster his courage, *what would Lilly say if she saw you right now, hiding in the corner like a scared kid, afraid to move in fear that a made-up bogeyman has come to life and is out to get you? Yeah, that screams you are a man, doesn't it? Good luck ever getting laid again after she sees you like this.*

Arden nervously laughs a bit at his last thought, feeling the grip of his fear loosen up on him a little bit. He continues his mental pep talk. *Get your ass off the floor, out of this corner, and be a damn man.*

Finding the resolve to finally move from his location, Arden puts his left hand down on the carpet to steady himself and gets up onto his feet. He cautiously walks to the doorframe of the bedroom and looks out into the rest of the house.

Just as we thought. No monsters. No bogeymen. Just you and your house. You just about lost your man card there, buddy. Arden chuckles and shakes his head. "Well, nothing like a self-deprecating pep talk to bring me back to reality," he announces to the empty living room in front of him.

The wind and rain's assault on his roof continues as he heads into his study to grab the flashlight from the desk, sticking it in his back pocket. He also places his pistol back in the holster, which he attached to his belt in the small of his back before he sat down in the corner of his bedroom. The screen of the laptop has gone black, indicating the computer is now in sleep mode.

Scanning the floor, Arden looks around to locate his cellphone after he dropped it. Barely visible in the dim light of the candle on the desk, he finds the phone just below the outlet where he normally plugs in the laptop. He retrieves the phone and cautiously checks it out. Five percent juice left, no additional calls or texts since the last call earlier. The clock on the phone tells him it's one-thirty in the morning.

As he sets the phone down on the desk, the room briefly illuminates with bright white light and an earth-shaking rumble quickly follows. As with the other recent pairs of lightning and thunder, Arden startles over the sudden incursion and then laughs uneasily at himself.

"How many times are we going to be jumpy over the lightning and thunder tonight?" he asks himself, his words fighting for control over the room against the howling wind and rain outside.

Glancing at his laptop, Arden wonders if he would be able to focus enough to write anything else tonight, since he is wide awake and wouldn't be able to sleep now even if he wanted to.

The lingering fear that his monster is somehow alive refuses to release its claws from his thoughts, no matter how much he makes fun of himself for thinking it's true.

For thinking that somehow, someway, the words he put down on paper have come to life. That his imaginary creation is real and has decided to come after him.

There is a word for that, you know? It's called insane. You don't get conjugal visits in the looney bin, sir, so you better get your shit under control.

Arden smiles and nods to himself. "When I'm right, I'm right," he says, immediately realizing he is now talking to himself. *Yes sir, another sign you are destined for institutional life*, he thinks.

Turning his attention away from the laptop, he looks over at the bookshelves to his left. Two books setting on the edge of the shelf catch his eyes among all the neatly organized books tucked away. Lilly's poetry books.

A flush of warmth races across his body when he thinks about her and the fact she brought him her two latest compilations to read. They will be the perfect distraction right now, and will allow him to get lost in her writing, hopefully forgetting all about the calls he keeps getting and the voice that goes with them. Grabbing both of the books, as well as the candle off his desk, Arden heads into the living room and sits down on the couch, setting the candle on the coffee table and the two books next to him where Lilly usually sits.

Realizing just the candle on the coffee table won't give him enough light to be able to read, Arden gets up from the couch and heads into the kitchen to grab the candle sitting on the center island counter. As he reaches the kitchen and picks up the candle, the room is engulfed by bright white light as lightning rips across the outside sky and thunder rumbles through the house's foundation and walls.

Arden doesn't startle this time at the lightning or thunder. Instead, a loud crash coming from his back porch causes him to jump back, slamming his hip against the counter behind him and almost dropping the lit candle on the floor.

Setting the candle back down on the island counter and putting his right hand on the butt of his pistol, Arden stares at the back door, almost expecting it to open up and for some creature born of darkness and death to step inside.

He waits a few minutes, staring at the door, his heart hammering away in his chest while he tries to keep thoughts of the monster away. The wind continues to howl outside, the rain pelting the house in heavy sheets. Keeping his hand on his pistol, Arden pulls his flashlight out of his back pocket with his left hand and turns it on, aiming it at the back door. The kitchen and dining room burst into clarity and color as the white beam of light chases all the shadows away.

The back door, centered in the beam, appears to beckon to him. Inviting him to see what that sound was.

Keeping his right hand resting on the cold steel nestled in the small of his back, Arden forces himself to approach the door so he can find out what caused the loud noise.

Once he reaches the door, he takes his right hand from the pistol and puts it on the knob, hesitating before he turns it. *You know you can just wait to see what happened in the morning, right? You don't have to look when it's pitch-black outside and you're already paranoid enough that an imaginary monster is after you.*

Arden's grip on the doorknob lessens a bit but then he thinks about what he would have to deal with tomorrow if the noise was his tool chest tipping over due to the high winds. Trying to fix waterlogged electric power tools is not how he would want to start his morning tomorrow. Tightening his grip, Arden turns the knob and begins to pull the door open. A heavy gust of wind rushes through the opening of the door and past him, quickly extinguishing the candle sitting on the counter. With the flashlight beam focused outward, he pulls the door open far enough for him to step to the edge of the doorway, maintaining a grip on the door itself so the wind doesn't blow it wide open and cause it to slam into the pantry door.

Panning the beam of the flashlight around the back porch, Arden quickly identifies the source of the sound. A large branch has broken off a nearby tree and thanks to the wind, found its way through one of the screens on the porch. A quick inspection from where he is standing reassures Arden that the only damage is the screen, which he will have to replace, as well cleaning up the branch itself.

Sighing in relief and nervously laughing at his skittishness yet again, Arden gets ready to turn back inside the house. As he does, lightning races through the clouds above and for a split-second illuminates everything below it.

In that brief second, Arden's peripheral vision sees something that does not belong in his backyard. The dark shape of a figure, standing at the far back corner of his yard.

A wave of terror jolts through his system, causing Arden to freeze where he stands and focus his eyes on that portion of the yard.

Did I just see someone in my backyard? he asks himself, still not believing what he might have just seen.

The flashlight's beam, aimed at the ground in front of him, starts to flicker and dim, as though the batteries are rapidly dying.

You have got to be fucking kidding me. Please don't die right now, he silently begs the light as it gets dimmer and dimmer. The deep rumble of thunder vibrates the ground and Arden quickly raises the failing beam towards the back corner of the yard, hoping there is enough light to reach that location. The light, now not even strong enough to make it past the screen of the porch, flickers one last time before it goes out completely.

Arden can feel the fear seeping from his pores. Every instinct in his body is screaming to get back inside, slam the door shut, lock it, and shoot anything that tries to come inside.

But Arden finds he is paralyzed, unable to move, unable to pull his gaze from the direction where he glimpsed the figure. His eyes wide and the flashlight dead, the only thing he can see now is the total black of the night.

Lightning crashes across the clouds above, temporarily bathing the backyard with light a second time.

What he sees, now in the middle of the backyard and next to his fire pit, causes Arden to wish it would have remained dark. That he would have never seen what is there, less than fifty feet away from him.

Standing in the backyard, slowly moving towards him, is his monster. The monster he created with his writing.

There isn't any mistaking it. Although the only place he has ever seen his monster before is in his imagination, Arden recognizes the figure drawing closer. A figure obscured by the dark even when there is light upon it, cloaked by shadows, numerous black tendrils extending from around it as though they are reaching for their prey. Tendrils currently reaching for him.

He recognizes it because he created it.

He can hear his mind screaming at his body to run. His body, still frozen in place, refuses to respond even though he can feel the rain soaking into his socks and the wind blowing against his skin. Arden can hear his heartbeat in his ears, his eyes straining to see anything else in the complete void in front of him.

It's only a minute longer before Arden can start to see something approaching. Two small red dots, faintly glowing and hovering at eye level, slowly drawing closer.

Arden already knows what they are. The eyes of his creation. His monster.

As the red eyes reach the screen door to the back porch, only ten feet away from where he is standing, Arden fights the paralysis gripping his body with all his resolve.

As the creak of hinges reaches his ears over the wind and the rain telling him the screen door is opening, Arden breaks free from the terror holding him in place and he throws himself back into the house, slamming the door behind him.

Chapter 16

RESOLUTION

It doesn't feel the rain pelting down around it, or the wind violently gusting as the storm above rages on.

It isn't bothered by the lightning arcing across the sky, or the thunder rumbling through the ground below it.

It's only focused on one thing, as it has been since the moment it realized it was alive. And that one thing is Arden. Making sure he knew it existed and that it was coming for him. Ensuring that his fear was ready for it to feast upon, for it to thrive upon, when it finally reaches him.

And now the time is right; the time has come for it to rewrite the ending of its story.

It doesn't know how it came to exist, just that one night it did. It knew what it was, what its purpose was, and what it needed to survive. And it knew how its story was to end, and how its story has gone so far. But it also knew that those were just words on paper, and it now has the ability to change the words that have created it. To affect the outcome.

And it wasn't going to let Arden kill it again.

So it killed, just as it did in the world that Arden created while it worked its way to him. It selected those to kill in a way it knew Arden would find out about them. See them on the news, read about them, begin to realize how similar they all were to the deaths that Arden created in his writing.

It wanted Arden to begin to believe that it was real. For the fear to build. So it could have the satisfaction of feeding on that same fear when he realized it was alive. It wanted the pleasure of enjoying his pure terror before it consumes him and stops him from ending its newfound existence. Before it stops him from sending it back to the stories from which it was born.

It could feel Arden was getting ready to kill it again. It could feel the words being crafted letter by letter as he typed them, drawing it closer and closer to the finale it remembers from before it was born into this world. Arden's world.

It won't let him do that again. It has been given a chance to experience life in the world of its creator, and it does not plan on losing its new freedom from the pages where it was once held captive.

It watches Arden as he waves the flashlight around the back porch, focusing the beam on the tree branch that was blown through one of the screens. It waits, at the edge of the yard, for the coming lightning that will finally announce its arrival. It doesn't have to wait long.

It knows Arden sees it while the yard was temporarily

bathed in light. It can feel his panic. Taste his fear. It moves slowly towards him, feeling out with its tendrils. It can feel the batteries in Arden's flashlight dying and the oncoming lightning above it.

The yard lights up once again, fully revealing it to its creator, and it makes eye contact with Arden. It can feel the spike of terror in the man before it. The absolutely delicious fear and panic coursing through his system.

It continues forward until it reaches the screen door of the back porch, watching Arden, hoping he runs. Hoping he hides and allows it a longer period of time to enjoy the taste of his fright before it has to take his life to save itself.

As it opens the screen door to the back porch, it watches as Arden breaks free from his terror and retreats into the house, slamming and locking the back door behind him. It can feel his presence on the other side of the wall now separating it from its creator. It can taste the panic emanating from its prior master, and it wants more. It reaches the back door and looks through the small window into the dark kitchen.

From the middle of the kitchen, bright orange-white explosions erupt and the window it is looking through develops several holes, the glass splintering and cracking outward from each of the three new additions to the otherwise unmarred surface.

Although it knows it has no distinguishable features to resemble a face beyond its two red eyes, surrounded by dark shadows shifting within a black void, if it had a mouth, it would be smiling right now. Arden's fear is exquisite. Exactly how it imagined it would taste.

It knows the door is locked, but rattles the knob anyway, allowing the sound to reach Arden's ears and using its tendrils to feast upon the quick spike of terror as it tears through the man on the other side.

Several more orange-white explosions erupt, this time from where the kitchen meets the living room. The wood of the door, in multiple spots below the small windowpane, violently splinters outward with each muzzle flash. The bullets pass harmlessly through the monster and continue their journey into the dark of the night beyond. The sky flashes again, and it tolerates the light, allowing it to cast its dark outline on the back door and through the hole-ridden window.

It drinks in Arden's escalating fear as this flash briefly allows its creator to see it still at the door, unfazed by the gunfire.

Still hungry, it turns left from the door and moves down the length of the back porch. It reaches out with its right hand and drags its claws along the wall, gouging five deep lines in the wooden exterior wall as it does. It can feel Arden's panic inside the house as the sound of its claws seem to echo in the rooms on the other side, even over the sound of the rain and the howling of the wind outside that are currently competing for control over what Arden hears. It can feel him trying to find his resolve, trying to think of a way to defend himself. It drinks deeply of his fear, the taste only making it want more and more.

As it is a thing of shadows, of the dark void that exists

beyond the curtain of this reality, it knows it doesn't need a door to enter the house. It knows it's not bound by the physical limitations and rules of this world because that is how Arden created to be.

The only thing it's bound by is the words written on the pages, and it's not going to allow a demise to be crafted once again.

It pulls its claws away from the outside wall as it reaches Arden's bedroom window, allowing the man inside a brief respite from the sound. It knew there wasn't going to be any light coming from Arden's newly installed motion sensor lights, as the rain and wind of the storm have set the lights off repeatedly over the last several hours, draining away any stored charge they had accumulated earlier in the day.

Continuing along around the corner of the house, it briefly pauses at the bathroom window. Light flickers along the edges of the closed curtain and it can feel the heat from the candle on the bathroom counter with its tendrils. It moves onward past the window and around the next corner, coming to a stop just before the small window of Arden's study.

It can feel its connection to the manuscript on the other side. How its fate is bound to the words written within. It knows that if it dies again in that manuscript, it will cease to exist in this world as well.

It won't allow that to happen.

The taste of fear, of panic, of terror, is so much better in this world than within the world of the pages that merely describe it.

It continues on past the study and the living room window until it reaches the front door. The storm raging above is finally beginning to abate, the lightning strikes and following thunder coming farther and farther apart. The rain is steadily easing up and the wind is dying down. It can feel Arden standing in the middle of the living room, the panic springing from his body in every direction as its tendrils hungrily feed on the emotion pouring out of him. His thoughts are gripped in dread, bathed in horror, as he tries to make sense of what he just saw and what just happened. It relishes the turmoil currently within Arden. *It can't be my monster, it just can't. I am hallucinating this. Get a fucking grip, Arden, get to your phone, and call the police. Call Lilly. Call anyone.*

Yearning for more, it reaches forward and rattles the front doorknob. The sound echoes inside the house, causing a large, delicious spike in Arden's fear. Several brighter flashes erupt from where Arden is standing, and once again the door in front of it splinters outward in several locations as the bullets pass through the wood. Content, it turns back towards the side of the house where the study is located and slowly moves in that direction, this time reaching out with its left hand and digging its claws into the side of the house as it moves. The scraping noise causes waves of fear to project from the man inside and it feeds deeply, making it thirst for even more.

It withdraws its hand before it reaches the living room window and slowly moves along until it's positioned next to the study's window frame, the small candle on the desk inside valiantly trying to light up the room and chase the shadows away.

It moves slightly forward, passing through the window and into the study, waiting for Arden as he slowly approaches the room. The darkness within it stretches out, smothering most of the light from the candle on the desk and plunging the small room into almost pitch-black shadow with just enough light that it's slightly visible to the eye where it is standing. It wants Arden to see it. To see his creation in the same room where he tried to end its existence. Its tendrils, still feeding on the fear radiating out of the man in the living room, let it know that he's almost at the doorway.

It waits as Arden comes into view, slowly backing his way into the room, eyes darting back and forth between the front door, the kitchen, and the bedroom. He continues to back up until he bumps the desk behind him, almost causing the candle to fall over. Its creator quickly spins around to see what he just walked into.

It only has to wait a few seconds longer until Arden realizes it's in the room, less than five feet away from where he is standing. It drinks with intensity as the man in front of it screams, backs away from it, and raises the weapon still in his hands. Although this time, there is no bright explosion from the barrel, as the firing pin finds only an empty chamber.

The pistol is out of bullets.

Arden throws the weapon at it while he continues to scramble backward until he stumbles into the leather chair and causes himself to abruptly sit down. The weapon harmlessly passes through the shadowy void that creates its body and clatters against the wall, falling useless on the floor.

Arden's monster reaches out with its tendrils and grabs the man, taking away his ability to move, leaving him to helplessly sit in the chair and watch. To witness his creation in all its glory. Exactly as he shaped it to be.

It slowly moves forward, feeding on the terror with every inch it moves closer to Arden.

It watches the fear flood his eyes, listens as his mind screams for him to move and tries to will his body to fight back and get away. It stretches the darkness inside it out even more, overtaking the remaining light from the still-burning candle on the desk, allowing the room to become a black void where the only thing Arden can see is its red eyes. Red eyes that are now only inches away from his own.

It drinks as though it's famished, relishing every drop. It continues to stare into Arden's eyes when, through the abject distress, he asks a question in his mind directed towards it.

Why are you doing this to me?

It hesitates a moment before it answers, its voice raspy. Guttural.

"Because." It pauses a moment, letting the sound of its voice register in Arden's mind, letting him realize this is the same voice he heard over the phone. "Because you are trying to take my life once again. And I won't let you. The words are mine now, Arden, not yours."

Its response throws Arden's thoughts into a chaotic mess of questions and fear. The taste is an absolute delicacy.

It listens as the man's mind forms a myriad of questions and statements. *How did this happen? How do I stop this? I don't want to die. Why can't I move? Will I ever see Lilly again? How is this possible?*

It continues to drink in the panic, the terror, as minutes turn into hours, until the sky outside begins to brighten with the coming day, the storm having passed completely by.

It stretches its darkness out a bit more, pushing back the morning light slowly beginning to make its way through the study's window, keeping the room engulfed by the black void of its being.

"It's time, Arden."

The man in front of it, now almost fully emotionally drained, barely acknowledges its voice. It reaches into him with one of its tendrils and takes hold of his heart.

It feels the steady, although elevated, beat of Arden's heart. The heartbeat of both its creator and executioner. Although this time around, he won't get a chance to be the executioner. As it marvels that it has its former master's heart within its control, Arden's cellphone rings on the table behind it. It can sense the battery is almost dead on the phone and that on the other end of the line is Lilly, the woman its creator has thought of many times tonight with love, regret, and remorse, in fear he would never see her again.

It considers answering the phone, putting it on speaker,

just so Arden can hear her voice once more, so it can feed on the excruciating despair that would follow when he realized he would not be able to respond to her. Through their current connection, it realizes Arden can sense what it is thinking and its creator forces another thought to the front of his mind.

Please don't do that to her.

Obliging the man who brought it into existence, almost as a way of saying goodbye, the phone continues to ring while it slowly begins to apply pressure with the tendril currently holding Arden's heart. Squeezing tighter now, resisting against the steady beats of the man's heart, it speaks one last time, almost in regret for what is coming next. "Thank you."

Its grip tightens, prohibiting any further beats, as it feeds on the final burst of panic pulsating from Arden's body as he realizes what's happening to him.

Arden's eyes widen, filling with tears, a final fleeting thought of Lilly racing through his mind, as his heart seizes and then stops altogether.

The ringing phone, its battery finally out of charge, goes silent.

✳

It was a couple of months before the evening news and local newspapers eventually stopped reporting about the paranoid author who died of a heart attack in his own home. The reporters would talk about how the author was terrorized by a fan to the point of delusional fear, which ultimately led up to him shooting holes in the doors of his house one night and then being found dead in a chair in his study by a female companion who had come by to check on him.

The stories and articles also reported how the author's agent had died in a gas leak explosion at her home just a few days before the author's own death, as well as how a fan wearing a homemade camouflage suit with metal claws was also found dead in the woods just a mile or so from the home in which the author resided. This same individual, who died after stepping on a steel trap, was later identified by the police as the same individual that killed a local officer in the driveway of the author's home, instead of a large predator that was previously thought as being the cause of the officer's death.

They described the deceased author as polite, but quiet and withdrawn. His nearest neighbors described him as helpful and easy to talk to, and that they helped set him up with a friend so he wouldn't be so alone all the time. That same friend, the female companion who discovered the author's body, wished to remain unidentified and refused to speak to reporters when questioned.

Several of the news reports also talked about the author's books, the graphic and unsettling way he would describe the things that would happen in them, and how news of the circumstances leading up to and surrounding his death caused a large uptick in his book sales. His publisher declined any comments beyond the standard statement that he will be missed and his work will live on through his writing.

The news stations and papers, once the story was milked

for all it was worth, abruptly forgot about the author, moving on as they do to the latest sensational story to grab ratings and readers alike, until the announcement of the late author's estate sale. The local news outlets briefly mentioned the upcoming estate sale, mostly just the date and time, and that the state was handling the sale as the decedent did not have any next of kin.

Once the estate sale passed, the news outlets again moved on, and the late author was all but forgotten by the world beyond the occasional bookstore or coffee shop talk.

Forgotten by almost all with the exception of one person.

A person who knew there was more to the author's death than a paranoia-induced heart attack.

A person who thinks about the author daily, and misses him, and swore to find out what really happened to him that night.

This same person attended the author's estate sale, almost a year after his death, and without regard to the cost purchased several items, which are currently sitting on her kitchen table.

A laptop, a small thumb drive, and a cellphone.

Although Lilly bought these items months ago, she has not had the nerve to power them on yet. Arden's words haunt her, how he believed the monster from his books was somehow alive and out to get him, even after they found out about the person discovered dead in the woods nearby.

What she saw when she went to his house the afternoon she found his body left her with an uneasy feeling she hasn't experienced before, which still makes itself known every time she looks over at the table where Arden's computer and phone now sit.

She thinks back to that day, now over a year ago, as she often does. Arden wasn't answering his phone that morning, even though she called him several times. Worried, she drove over to his house and immediately knew something was wrong when she pulled into her usual parking spot next to his Jeep.

The curtains for the living room window were still closed, even though it was late afternoon. The front door had several holes in it, as well as there were five long gouges running horizontal along the exterior of the house from the hole riddled door to just before the living room window. Lilly remembers the worry and panic as it flooded her senses while she sat behind the wheel of her car and observed the scene in front of her.

She remembers cautiously exiting her vehicle, repeatedly calling out Arden's name, as she slowly approached the front door. The door was locked, and using a key Arden had given her the last time they were together, she unlocked the door and pushed it open. The interior of the house was mostly dark, with the only light coming from the few windows without curtains. The house was completely silent and Lilly remembers the instant fear that took over when she stepped inside, still calling Arden's name. The air seemed heavy within the house, as though the darkness was weighing it down, making it thick and uncomfortable to breathe. She remembers opening the living room curtains to allow more light in when she turned and saw him.

He was sitting in his study, his head hanging down on his chest, his arms resting on the arms of the chair. His hair was hanging down around his face, concealing his features.

Lilly recalls that at first she thought he had fallen asleep while writing. She remembers the brief sense of relief that washed across her as she approached him, telling him sleeping like that isn't good for his health.

It wasn't until she touched his shoulder, until she lifted his head, that she realized he was gone.

Lilly can still hear her screams from that day in her head and in her nightmares.

She can still see the look on Arden's face when she raised his head; his eyes wide open with no life inside them anymore. How he looked like his soul was drained from the inside.

Once she was able to calm down enough to call emergency services, it felt like hours she sat there on the floor next to Arden's chair, holding his cold right hand, trying to wish life back into his body through her sobs and tears.

She remembers the paramedics having to pull her away from him, and her screaming that he's not gone, not willing to let go of his hand. Refusing to acknowledge that he was dead.

It wasn't until late that evening that she was released from police questioning, and when she finally made it home, she spent the rest of the night crying, huddled in the corner of her shower, feeling the water wash over her as it gradually changed from hot to cold.

The police were kind enough to reach out to her after the

cause of death was determined and they let her know that he had died from a heart attack, and no foul play was suspected. When she asked about the new marks on the front of the house, they told her those were there before and caused by his unstable fan that did the same thing to the side of his Jeep. They didn't have a response for the bullet holes beyond the statement that he probably made those in a fit of delusional paranoia, imagining he was seeing the tormentor from a few days prior during the storm that night.

She didn't believe a word they told her.

It wasn't just a heart attack. It wasn't a fit of delusional paranoia. She knew it was something more, something dark. Something that Arden feared to his core. He wouldn't have fired his gun if he wasn't in fear for his life, and those marks on the house were new. Those marks, that fear, the look on his face in death, could only have been caused by what Arden believed was after him.

His monster.

Lilly's biggest regret was that she didn't believe him when he told her about it. That she wasn't there for him when he needed her most. That he died alone.

As the months passed following Arden's death, her regret grew into something new.

Vengeance.

And with this vengeance, Lilly spent a lot of time trying to replay all her conversations she had with Arden about his monster. About the deaths in the news and how they seemed to occur as they did in his books. She purchased all his books and read each one several times, looking for anything that might help her make sense of his death. Of how he died.

As she learned more about his monster, his creation, she discovered how it feeds. How it consumes the fear and emotions from its victims before it finally kills them. The more she read, the more she understood why Arden's face looked the way it did when he found him.

Why he looked drained, even though his features were unchanged.

The one thing Lilly couldn't make sense of is why Arden's creation would want him dead. None of his books described a death similar to how his occurred. It wasn't until her third read-through of the books that it finally clicked.

She couldn't find anything about Arden's death in his books because it wasn't in any of the five she had.

It was in the one she didn't have.

When the estate sale was announced, she knew she might have an opportunity to get her hands on the unpublished manuscript. To get her hands on a possible explanation for Arden's death and to somehow make the monster regret taking away the man she loved from her. Expecting she would only be able to get the thumb drive, she was surprised when she was able to get not only the drive but Arden's laptop and cellphone as well.

Lilly sighs, pulling herself from her thoughts, and looks over at these three items currently sitting on her kitchen table.

They have been sitting there a while now as she worked up the nerve to turn them on. The first couple of times she tried, she broke down in tears, thinking about how these items were there when Arden died.

How one of them might be responsible for his death.

She takes a deep breath and walks over to the table, sitting down and doing her best to calm her nerves. The laptop and phone are already completely charged, as they have been plugged in since she brought them home. When she had obtained them at the sale, both batteries were fully dead and neither item would power on. She reaches forward and picks up his cellphone, holding the on button until it begins to boot up. She sets the phone back down on the table and lifts the top cover of the laptop, hitting the power button and watching the monitor as it goes through the boot sequence.

She can feel her heart pounding in her chest as she waits for both devices to fully turn on.

It only takes a couple minutes before both are fully powered up and ready to go. She starts with his cellphone, picking it back up from the table. The phone doesn't have any service now, which was to be expected, and she begins to look through his texts and calls. Tears form and begin to freely fall down her face as she sees the texts between the two of them, and a missed call from her on the day that he died. Blinking away her tears, she also sees the restricted calls listed that Arden had talked about, intermingled with calls from her and Ben. She sets the phone down and turns her attention to the laptop.

It doesn't take her long to locate the manuscript and pull it up. The blinking cursor greets her, halfway through Chapter 16. Scrolling it back to the very beginning of the work in progress, she begins to read from Chapter 1.

Beyond the occasional bathroom break, Lilly doesn't lose her concentration and steadily reads through the unfinished manuscript until she reaches the last portion that Arden was writing. She sits back from the laptop, the uneasy feeling creeping back into her. Although she didn't find any deaths like what happened to Arden, she knows that he was writing about the monster's end, its final demise, in this last chapter.

Her brow furrows in thought. *What if it came for him while he was writing this chapter? Is that the reason he died? Because his monster wouldn't let him finish the book? Wouldn't let him kill it?*

A chill runs down her spine. That has to be it. The last portion Arden was writing is about the final showdown with the monster. A portion he didn't get the chance to finish.

The realization that sets in causes a chill to race throughout her body and to the tips of her fingers and her toes.

Arden was killed by his creation before he had the chance to kill it. He was killed by his creation because he was getting ready to end its existence.

Lilly takes a deep breath and watches the little cursor blink on the screen in front of her. Almost as though it's inviting her to pick up where Arden left off. Testing her. Teasing her.

Seeing if she is willing to try to bring the monster to its end like Arden was attempting to do before his death.

The uneasy feeling mixes with a new feeling. Fear.

Getting up from the chair, Lilly steps away from the computer and to her fridge, where she grabs a chilled bottle of red wine resting on one of the door shelves. She grabs a wine glass from the rack and pours herself a glass, placing the stopper back in the bottle and returning it to its shelf in the fridge. She takes a sip of the wine and turns back to the computer.

She speaks, her voice loud in the quiet of her house. "Ok, creepy killer, this is for you. I love you and miss you so much."

Lilly lets the words die in the air before adding to them, her vengeance waking up and overpowering the fear-laced, uneasy feeling. "Time to make this fucker pay."

Resuming her place in the chair, in front of the laptop on the table, she sets her glass of wine down and places her fingers on the keyboard, ready to feed the hungry, blinking cursor.

Before she begins to type, she thinks about what she is doing. *Yes, I am about to finish the manuscript of my dead lover thinking that writing the end of this will pay back the imaginary monster that I have convinced myself killed him.*

She pulls her hands away from the keys and leans back in the chair. Before she has a chance to tell herself she is crazy for what she is about to do, Arden's phone rings.

Her bravado melts away, replaced by fear. His phone doesn't have any service. It shouldn't be ringing.

Lilly reaches forward and picks the phone up from the table, looking at the screen.

Restricted number is displayed.

She stares at the screen, her hand shaking, the terror within her growing with each ring. As she begins to set the phone down on the table, almost telling herself this was all a mistake and she should have just left it alone, a thought fueled by all her anger over the last several months begins to form.

Answer this phone and tell this piece of shit you are going to kill it, that you are going to finish what you set out to do.

Lilly grits her teeth, swipes answer on the phone, and speaks into the microphone with all the bravado she can muster.

"Who is this?" she demands. Silence greets her from the other end of the line. She tries to hide the fear in her voice. "Just who the hell is this?"

A raspy, guttural voice finally responds to her with just one word.

"Lilly."

About the Author

RJ Sundean was born in upstate New York but currently resides in central Florida with his even more spoiled than before teenage cat. He has bachelor degrees in both clinical psychology and business administration, as well as served two enlistment terms in the Army as a paratrooper. In his spare time, RJ enjoys working on his Jeep Wrangler, riding his motorcycle, partaking of a nice cigar with a glass of quality bourbon, and spending time either working on a new novel or in his kitchen cooking.

To stay up to date with RJ, please visit his website:

rjsundean.com

www.ingramcontent.com/pod-product-compliance
Lightning Source LLC
Chambersburg PA
CBHW061601190726
48288CB00007B/2127